Rebecca's Return

This Large Print Book carries the
Seal of Approval of N.A.V.H.

REBECCA'S RETURN

JERRY S. EICHER

THORNDIKE PRESS

A part of Gale, Cengage Learning

Detroit • New York • San Francisco • New Haven, Conn • Waterville, Maine • London

GALE
CENGAGE Learning™

Copyright © 2009 by Jerry S. Eicher.

Adams County Trilogy #2.

All Scripture quotations are taken from the King James Version of the Bible.

Thorndike Press, a part of Gale, Cengage Learning.

Thorndike Press® Large Print Christian Fiction.

The text of this Large Print edition is unabridged.

Other aspects of the book may vary from the original edition.

Set in 16 pt. Plantin.

Printed on permanent paper.

LIBRARY OF CONGRESS CATALOGING-IN-PUBLICATION DATA

Eicher, Jerry S.
    Rebecca's return / by Jerry S. Eicher.
        p. cm. — (Thorndike Press large print Christian fiction)
    (Adams County trilogy ; no. 2)
    ISBN-13: 978-1-4104-1676-6 (alk. paper)
    ISBN-10: 1-4104-1676-3 (alk. paper)
    1. Amish—Ohio—Fiction. 2. Amish Country (Ohio)—Fiction.
    3. Large type books. I. Title.
    PS3605.I34R43 2009b
    813'.6—dc22   2009009202

Published in 2009 by arrangement with Harvest House Publishers.

Printed in the United States of America
1 2 3 4 5 6 7 13 12 11 10 09

Rebecca's Return

CHAPTER ONE

John Miller knew he loved Rebecca Keim, and yet he was afraid.

In the predawn darkness, John walked across the graveled parking lot of Miller's Furniture, digging in his pocket for his keys. Even with his glove off, his fingers still kept fumbling, his mind on Rebecca. Why hadn't she returned yet?

There had been no word, no phone call, and no letter. Miller's Furniture had a phone in the building just outside the backdoor, and its ringing could usually be heard from the front desk. Was he expecting too much that Rebecca should call him? But then where would she have called from since Leona, Rebecca's aunt, could hardly be expected to have a telephone close to her home.

Even so, she surely could have found a way — and that was what bothered him.

They had become engaged right before

she left to help care for her aunt's family in Milroy while Leona gave birth. That was only a few weeks ago, but to John it was an eternity. He had seen her only once since their engagement. That was on the night she told him she was leaving for Indiana to help with the newly arriving baby. It had been a sudden decision made by her mother, Leona's sister, and according to Rebecca, it was a surprise to her also.

That was a reasonable explanation, but did Rebecca need to seem so happy about leaving? Wouldn't she miss him? And yet, going to help an aunt with a new baby was a good thing and a sign of trust and status.

He was sure there was something more going on with Rebecca. The gnawing fact hung around him like a sweat fly in the summer. Like the fly, the thoughts of trouble would land on him, and he would swat them away, but they always seemed to find a place to land again, and he would swat again.

Was he afraid of somehow losing Rebecca? But why would that happen? The idea had no basis. Yet the doubt persisted.

Had the baby come already, he wondered. There was really no way of knowing unless he asked Rebecca's family on Sunday, but he would feel awkward doing that.

What was he to do? Walk up to Lester,

Rebecca's father, after church and ask, "Has Leona's baby been born?" Maybe he could get his mother, Miriam, to ask Rebecca's mother.

No, he wouldn't do either of those things. Surely Rebecca would contact him soon. He tilted his brimmed hat sideways to keep it from blowing away in the wind. There was no snow expected today, for which he was glad. Even though he worked inside most of the time, both as a sales person and all-around handyman, winter always came too soon for him.

With his fingers finally around the keys, he pulled his hand out of his pocket and transferred the ring to his other hand. Placing his glove back on the exposed hand, his fingers warmed quickly in the fur lining. Pausing at the door, he brushed the frost from the knob and inserted the key.

As he walked through the door, the warmth of the store welcomed him. The outdoor furnace could burn all night on low when well-stocked with wood. Now though, the furnace would be in need of fresh fuel.

John's uncle Aden was already in his office, light from a gas lantern shining out into the main room. When John glanced in, Aden said without looking up, "Fire needs making." He was reading from the current issue of the *Adams County Crossroads,* an official visitor's guide to Adams County, Ohio, in which Miller's Furniture and Bakery was prominently featured.

"It's pretty warm still," John said. "The furnace keeps up the heat, even on cold nights."

Aden, his brown eyes framed by black hair and a dark beard that came down over the first button on his shirt, glanced up and answered, "Ya, it's a good furnace. Does pretty good unless we get subzero weather. I have to come out during the night once or so to add wood."

"How cold is too cold in here before there's damage to the furniture?" John asked, curious.

Aden wrinkled up his face. "Don't really want to find that out but maybe below forty. Just to be safe, fifty or so."

"Sales are pretty good this year," John said.

"The Lord has blessed us, especially our year-end sales," Aden agreed, not looking up from his *Adams County Crossroads.* With Christmas only two weeks away, business was brisk. Even the slowing economy seemed not to have affected the tourists from Cincinnati, a bastion of conservatism and old money.

These were people who valued the Amish traditions, admired their industriousness and the quality of the finished product to the extent that they readily passed up names like Widdicomb and Lane to invest in the unnamed brands created by the Amish. In a sense, *Amish* was itself the brand, produced in little shops and crannies of the various Amish communities located in Ohio, Indiana, and Pennsylvania.

Here on Wheat Ridge, there was no Christmas sale, as there were no Sunday sales, in deference to the sacred nature of the holiday. There was a year-end sale though, serving the same purpose but avoiding the impropriety.

"I'd better see to the furnace," John said, stepping out of the office and following the hallway to the outside door where the garage-type structure housed the furnace.

Stacks of wood lined the north wall. More was outside, now snow-covered. John calculated that there was enough inside, high and dry, until a thaw arrived and allowed more wood to be moved in. If not, then the snow-covered wood could be moved inside and stored until it dried from the heat of the furnace.

Opening the large steel door, he stirred the embers with the long fire rod. Under

11

the rod's encouragement, the ash filtered down into the ash box below. The embers left on top glowed with a red intensity. John removed the sliding ash box, took it a distance away, and carefully spread the ash on the ground.

John took care to keep the pile of ash thin enough, so it would cool fairly rapidly. Piled thick, the coals could be kept alive for days under the ash. If a wind arose at night and blew the ash off the top, the live coals could start a fire where it was not wanted.

With the ash box back in the furnace, John piled the chamber full of wood, setting the last two pieces in vertically in front. He then went to the thermostat and set it to its normal setting for daytime comfort.

When John returned to the office, Aden was still reading his *Adams County Crossroads.*

"What's on the list to do before we open?" John asked.

"The lists of shipments from yesterday's sales are on the counter, left side," Aden said. "Those need to be packed up. Roadway comes at one."

"Is Sharon coming in?"

"Yes, around nine or so. She'll dust the furniture and take care of the customers."

"I wouldn't want to do the dusting anyway."

Aden chuckled. "Neither do I, but we do what we have to do."

"You're right on that," John agreed.

"Say, how's that girl of yours?" Aden asked, without looking up.

"Same as always, I guess," John said, hoping the conversation would end there. With Rebecca absent and no word from her, John felt uneasy when asked about their engagement. And then too, there were those nagging doubts about Rebecca.

"She's still taking care of her aunt's baby in Milroy?"

"Yes."

Aden shrugged his shoulders. "Ought to be back soon, eh?"

John said nothing, which just made things worse.

"Oh, you don't know?" Aden asked, surprised. "She hasn't called?"

"She probably didn't have time," John said, convincing no one.

"Maybe she has someone she's seeing in Milroy? Someone you should know about?" Aden's twinkle was gone.

"Why would she?" John snapped. "We just got engaged."

"You ever ask her?"

After a hesitation, John said, "Yes."

"What'd she say?"

"There's no one else."

"Was she telling the truth?"

"You know something I don't?"

"No, just asking." Aden shrugged his shoulders. "They came from the old community. Did you ever talk to anyone from there about her past?"

"No," John replied, "it didn't seem necessary."

"You going by your own feelings then?"

"Yes."

"Not the best choice, especially when you like the girl."

"Well, I do."

Aden turned to his nephew. "Well, don't lose your head just because you've lost your heart."

"But she's . . ." John said, searching for words, "wonderful."

"Wonderful is as wonderful does," his uncle said gravely. "Like the good book says, 'Beauty is vain, but a woman that feareth the Lord, she shall be praised.' "

John numbly nodded his head in agreement, then reached for the stack of invoices to begin the packing.

CHAPTER TWO

How am I to figure that one out? Is my uncle right with his concerns about Rebecca? Why has she not contacted me from Indiana? When is she coming home? John pondered the situation, the invoices in hand. Noticing that his uncle was watching him, John walked toward the storeroom to begin the packing.

He hoped to be finished by opening time, but if the packing took longer, perhaps he could continue it between waiting on customers. John got to work, forcing himself to stop worrying about Rebecca.

At exactly five till nine, time for the first customers to show up, a dull thud was heard from the direction of the highway. It was a solid sound, a boom as if a barrel were covering it.

Pausing from securing a rail-backed oak dining chair in its cardboard crate, he stood up straight and listened.

"You hear that?" John hollered to Aden, who was still in his office.

The muffled answer was unintelligible, at least from where John stood.

John finished the wrapping on the inside of the crate, making sure there was no room for movement that could break the delicate spines on the chairs.

Hearing the door open, John glanced up. It was Sharon, Aden's sixteen-year-old daughter and his cousin. She was tall for her age and had blue eyes that twinkled in the same way her father's did . . . but they weren't twinkling now.

She stood in the doorway holding the exterior door open, the vapor from the outside cold wrapping itself toward the ceiling. "There's been an accident on the highway," she said, clearly shaken. "They need help."

"How bad is it?" Aden asked, coming out of the office.

Sharon's blue eyes flashed with concern. "I don't know. I just saw it as I was coming in. The car is off the road and in the trees."

"I'd better call it in," Aden said. "John, you can go on down to see if you can help. Sharon and I will stay here to watch the store."

Sharon held the door open for John.

"There's no use me going," she said. "I can't do anything."

"Have you got your buggy blanket?" he asked. "The blanket might keep the people warm, if they're hurt."

"Yes, it's in my buggy, on the seat."

Walking quickly John gathered up the blankets from both his buggy and Sharon's and ran out the driveway. Halfway there he heard the cries for help coming from the car, hidden out of sight over the slight knoll toward Highway 41.

It was clearly a woman's voice, and John quickened his pace. As he came to the blacktop, he quickly looked for tire or skid marks on the pavement but noticed nothing unusual. In the ditch though, a single set of marks disappeared over the knoll. Apparently whoever it was had not tried to stop.

Following the sound of the cries, he went to the ditch and jumped across to avoid the slush at the bottom. Cresting the knoll, John saw the car off to the side in a clump of trees. The trees' barks were peeled away, and the blue, four-door Chevy Impala lay where it had fallen beside them. Still upright, its front bumper nearly pushed halfway into the engine compartment, the driver's side door was crushed inward.

The woman was clearly disheveled and

frantic with fear. Her head was thrown back against the top of the seat. She saw John and cried, "Please help me . . . Please. Please help me."

He approached, uncertain what to do. The English were very particular about accident scenes, he had heard. A person could get into real trouble trying to help or move injured persons without the proper training.

"Please help me," the woman cried again, her eyes glazed with fear.

John had never seen anything like this and searched his mind for solutions. Carefully he examined the woman's condition, while standing close to the car door. There was no blood, although the woman was obviously trapped. John could see that it would be impossible for him to open that crushed door. The only other way out was through the passenger side door on the other side, and that was out of the question because it was lodged against a tree.

With the woman's eyes on him, looking through him as if he were not there, John spoke quietly, "There's help on the way. They will get you out of here."

"Oh, help me . . . Please help me. Somebody help me. I'm going to die." The woman's voice was raspy by now.

"You have to breathe," John said, seeing

that her breath was coming in short jerks, her body shivering. "Here's a blanket." He unfolded one of the blankets and offered it through the broken window. The woman made no effort to take the blanket, so John reached in and laid it gently over her. She closed her eyes, pressing her head back against the headrest, drawing in deep breaths.

"What's your name?" he asked. Cars were stopping along the road now. John could hear their tires crunching to a halt, but the sound he was listening for was not yet wailing in the distance.

"Cindy," she told him weakly, trembling under the blanket.

"What happened?" John asked, wanting to keep her conscious. The woman's breathing was slowing down and she looked like she wanted to drop off to sleep. What that meant, he wasn't sure, but it couldn't be good.

"I fell asleep. Up too late last night," Cindy said through drooping eyelids.

That would explain the lack of skid marks. Hearing someone behind him, John turned around. Two people were standing on the knoll, and a woman was approaching.

"I'm a nurse," the woman said. "Let me talk to her."

John was more than glad to step away from his spot by the window. "Her name is Cindy."

"Help is on the way, Cindy," the nurse said soothingly. "Is there someone you would like us to call?"

"Yes, call Maggie," the trapped Cindy said.

"Is she family?"

"Just a friend."

"Can you give me that number?"

"Yes," John heard Cindy say, but missed the numbers. The nurse got out her cell phone and punched in the numbers rapidly.

When the nurse stepped away to make the call, Cindy was left unattended. John saw her head go back against the headrest, her eyes rolling back into her head. Afraid this meant Cindy was going into shock, he started talking to her again. "The ambulance has been called. They're on their way. Just hold on a little longer." Cindy seemed not to hear him.

Flipping the cell shut, the nurse came back. "She's not answering, Cindy." The the nurse stuck her head in through the smashed window, little jagged pieces of glass above and below her. Cindy didn't respond.

"Uh-oh," the nurse said. "Cindy, wake up. Cindy, just a little longer. Hold on, dear."

She took Cindy's hand and lightly shook her shoulder.

Cindy snapped forward as if she was awakening from sleep. "Come on, *breathe*," the nurse said in her ear. "Just hold on."

John turned toward the road when he heard the sound of sirens. "They're coming."

"Thank God." The nurse continued shaking Cindy's shoulder every time she seemed to be on the verge of dropping off.

The fire department truck from West Union arrived first. They were all young men, moving quickly and cautiously down from the knoll and toward the car. Right away they determined that they needed the "Jaws of Life." While those were being unloaded, a temporary oxygen mask was fitted on Cindy. Immediately Cindy laid her head back on the headrest, seeming to relax considerably.

As the firemen began their work, John noticed the tool they used to spread the metal apart. A fireman inserted it between the door hinges and turned it on. To the groans of creaking metal, it created a space where they could use a pair of giant snips to cut through the metal that was in the way. John watched in fascination as they used a smaller version to snap off the main arms of the door.

John walked back up the knoll, hearing more sirens and seeing a state patrol car following an ambulance up the hill from 41. John waited until a stretcher was taken down to the site and Cindy was slid on to it before deciding that he really should get back to the store.

When he walked in through the doorway, Aden was taking care of customers. Sharon, clearly in over her head, was showing a young couple the grandfather clocks. Relief showed all over her face, at the sight of him.

"Anything serious?" Aden asked John, interrupting his conversation with the customers. All eyes turned in John's direction.

"She's conscious," he answered. "A woman, the only person involved, was injured. They just took her out on a stretcher. She said she fell asleep while driving to work."

"That's too bad. Good that it's not worse," Aden said, turning back to his customers. The place immediately fell back into its normal routine, as if the world, having paused in concern, now continued on.

John stepped over to the grandfather clocks to help Sharon. "Can I be of assistance?" he asked.

"Yes," Sharon said, almost gushing with relief. Then turning to the customer, she said, "This is John Miller. He can answer your questions much better than I can."

"I'll try," John told the young couple. "So what are you looking for?"

Their foyer needed a clock, they told him. It needed to be somewhere between eighty and ninety-six inches tall, fit into an alcove that measured forty-two inches wide, and have an elegant design but not too fancy. He got a tape measure from the counter and had a sale in ten minutes, arranging for shipping into the suburb of Delhi Hills on the southern edge of Cincinnati.

After they left and John had a moment to relax, he was annoyed to find that the troublesome thoughts of Rebecca were back in his mind. The accident he had just witnessed heightened his sense of uncertainty. The world was a dangerous place, he thought, able to change drastically in a moment of time.

He wished he knew when Rebecca was coming home. But what if his feelings of doubt were justified. What if she *did* have a secret in Milroy? A boy she had loved. Or still loved. What if she told him something he'd rather not know? Something that would break up their engagement. Was the Rebecca he loved even capable of something that bad?

His head spinning, John pushed the difficult thoughts away as he turned to help another customer coming through the doorway.

CHAPTER THREE

Rebecca, riding in the backseat of the twelve-passenger, silver Dodge Caravan, was squeezed between chubby Amanda Troyer and her husband, David, whose stringy growth of hair on his chin was trying unsuccessfully to form into a full-length beard.

In the seat in front of them were Roy and Dorothy Miller and their four-month-old Elizabeth. Both couples were young, traveling to visit relatives on Wheat Ridge during Christmas.

Rebecca had known both couples from her growing-up years in Milroy, as well as the older couple on the front bench seat, James and Laura Miller and their daughter, Susan. In the front seat beside the driver was James and Laura's son, Andrew, a boy of twenty or so.

Rebecca had heard something to the effect that Andrew had his eye on one of her cousins on the Keim side. In fact, he might

25

well be going to visit the girl, she figured, instead of just writing a letter to begin a possible relationship. It could make for an interesting upcoming Sunday evening.

Andrew hadn't said much during the entire trip. The silent type, he had barely glanced at Rebecca when she had boarded the van at her aunt's place. Not that Rebecca cared one way or the other, but it started her thinking about John.

Rebecca breathed deeply. Leaving Emma's she had been certain everything would be okay. She would tell John about her promise to Atlee, if he wanted to know. If John didn't want to know, that was fine too.

She had been honest with herself on this trip to Milroy. Yes, she had loved Atlee, loved him deeply, but that was over. Her heart had grown since then. It had grown larger with new places for love and affection. John could fill those places now. And she very much wanted John to fill her heart, to look at her with that intense desire shining in his eyes the way he did that day he proposed.

The fear of the past, so haunting before her trip, now seemed to recede into the distance, driven away by the light. She smiled thinking about it.

"A penny for your thoughts," Amanda

whispered, her midsection vibrating vertically with each bump in the road. "What's that sweet smile about? John waiting for you?"

"How do you know about John?" Rebecca whispered back, feeling a flush of red on her neck.

"Oh," Amanda replied with a grin, her voice going back to its normal tone, "birdies fly from tree to tree, you know."

"Well, yes, they do," Rebecca agreed. "And yes, I suppose I was thinking about him. I don't know if he's expecting me back this Sunday or not. I haven't let anyone know."

"Well, you should have, but they can probably figure it out," Amanda allowed. "Your mom knows the baby was born, doesn't she?"

"Yes. I wrote her the day after."

"But no one might have told John," Amanda stated more than asked.

"Perhaps not. I don't know." A cloud crossed Rebecca's face. "I guess I should have made more of an effort. There was just so much going on."

Amanda answered, "Either way — he'll be so happy to see you, it won't matter. How were you supposed to let him know? You weren't gone that long?"

"About three weeks."

"That's not very long."

"I guess I could have called or written him. I'll have to tell John I'm sorry."

"Did you have his address?"

"There never was a reason for it before."

"You've never mailed him anything, not even a card at Christmas?"

"I just gave it to him."

"*Ach vell,* don't worry about it. Like I said — boys. They're just so glad to see their girl."

The van slowed and made a turn onto a narrower road.

"Is this your road?" Amanda asked.

"Yes," Rebecca said, as the driver took the van around a sharp turn, "our place is up here on the left."

"So we'll see each other on Sunday then?" Amanda asked hopefully. "It would be good to see another familiar face."

"Are you going to our district?"

"I don't know." Amanda's face fell. "If not, maybe I'll see others I know from Milroy."

"There's quite a few, I think," Rebecca said, as the van slowed down to turn into the Keim driveway. "My, but it's good to see home again."

"It's a nice place here," Amanda told Rebecca in approval. She then motioned for David to move, as the van came to a stop, so they could let Rebecca out. Both David and Amanda squeezed down the right side and stepped completely out of the van. Rebecca followed.

David went to find her suitcase, while Rebecca paid the driver for her share of the trip. When she was done, her suitcase was sitting on a bare spot of the frozen ground. David and Amanda had already climbed back into the van. As the van drove down the road and out of sight, she was left alone in the driveway, the sense of home closing in all around her.

CHAPTER FOUR

Even though little time had slipped by, Rebecca felt as if she had been away from home a very long time because of all that had happened. Her heart felt aged and wise, having grown by leaps and bounds in such a short time.

"Thank You, Lord," she whispered, bending down to pick up her suitcase. "You have been so good to me. You used that trip at just the right time to bring me to my senses. Emma was so wise. Such good counsel. You must have known exactly what I needed."

The kitchen door opened slowly, and her mother stepped out, breaking into a smile at the sight of Rebecca. "I *thought* I heard something. Oh my, it's so good to see you home." Mattie came toward Rebecca, a food-stained apron around her waist, and reached for the suitcase after giving her a quick embrace.

"Thanks, Mom, but I can carry it," Rebecca said. "Where is everybody?"

"Oh, the usual for this time of the day. Dad's in town getting a part for the hay rake. It broke down last fall, and he's getting ready for spring. Hopefully the dealership has it. The children are still in school. So, you were able to come on a load instead of the Greyhound?"

"Yes. I only found out on Sunday, but by then my letter to you was already sent. Anyway, I figured you were expecting me about this time."

"I was, but I thought maybe tomorrow. So, how's baby Jonathon?"

"Hungry and still angry, I think. He didn't seem to be too happy to be a part of this world."

Mattie chuckled. "They're all like that, at least mine were. It takes a little adjusting sometimes. Then we learn to appreciate what *Da Hah* has in store for us. Is Leona okay?"

"She was up working some on Wednesday already. I told her it wasn't necessary, but she insisted. Said she needed to get in shape as soon as possible."

"That's like Leona."

"It's like you too," Rebecca chided.

"Well, we *are* sisters. It would have been good to see her again myself. So how was it, running a whole household all by your-self?"

Rebecca pulled in her breath at the memory. "Scary at first. Thankfully, I had a few days to start in slow with Leona help-ing. That was a wise idea to go early. I think Leona appreciated it too."

Mattie nodded. "That's what I was think-ing, with it being your first time and all. Now you're an experienced baby maid — in much demand. Even around here, if you want to."

Rebecca wrinkled her face. "That many diapers in that many days — I don't know about that."

Mattie laughed. "It doesn't pay much either. Not nearly as much as housecleaning for the English does. I guess that's why most of us only do it for family. Come on inside and get settled in. There's no sense in talk-ing out here in the cold."

"Has John asked when I was to come back?" Rebecca asked, looking worried.

"No, I assumed you would let him know. You didn't write him when you wrote me a letter?"

Rebecca made a face. "I didn't have his address, but I know that's a poor excuse. There was so much going on."

"That is a poor excuse."

"I know," Rebecca said, "but I am glad I got some things solved. It was a busy time. Maybe if I explain it all to John, he'll understand."

"He probably will, although it's not good to leave a boyfriend without news for long."

"Mom, there's something I should tell you about what happened though."

"Oh?" Mattie hesitated at the kitchen door.

"Do you remember Atlee from Milroy?"

"Yes. You and he were close at one time, weren't you?"

"Yes. But even more than that," Rebecca said, then hesitated. "I finally figured out that I really did love him — in the sixth grade."

Mattie glanced at her and asked, "Now where did that come from? You surely don't anymore, do you? That was a long time ago."

"It was," Rebecca allowed. "But it troubled me. I didn't quite trust my heart."

"Your heart was not then what it is now. If you let Atlee fill it — what there was to fill — now you can let John fill it. He is much better for you."

"I know that now, but I didn't *let* Atlee fill it. He just did," Rebecca protested.

Mattie shrugged. "One never knows how such things happen. They just do. You can open and shut the door though. And now with John, you must simply shut the door on memories of Atlee."

"Yes," Rebecca replied, "Emma said the same thing. But I didn't know that before I went to Milroy."

"Why? What happened in Milroy?" Mattie asked, now suspicious. "Surely you didn't see Atlee? Surely he would not have sought you out."

"No, Mom, it's not like that. I went down to the Moscow bridge, where we used to go. I was trying to deal with something between us. Then Atlee did stop by — he was visiting relatives."

"And what happened?" Mattie asked.

"Nothing to be alarmed about. He's gone Mennonite . . . but you knew that. He's getting married. I think talking to him was good. It helped me realize how much I really do love and need John."

"Good," Mattie said, relief in her eyes. "All of us had thoughts and feelings when we were very young. But it's not the same when you're older. Real life starts when we grow up."

"And that's how I feel now, Mom — grown up somehow. You think John will be too upset?"

Mattie smiled at her daughter and then

said, "I don't think so. Now get yourself unpacked. I suppose Matthew will be glad for your help in the barn. I do think the chores are still a little too much for him. I could use some help myself in the kitchen too."

"What are you making?"

"Cinnamon rolls. Now hurry and get changed. You can lay your clothing on the bed for now. Hang them up later. That way you'll have time to see if any of them need ironing."

"I'll be right down," Rebecca said, heading for the stairs. As she opened the door to her room, she stood still for a moment, the feelings flooding her. This was her room, her place where she came when she needed to be alone. Here she wept when tears were needed, where no one else would see. It was the heart of home.

Walking to her bed, she gently ran her hands over the quilt. The square cross-stitch design soothed her eyes, and the soft feathery strings brushing against her fingers moved her.

She felt tears sting her eyes. *I am being silly,* she told herself. *It's just a normal room.* Still she stood there for long moments, taking in the sensations of home. Hastily, to make up for time already lost, she lay her clothing from the suitcase out on the bed, changed into work clothes, and dashed downstairs.

CHAPTER FIVE

Luke Byler was sitting in the New Holland front-end loader, his plans of finishing early with the chores running through his mind. The melting snow from the storm a few weeks ago had turned the barnyards muddy. He could see the front barns where the cattle gathered to feed, their split hooves keeping the dirt mashed to a gooey mush from the constant tramping.

Emma didn't like to see her cattle with mud caked on their undersides, becoming unsightly and unsanitary specimens of fattening beef. The solution was to move the round feeding bins to another spot, allowing this section of the barnyard to dry out. From what he could tell of the weather, winter was just beginning.

In Luke's pocket was the letter Emma had put out to mail, and which he had retrieved. The letter burned in his pocket, begging to be taken home as quickly as possible. Yet danger lurked around the envelope, like stinging, flying wasps protecting their nest in the summertime. It had no doubt been wrong for him to have taken the letter from Emma's mailbox. It was, after all, Emma who gave him work, paid him well, and even gave him a little extra at times.

Fear of the consequences and yet delight at the cunningness of his actions had been playing themselves out in Luke's mind all day. *What if I get caught? Yet how could I get caught? Mail gets lost all the time, and Emma would simply conclude that was the case, if she concluded anything.*

Perhaps the letter would never be missed, and was it not his right to have the letter anyway?

Had that not been his right, his family's right all along, to inherit what was theirs?

With the letter in his pocket, the future could well be secured for them all. Emma was surely giving the farms back to their rightful owners. Now his mother would no longer be able to blame him for holding back, for being a part of the fault that the three family farms were slipping through their fingers. No longer could she blame him for letting his enjoyment of Susie Burkholder blind his eyes to higher and nobler places.

Luke sighed, thinking about the money that would come his way. Then he thought again of Susie. *Funny how she seems to require so little. She just wants attention and affection from me. So why am I so concerned about money if Susie isn't?* His father, Reuben, didn't seem to care much for money. In fact, most of the men he knew didn't care about it either. Or did they?

Maybe there was something he wasn't aware of, some secret passion missing from his constitution. His mother, Rachel, seemed to think so. Luke could see her disappointment in the way she looked at him when they had conversations about money and farms. The accusation was there, the blame that he didn't care enough about what really mattered in life — security.

But *did* it really matter? He so easily could just have let it go. Yet here was the letter in his pocket, surely promising otherwise.

Thoughts of last Sunday with Susie, her eyes glowing with the pleasure of having him in her parents' house, crossed his mind. How she brought out the cookies and brownies on a plate, just a plain white one, nothing fancy. He could tell that she was delighted from the way the cookies lay against each other, the brownies touching just so, the crumbs brushed off the plate and out of sight. Susie cared deeply about him.

It all felt like the old buggy blanket he used. Worn? *Yes.* Poor? *Yes.* But comfortable, at ease, and having a place in his life. Why disturb it, uproot it like a weed in the garden? That's what this letter now felt like — a danger with its claws out for him, drawing him away to who knows where. Why not just put the letter back and forget it?

Then he remembered his mother, what she would say and how she would look if he told her that he had a letter, gotten it out of Emma's mailbox, and then put it back. *Luke,* she would say, *I can't believe what you've done.*

Her eyes would say, *You are as worthless as your father. A hopeless wreck of a man, who will settle for anything as long as your bed is warm and food is on the table. Never mind that the food is meager and stringy and the bed is covered with hand-me-down quilts your mother made for her wedding night.*

Lift your head higher, she would say, without saying a word, her eyes flashing at him. *Remember Rebecca,* she would say, as he was even thinking now, the image of her going through his mind.

Luke touched the letter in his pocket. He would take it home as soon as he could, let

40

the chips fall where they may. Susie would still be Susie, there for him if he needed her, but there was no reason to let that stop him from walking through a door if one should open. If it was open, he would walk through it.

Letting his breath out, Luke turned the key on the New Holland, waiting while the timer ran down, indicating it was warming up. He then started the engine. It roared to life, black smoke pouring out for a few seconds. Slowly he drove out of the barn, refraining from going too fast until the engine was thoroughly warmed up.

Once through the gate, he got to work on moving the feeding bins with a vengeance, urgency now pushing him on, the news in his pocket needing to be told at home.

The cattle followed him around, seeming to enjoy the spectacle of the semi-airborne feeding bins bouncing across the ground. A few times he had to slow down lest he hit a cow with a steel bin. The delays were frustrating, but broken legs or ribs on the cattle would not be easily explained and would keep him here till late in the day.

With all three bins finally moved from the slippery mud and restocked with new hay, Luke went into the house. He told Emma that he was done for the day and was leaving. For a moment he thought his eyes would betray him with their guilt. Then he got his emotions under control, remembering what was at stake.

With the horse harnessed, Luke was on his way, taking care to drive at the proper speed out of Emma's driveway. On the way home, his courage faltered again, the seriousness of what he was doing pressing in. Should he return the letter to Emma's mailbox?

No, having left the farm, Emma would surely see him returning. And there would be his mother's wrath to contend with if he faltered now. She would surely find out. In her presence, he would give himself away. His guilt before her would betray him even more than his guilt over taking Emma's letter.

Arriving home, Luke saw his father come out of the barn and pause to watch him drive in.

I'll have to wait to see Mother. He wants me to do something with the chores.

Pulling up, Luke jumped out to unhitch. His father came over to the other side of the buggy to help with the traces, saving Luke from having to walk around.

"I'm glad to see you home early, Luke," he said. "I have to go into town. The water main broke during that last storm we had. I only found it today. Wasn't sure how I was going to feed the cows yet. But this really helps out."

"How many bales have to go out yet?"

"Only one to the back pasture. I was getting ready when I noticed the wet ground on the west side. The cattle in the upper pasture are already done. You ought to get right to it before dark."

"I have to tell Mom something first," Luke stated hastily. "It shouldn't take long."

"Just get right to it then."

"How are you going in? You could use my horse."

"I'm already harnessed up." Reuben motioned toward the barn. "I need a fresh horse anyway. Have to get to the supply place before they close at five."

"Want me to help you hitch up?"

"Sure, I'm in a hurry."

Assuming that his father was using his double-seated surrey to bring materials home, Luke went over to pull the buggy out. His parents' surrey was parked inside the barn during winter because they typically used their single buggy for most trips — it was small and light and had just enough room to fit the two of them.

After pushing the barn door open, he

brought the buggy out by the time his father returned with the horse. From there it was a simple few minutes to get the horse under the shafts and his father on the road. As the buggy turned south on the paved road, Luke walked toward the house.

His mother was in the kitchen, preparing a salad. Peppers, tomatoes, and cauliflower lay on the counter, waiting to be added.

"I've got something you'll be interested in," he announced, sure no one else was in the house, but glancing around just to be sure.

"There's no one here," she told him, wiping her hands on her white apron. "What is it?"

He sat down at the kitchen table, producing the letter from his pocket, "A letter to Emma's lawyer. She just took it out to her mailbox this morning."

"Really?" Rachel took a seat and reached for the letter. Once in her grasp, she turned it over carefully.

She walked over to where steam was rising from the teakettle and ran the edge of the envelope over the rising vapors, carefully removing the torn pieces of paper. Opening the envelope, she removed the letter and returned to her seat. Unfolding the paper, she read out loud.

Dear Mr. Bridgeway, Esquire,
Please, first of all accept my gratitude again for your consenting to visit with me here some two weeks ago. In a continuation of our conversation, I have arrived at a final decision on the disposal of my assets. Due to my continued serious illness, I wish to deal with the money appropriations to my family first and the three farms given out according to my wishes.

You can determine the amount given to my relatives by tripling the percentage basis used by my brother, Millet, in his will. From the list I gave you, please have this amount given to each relative.

At this, Rachel paused. "I still have a copy of my father's will. We can easily figure out how much that amounts to."

"Okay, so go on. I want to hear about the farms."

Rachel, finally proud of Luke, continued reading.

Then please name Rebecca Keim, of Union, Ohio, the daughter of Lester and

Mattie Keim, as the primary beneficiary of all my property.

Rachel gasped. Luke stood up straight.

This is all contingent upon the same clause that Millet had placed when he first had your father draw his will when I was still in my early twenties. The clause being that Rebecca Keim must not under any circumstances marry a non-Amish person. Amish is to be defined as a church which does not allow for the driving of motor vehicles. She may, as I have, remain in an unmarried state, if she so wishes.

I am aware that there are considerable assets involved and that my brother did not have as many when he made the gesture toward me out of his deep concern for my well-being. Yet he remained true to his promise, even when his possessions increased, believing that he was under the Lord's blessing.

I will proceed under the same belief and would appreciate it if you would notify Rebecca Keim of this decision by certified letter as soon as convenient. I will

not need to be notified of this cor-
respondence between the two of you but
will wait for you to contact me to sign
any necessary papers.

Sincerely,
Emma Miller
Milroy, Indiana

Rachel's face was white. "She's doing it,
and this time it's not even in the family."

Luke's mind was whirling. He barely
heard his mother. He simply said, "I have
to go do the chores." His body felt strange,
out of focus. But before he got to the door,
he turned and said, "Get that letter sealed
again. I'll drop it off in the mail tomorrow.
Emma will never miss it."

When his mother didn't reply, Luke
looked at her.

"We're not mailing it," Rachel declared,
her lips bloodless.

"We have to!" he said.

"Do your chores," she said, rising and
returning to her salad. "The Lord will help
us somehow. We'll yet overcome this evil.
We have to."

CHAPTER SIX

John, his mind continually wandering to thoughts of Rebecca and when she might return, forced himself to the task at hand. He was in the middle of showing a mid-sized cherry wood chest, finished in a natural stain with recessed hinges, to a young couple who had just walked in a few minutes before. They would be, he hoped, his last customers of the day.

"We're looking for something for our daughter for Christmas," the lady told him, her blue eyes sparkling. Bending over the chest, she ran her fingers over the heavily grained cherry. "Perfect for Candice," she half whispered, affection in her voice.

"How are you getting it home?" Candice's father asked, standing back from the chest in question, more interested in the price tag at the moment, which he couldn't seem to locate.

"That's why I had you remove the backseat of the Navigator this morning," she said. "I thought I might find something exactly like this. They have wonderful things here."

He nodded, then asked, "Sure this fits? I still want that Panasonic screen. Today — if possible."

"They don't sell those here. Do you?" she asked, glancing at John.

"No," he said, not certain what a Panasonic screen was, but assuming it had to do with television.

"See," she told her husband, triumphantly, "you can get the Panasonic on the way home. Probably at Circuit City. With the size you want, it has to be delivered anyway. This now," she said, her fingers following a V-shaped grain of dark cherry halfway across the top, "is the thing of dreams. It goes with us today."

The man chuckled, glancing at John. "You watch football?"

"No," John shook his head and replied, "not really."

"Thought so." His chuckle turned into a grin. "Watching the game on a new fifty-eight inch plasma is a dream."

"Just ignore him," the woman told John. "*This* is what we want. A real Amish hope chest for Candice. A quilt for her too. Just to start things off. A real jump-start to her *hope* life. Perhaps one of those." She motioned across the room with her eyes. "From there Candice can come up with her own ideas. Isn't that right?"

"What is Candice going to do with a hope chest?" he asked. "She's only five."

Her eyes regained the sparkle John had seen earlier. "You Amish have hope chests, don't you?" She directed the question to John.

"I'm not sure." John found himself searching for an answer. "My older sister had a cedar chest."

"There you go," she pronounced in victory, turning in her husband's direction. "That's what I want for Candice — what the Amish girls have. Something to keep her in touch with reality. The way things are messed up in this world — just look at the political situation. This is the perfect touch. A real Amish hope chest. Right in her own room."

He shrugged. "I suppose she can use all the help she can get."

"We'll take it," she announced with zest, turning toward John. "Let's get it paid for and then packed into the Navigator. I've got some blankets to use so it won't get scratched on the trip back home. You will help load it, won't you?"

"Sure," John assured her. "We have shipping too, at an extra charge if you want that. It then comes right to your door."

"I thought the blankets were for the screen." The husband was protesting the inevitable. "Why not ship this? Then we can have the screen home by tonight."

"The screen can ship," she told him firmly. "There's nothing special about a new television. This," she said, running her hand over the cherry grain again, "I want to bring home myself." She smiled, but her husband was still looking for the price tag.

"Will that be all then?" John asked, clearing his throat and remembering her interest in the quilt but not wanting to push too hard. He flipped over the tiny price tag and busied himself writing the size and price on his clipboard. He saw the husband register the price and wince.

With that look, John figured the big screen he planned to purchase must have just gotten a few inches smaller and might get even smaller if the quilt was still in play. Feeling sympathy for the man, he was about to walk toward the checkout counter.

"The quilt," she exclaimed into her husband's ear. "Can't forget that. Could be a long time before we get up here again. We can't give Candice an empty hope chest for Christmas. What a horrible start to a dream — with an empty chest. Show me what you have," she said, glancing in John's direction, her eyes still carrying the alarm of her just spoken thoughts.

John avoided the man's eyes, fell into his responsibilities as the salesman, and followed the wife over to where the quilts hung on a rack. The first one she stopped at had a floral arrangement design. The center was dominated by a flowerpot. Its flowers protruded up and down, past the sides, and everything was held visually in place by two circles.

"Don't think so," she muttered to herself, "a little overdone. Let's see . . ." She moved over to the next quilt, nestled closely beside its companion. Her eyes ran over the cross in the center, its crossed arms of equal length, ends flaring with eight-sided stars. Another larger cross outlined the smaller one, the sort which graced the Christian shields of the knights of old. Beyond that was a repeat of an even larger version, going all the way to the edges of the quilt.

"No," she said in John's direction, who was waiting respectfully, his tablet ready. "Most certainly not hope chest material."

John nodded because he agreed, sale or

no sale, the truth was the truth. The husband, having done his own evaluation agreed for other reasons. "I think you're right. Maybe this one over here . . . Now that's perfect. Take a look at this one."

She turned toward her husband and crossed the short space between the two racks to the quilt in question. Coming in close and then stepping back, she said nothing as she looked the quilt over. The center had a circle of squares, overlaying each other like fallen dominoes. Each square was made of multicolored squares within squares, and a six-sided, solid-lined hexagon surrounded the circle of squares. An outer border, made of many brightly colored rectangles, finished the design perfectly.

"That's it," she said firmly. "Perfect. The patchwork of life. So many different colors and ways of putting it together — then overlapping each other. We'll take it."

"I think it's nice too," the husband agreed, then tried quickly to cover up his pleasure at the lower price by a half-hearted protest. "It could be quite mature for a five-year-old. But I suppose Candice will grow into it."

"It shows her where to go," she said, standing in front of the quilt, her face contented.

The husband was obviously in a leaving mood. "So let's get this stuff into the Navigator, then on the road."

John wrote the price and description on his tablet, copying down the name of the maker of the quilt, which was how they kept track of quilt inventory. The price varied with each quilt, both from Aden's evaluation of its intricacy and from the quilter's own report on the time it took to make. This one had Mrs. C. Kemp's name written on the back of the price tag.

Excusing himself, John went into the storage room at the back of the store. Finding a box and a step stool, John returned to where the quilt hung. All the quilts were fastened by their upper edges to the frames, a little out of reach of even someone of his height.

Asking both of them if they would stand on either side of the quilt to keep it from brushing the floor, John undid the snaps on top and released it carefully. The folding process began even before he was off the stool. "Makes it easier with help," John said to express his thanks. Taking the half-folded quilt, he completed the task by himself.

When the woman noticed the tag on top of the quilt inside the open box, she bent over to look at the name. "Who is Mrs. C. Kemp? Is she the one who made this?"

John nodded.

"Can you give me any information about her? What she's like?"

"Sure. That would be Clara Kemp, about sixty years old, I think. Her husband died of cancer some years ago." John searched his memory. "Five years, now," he concluded. "She lives by herself just outside Unity. Still keeps up the small farm her husband left her. Most of her income comes from these quilts though."

"She's Amish?"

John nodded, smiling and thinking of Clara sitting in the back row in church on Sundays. She often held a grandchild in her lap when one of her daughters needed help. Clara was as faithful and upbuilding a member as they came.

"Oh. That's perfect!" she exclaimed, delighted with the news. "What an excellent role model for Candice. Hardworking woman, no doubt. Suffering her share in life. She must have a heart of gold — working with her hands." She stroked the quilt lovingly, as if to reach out and touch the woman who had stitched the delicate threads in each design.

"Clara is a godly woman," John agreed because Clara was just that, and he felt it was appropriate to mention it. Pride was a great pitfall, he knew, and praise could knock a person down quicker than anything. But Clara wasn't there to hear him, and so he said it.

Lifting the box, with the quilt bulging out of the top, John walked to the back counter. "They're ready for checkout," he told Sharon. "A chest and one of Clara's quilts. It's the last one I think. You might want to tell your mother we need more."

She reached for the invoice. "I'll see that mother gets told. I think Clara's working as hard as she can already."

"Maybe one of her daughters can help," John suggested, although he doubted whether they had time. As his memory told him, all three of them had large families.

"They're all busy." Sharon confirmed his thoughts. "I heard her tell mother that the other Sunday."

John filed a note in his mind to tell Aden later that the price of Clara's quilts needed to be raised, then went back to where the husband was ready to begin loading the cherry chest.

At the counter the wife waited while Sharon copied the numbers on the ticket and added them up with their solar-powered calculator. "You have a hope chest?" she asked as Sharon was writing the total on the bottom.

Sharon chuckled. "Do I have a hope chest? Don't know if it's a hope chest or not. It's a cedar chest."

"Why cedar?" she wondered more than asked, "John mentioned that back there too."

"Keeps things nice," Sharon volunteered. "Something about the cedar wood — I think. Mom says it preserves clothing — almost makes them better. It might even keep the bugs out too. I'm not sure."

The thought crossed her mind in horror. "But the one I just bought was cherry. I'm sure of that. John just said —"

"Oh," Sharon replied, quick to assure her, "all our chests are cedar-lined, even when they have different wood on the outside. You get a different look that way, but still the full benefits of the cedar."

"Oh," she said, sighing deeply, "that's so good to hear. Here I thought I had just made a drastic mistake. Me and my haste. I do so want Candice to have a proper chest. She's my daughter."

"They're all wonderful chests," Sharon said, speaking from personal experience. "The different wood can make it more expensive, so we have simple cedar." Sharon wrinkled up her face.

"Well," the wife ventured, "I guess I don't own a furniture store. I get to buy the nice wood instead of sell it."

"Cedar is nice," Sharon assured her, handing the bill across the counter.

She wrote out the check, gave it to Sharon, and laid the pen on the counter, finishing just in time to see John and her husband come through the front door.

"All set," John announced. "Hope you like everything."

She assured him that they would, and with thanks all around, they left.

It was then that thoughts of Rebecca returned.

CHAPTER SEVEN

"You're going to have to take care," Mattie said mildly when Rebecca showed up in the kitchen. "Rushing down those stairs like that. One of these days you're going to trip, fall right down, and break something."

"I'll try — to slow down, I mean. I'm just in a hurry to get busy I guess."

"I could use the help." Mattie motioned toward the dough on the kitchen table. "Roll that out. The pans are still in the cabinet. You can probably get them in before chore time. I need to start supper. With your help, I guess I won't be late. Just took on a little too much this morning."

Rebecca chuckled at the familiar sight of her busy mother.

"I know. I'm always busy," Mattie said, looking for the correct cooking pot for heating the canned corn. "You don't have to laugh."

"It's just good to be home," Rebecca said,

letting the feeling of it all flow through her, the rhythm and pattern of its work was comforting at the moment. Opening the drawer, she found the rolling pin and set to work on the dough.

Glancing up when the clatter of buggy wheels sounded outside, Mattie said, "The children are home." Moments later the door burst open, and a rush of small feet filled the living room.

"Rebecca's home," ten-year-old Katie said, sticking her head into the kitchen. "Yummy — cinnamon rolls!" Tall for her age, she had black hair like Rebecca. Her sisters were right behind her.

"Hi, girls," Rebecca told them and glanced their way.

"Why are you home?" nine-year-old Viola asked.

"Now be nice," Mattie told her. "You ought to be glad. She's finishing the cinnamon rolls."

"I don't know how to do that anyway," Viola said dryly. "She'll just boss us around now that's she's home."

"That's because you need bossing. I can't be everywhere at once," Mattie said.

"You can help by putting these in the oven," Rebecca said. "Practice is what you need. The sooner you start the better."

"See," Viola declared, "that's what she does."

"It's good for you," Mattie stated simply. "Now listen to what she says."

"I'm still in my school clothes," Viola protested.

"It doesn't matter." Mattie said. "You'll hardly get those dirty. You're just putting pans in the oven."

Viola made a face and joined her sister in front of the kitchen table, arms stretched out to keep the proper distance between the pans and her school dress.

"You're just afraid James will see your dirty dress tomorrow," Viola taunted Katie as they stood there.

"I am not," Katie retorted.

"Yes, you are. I saw you smile at him today." Viola wrinkled her face into a fake smile, her features contorted, her head tilted sideways.

"I was not. I was smiling to myself."

"He's in your grade. He sits right across from you," Viola stated, as if that proved it all.

"Be quiet, girls," Rebecca said. "The oven is ready. I'll open the door."

"She's so bossy." Viola made another face.

"And you are the pest number one," Katie

informed her. "Like a little insect. Buzz, buzz."

"I am not!" Viola retorted. "*You* are. You little worm — wiggle, wiggle."

"That does it," Mattie said. "I think one little girl needs something."

Without further ado, Mattie took Viola by the hand and disappeared into the bedroom. Sounds of solid whacks soon came, followed by muffled cries.

Rebecca and Katie said nothing, solemnly transferring the pans of cinnamon rolls to the oven and taking no pleasure in the event in the bedroom. They accepted it for what it was, the necessary ebb and flow of growing up into something resembling civilized human life.

Letting the oven door shut gently, Rebecca made sure the temperature was right. "There. That's done."

Behind them, Mattie appeared with a tear-streaked Viola in tow. "Both you girls go change. And no more arguing. Is that understood?"

Katie nodded, heading for the stair door, careful not to look at Viola lest she mistake the gesture as hostile. Viola only sniffled, going over to wet her hands in the kitchen sink and running them over her face. She pulled a piece of paper towel off the roll on the countertop to dry herself, dropping the crumpled result in the wastebasket in the corner.

The younger sisters, Martha and Ada, were already coming down the stairs, having changed into work clothing. With her back turned to the kitchen, Viola must have thought her actions were hidden. She made a face — just a quick, deep contortion — without turning around.

Maybe it was that Mattie was watching, expecting that sort of thing, or the brief dark looks on Martha and Ada's faces. Mattie turned around, exclaiming in an exasperated tone, "I told you to stop that. I guess you haven't had enough yet. Let's go see about this again."

"I'll behave — I will," Viola protested. "I didn't mean it."

"If you don't watch it, you'll get spanked for lying yet," Mattie pronounced, unpersuaded. "That was not a nice face."

"I was teasing," Viola insisted. "They were laughing at me."

"I don't think so," Mattie told her. "I could see them."

Second-grader Martha and first-grader Ada adamantly shook their heads when Mattie glanced at them for confirmation.

"They were *going* to," Viola proclaimed.

"Okay — this is enough." Mattie was tired of the conversation. "Your attitude is bad. When you get spanked, you don't make faces at other people. It's not their fault. It's your own fault. And don't be changing your story."

"I didn't," Viola insisted. "They just want to see me spanked again."

"No, we don't," Martha and Ada said together.

"Yes, they do," Viola quickly added. "They don't like me."

Mattie was already moving, taking Viola along by the arm, ignoring her remark.

Preparing warm water in the sink, Rebecca squeezed a few drops of Ivory liquid soap in and shut off the faucet. "Use this water," she told her sisters. They already knew how it was done, but conversation was needed at the moment. Normal conversation on normal things to give one the hope that things would again be normal.

The front door opened as Martha and Ada were wiping the table down. Rebecca was doing a quick check on the cinnamon rolls in the oven, when Matthew walked in. "Awful quiet in here," he commented, standing in the kitchen door opening.

"Viola's getting spanked," Martha said soberly.

"Two times," Ada echoed.

"A tough cookie," Matthew said.

"Maybe this one will be enough," Rebecca told them comfortingly, sincerely hoping that it was.

"Two times." Matthew whistled under his breath. "Who likes whoopings that much?"

"We learn different," Rebecca said, venturing a guess.

"But that's a hard way," Matthew replied, a bit puzzled. Still thinking about it, he glanced toward the bedroom door where the sounds of discipline were subsiding.

"You learn hard in some things too," Rebecca reminded him.

Lost in his own world, Matthew's face brightened. "It's because she's a girl," he pronounced. "*Girls* learn hard."

Rebecca glared at him. "You have your hard spots too."

He ignored her.

"He turned red today," Martha whispered quietly in Rebecca's direction, just loud enough for Matthew to hear, though he pretended not to.

"As she walked by him, his ears turned pink," Martha added, chuckling at the memory.

Matthew still was pretending not to hear, his ears still red.

"He's just growing up," Rebecca whispered back to Martha, making sure it was loud enough to carry to Matthew.

"It's not my fault. Like a whooping," he finally protested, anger flashing in his face.

"Maybe it's not totally Viola's fault either," Rebecca said, raising her eyebrows in his direction.

He was still pondering that when Mattie returned with Viola, the tears dried this time.

"Tell them," Mattie said simply, her words at a minimum. The afternoon was slipping away and supper was still not done.

"Sorry for the face," Viola said, her eyes on the floor.

"Okay — that's better," Mattie sighed. "Now let's get busy with supper. Rebecca, you and Matthew need to start chores, don't you?"

Rebecca glanced at the clock and nodded.

"I'll get changed," Matthew said, leaving for the upstairs and carefully shutting the door behind him. Viola took a seat at the kitchen table, catching her breath as the others went about their work. Slowly she came back into their world, and the minutes went by without further comment on the incident.

CHAPTER EIGHT

Through the kitchen window, Rachel could see Luke open and shut the barn door and begin the chores for the evening. There was no sign of Reuben yet, but she had no doubt he would be returning soon from town, hopefully with the correct part for his broken water main.

God, she prayed, *don't let Emma destroy our lives. Luke deserves better than this. Remember my child. Please. Even if You don't remember me.*

Rachel's salad bowl was on the table. The teakettle whistled loudly, its steam pushing out of the nozzle in a solid funnel and disappearing into nothing inches from its exit. She no longer knew why it was turned on, and so she walked over to flip the gas burner off.

Glancing at the letter still on the counter, she opened it again, willing the words to not be there. Surely there must be some mistake. But without reading, Rachel felt the searing fear accompanying the words. Emma was giving the farms away to someone else.

Not only someone else, but someone not even in the family. Surely it was not true . . . but it was.

Rachel's eyes caught sight of the salad bowl, distracting her. The salad was still not completed. Although she had prepared the lettuce and put it into the bowl, the peppers, tomatoes, and cauliflower sat on the table, yet to be added. Pulled toward it by her ingrained discipline, she began chopping the items into suitable sizes, her mind hazy and stumbling over a thousand chaotic scenarios.

Why would Emma choose Rebecca Keim as the heir? It made absolutely no sense from any angle. There was no family connection, no distant cousins either. How did one go dropping money on people without a reason?

What was the part about not marrying Amish? Rebecca was already dating someone. Was he Amish?

M-Jay's will had said nothing about Emma marrying Amish. Rachel knew that because she had been there when the will was read. Every word from the lips of that fancy lawyer had sounded in her ears. She clearly remembered him telling them all what was and what was not to be.

Had the lawyer lied? But how could that be? Lawyers from the English surely did not lie. They have judges who oversee such matters.

She searched her mind, hoping to find some tidbit of information that would shed light on the subject, some dropped reference from her English neighbors, or some article she had read in school.

Nothing Rachel thought of made any sense.

Her knife easily sliced through the tomatoes, its cutting edge kept to a fine sharpness. Caught up in her vigor, the pieces fell to the side in all shapes and sizes, their red juice spreading into a little pool on her chopping block.

While slicing the next tomato, the knife found her finger, making a long cut and laying open the skin. The pain never registered, blocked by her already overtaxed senses. It was the blood that caught her attention.

She jerked her hand away, dropped the knife, and pressed the wound together with her fingers. More concerned with the contamination of her tomatoes than with the injury, she carefully separated the blood-splattered ones.

Still holding her wound, she washed the finger under the kitchen sink, only then going to the bathroom for a bandage. *God is smiting us.* The thought stung stronger than the pain under the freshly applied bandage. *It's as plain as day. I can't even cut tomatoes anymore. Something I've been doing since I was a girl. We must have sinned greatly. That's what He's trying to tell us. He wants the sin atoned for. There can be no other reason for this terrible trouble.*

Cleaning the table of the contaminated tomatoes, Rachel placed them in an extra bowl. Moving through the kitchen, she caught a glimpse through the kitchen window of the returning Reuben. She shook the bowl to hide any red stains, making sure the color blended well with its surroundings. The thoughts continued. *The water pipe. It was God's judgment too.*

There was no doubt in her mind that God, reaching all the way down from the lofty heights of glory, had used His mighty finger to pop that pipe wide open. How else to explain what Reuben had found today — the very day, he claimed, it had occurred. It would normally take days before Reuben found such a thing. The whole lower pasture could well be under water before he noticed it, yet today he had walked back and discovered what God wanted him to see.

A ruptured pipe, so innocent and yet done to send them a message of displeasure from the One who knew everything. Rachel shud dered. The sting of her thoughts reached deep into her soul, much deeper than the pain of her finger. She searched desperately for answers. *How was this then to be atoned for? Yet it must be for much was at stake. The sin or sins must be found and cut out.*

Rachel hurried through her supper preparations, already behind schedule, pondering the situation. It came to her rather quickly. Her mind sized up the offered thought. It was perfect. She moved even faster now that she knew the solution. Endued as if with holy zeal, she believed the letter's contents were no longer about lowly concerns of money. She was laying her hands on information regarding the lofty laws of the church. She knew the money itself was as dirt in the eyes of her husband, not worthy of mention in the hallowed halls of his sanctified mind. But the law of the church — well, that was something Reuben wouldn't be able to ignore.

Was Reuben, as deacon, not charged with their enforcement and held accountable for holding their place? Did not the wheels of his buggy travel miles on many a Saturday afternoon and evening, all while there were duties to be done on the farm? Didn't Reuben take his duty seriously to seek out those who strayed — rebuking, calling, exhorting them back to the fold? For once, what had been a chafing in her life turned into pleasantness.

How like God, she thought, *to supply a way of escape in time of trouble.* She, who desperately needed to find sin in the church, was married to a deacon.

Rachel sat the finished salad on the counter, hope swirling in her for the first time since reading the letter Luke had brought home. Maybe this would be easier than she had figured. Reuben — who would have thought it — was now her best hope.

What to do with the letter though? Should I keep it? Do I need it now? Why not just mail it as Luke wanted and do away with the risk?

Pondering the option, Rachel wanted to be certain. What was right or wrong did not enter her calculations, only what was best for her. She would keep the letter, she decided. Emma would think the letter got lost in the mail. Never being the wiser for it, this might buy some time before the lawyer began his work.

After going to the basement, she returned with cans of beef and corn, the corn from the summer prior, the beef from a steer they raised on the farm and butchered that fall. Tonight's supper would be simple. The salad was made, but there would be no dessert. They would survive.

By the time Luke came in, with Reuben not far behind him, everything was ready. The beef was steaming in its own juice, and the corn was hot. Luke said nothing as he came in from the utility room, leaving his shoes as well as his boots outside. She saw his eyes searching for the letter. *Surely the boy didn't expect to find the letter in plain sight. Does he think I'm stupid?*

"Supper ready?" Reuben asked, not waiting for an answer as he went to wash up. Rachel didn't respond as the steaming items on the table were an obvious answer. Luke, drying his hands on a towel, tried his best to look comfortable and then found his usual place at the table.

"No dessert?" Reuben asked, pulling out his chair, scraping the legs on the hardwood floor as he sat down.

"Not tonight," Rachel stated simply. "I'll make — oh, maybe pies for Sunday. Did you fix the water pipe?"

"I'll dig it up," Reuben said, "maybe tomorrow. At least the hardware store had the parts. You never know nowadays. Stores don't like to keep things in stock."

"Isn't it a bad leak?" Rachel asked, seeing Reuben stiffen. *Probably expecting me to badger him.*

"Let's pray," Reuben said quickly.

Trying to put off the lecture, she thought as they bowed their heads.

Reuben led out in a German prayer. Rarely did he pray in silence anymore. Rachel figured this came from knowing many of the German prayers by heart because he read them in church so many times. That Reuben might like the words or their meaning had not occurred to her. This frequent, out loud praying had not been practiced in their early years of marriage. It began soon after the deacon ordination and so was only explainable in her mind as driven by the ego of his office.

Reuben lifted his head from prayer, letting that be his answer for now, she figured, since what else was there to say. The water line was not dug out, and Reuben sure wasn't going back out in the dark to do it.

"It'll wait — I suppose," Rachel said. "Luke might be able to help you in the morning."

"I suppose," Reuben allowed. He took the spoon and helped himself to a generous por-

tion of meat before passing the bowl on to
Luke.

CHAPTER NINE

John pushed himself away from the table, his plate scraped clean of his mother's Friday night tradition, meatball stew. It came from a recipe that had been in the family for years.

Dessert was Pennsylvania-style Hustle Cake. It must have been baked today because John had not seen it last night. He looked at the cake's appealing freshness, contemplating a large piece.

"*Goot essas* as usual," John's father, Isaac Miller, commented to no one in particular.

Miriam only nodded her head, not expecting anything less from herself or more from Isaac. After all these years, her husband didn't always voice his thoughts, but they knew each other's roles at suppertime. She, her good cooking, and he, that it was to be enjoyed.

To Isaac bad cooking was only a faint and rare memory from his 1-W service in the late sixties. Before and since then, he had been surrounded by his mother's and now his wife's excellent touch in the kitchen.

Age had left his body round in the middle, the work in his harness shop not supplying much physical exercise. His forceful Sunday sermons, which he had been delivering since his ordination in his early thirties, were his only form of exercise.

Isaac's weight worried Miriam, although why she didn't worry about her own tendencies in that direction was not certain. It could have been that Miriam's family had little history of heart trouble, while Isaac's did. To be left alone, to spend her remaining years without Isaac, was often on her mind.

"Go easy on the cake, Isaac," Miriam told him. "You're getting older."

"Ach, du denkcht zu feel," he told her, smiling broadly. "The good Lord has many years for me yet. Don't worry so much."

"I can't help it. Heart trouble runs in your family."

"One little piece of cake won't change that," he allowed, cutting himself a generous portion.

"If that is a little one," she said dryly, "what would a big one be like?"

"Big," he said, still smiling.

"John at least knows better," she retorted, glancing at the smaller piece John was transferring to his plate.

"He looks thin," Isaac said, not looking at his son. "Underfed."

"You should think about exercising," she said. "The bishop just got himself a walking cane, so he can go out in the evenings. I think you ought to try it yourself."

"That's because he doesn't preach as hard as I do. It's easier for him. I have to work on my Sundays. Why preach and walk too?"

"So," Miriam asked, "you think your preaching hard gets you special favor with *Da Hah?*"

"Well," he said, as he cut a small piece of cake to fit his mouth and lifted it reverently upward. The spoon was steady, but the piece wobbled under its own weight, toppling back onto his plate.

"See," she exclaimed gleefully, "even *Da Hah* thinks so. He's on my side."

"It just fell off," he retorted, pretending indignation, getting the piece into his mouth on the second try, chewing it carefully, and savoring its sweetness.

"What's wrong with you, John?" she asked, abruptly changing the subject, turning toward her son. "Your piece is so small — don't like it?"

He shook his head. "No, it's not that."

"You don't look well." She studied him, placing her hand on his forehead.

He knew the familiar gesture, but wished his mother would stop it. He was a grown man now.

"You worried?" she asked.

"She hasn't written," John said, thinking that was explanation enough. "Or called," he added, just in case it wasn't.

"She's fine, John," his father told him, getting in on the conversation, the last of his cake heading toward his mouth. "Babies take time."

John figured now was the time to tell his parents his news.

"I asked her a few weeks ago to marry me."

"Oh?" was all his mother said.

"Said yes?" was Isaac's response.

John nodded.

"It's good you do have the eighty acres then." Isaac pushed his plate away. "When will you start remodeling?"

"This summer maybe . . ." His parents' confidence was disconcerting to him, making him certain his present fears were best left unsaid.

"She's a nice girl," Miriam added. "Always thought so. Good family too. Set a date yet?"

"Next spring — maybe." John said it easily enough, even with how he was feeling.

"Our only boy," Isaac commented, nostalgia in his voice. "Even they grow up."

"Makes us all old," Miriam said. "Exercising holds it off . . . a little at least."

Isaac refused to take the bait. "So she's not let you know when she's coming back."

John shook his head, not trusting the sound of his own voice. It was embarrassing how this girl was getting to him, and he wished not to show it. He should be confident and not so worried.

"It's all the work," Miriam said, as if reading his thoughts. "Rebecca had a lot of things to do. Women work hard when babies come."

Isaac pretended to glare at her. "We men do nothing?"

"Scarce little — *afterward.*" She squinted her eyes at him.

"I did change a few diapers though," he reminded her, unoffended.

"I suppose so," she allowed. "So what should John do?"

"Ah. She'll be around soon," Isaac said, his voice reassuring.

The comfort did little for John.

Miriam must have noticed. "Have you thought of going over to her parents' place?"

"Now?" he asked, trying to keep the feeling out of his voice.

"Well, why not?" She shrugged her shoulders. "They might know something."

"Maybe she's already home," Isaac said, adding his opinion.

"How would that look?" John asked. "Home and not letting me know."

John waited for Miriam's response, trusting his mother more when it came to these matters. His father was a good preacher, holding the congregation spellbound with one of his Sunday morning stemwinders, but here his mother was the knowledgeable one.

"I think you should go and find out," she said. "That is, if you have to know."

Isaac, noting his son's face, said with a grin, "Glad my time of courting is over."

"Don't want to do it again?" Miriam asked, pretending she wasn't listening for his answer.

"Nope. You're staying with me till the end."

"*Da Hah* told you that too?"

"No," he allowed, "I just need you."

Miriam smiled at that.

John cleared his throat. "Maybe I'll run over. It's almost dark, but it's still early."

"Whatever you think," Miriam told him,

81

getting up to clear the table.

"I'll go now," John said and got up to leave.

Well after John had left for the barn, Isaac asked, "What'd you think about that?"

"I knew something had been bothering him. Wasn't sure what."

"You think Rebecca's good for him?"

"You heard what I said. You were right here."

"I know. He was here too."

"I think she's a nice girl."

"You ever hear anything about — before they moved here?"

"No. They came from Milroy."

He said nothing, staring off into the distance.

"You heard anything?" She was alarmed again.

"No, but that's strange too. There's usually something."

"You should know. You're a minister."

"Sometimes ministers don't know everything."

"So what *do* you know?" she asked undeterred.

"Not a thing," he said puzzled. "Family came with a perfect church letter — never made trouble either."

"So what's wrong with that? You should be happy."

"Nothing to do with happiness."

"You worried then?"

"Don't know — just strange, that's all."

"You think *Da Hah* will have trouble for us then?"

"That's in His will — only He knows."

"But you feel it?"

Isaac shook his head. "It's all in His will. He will give us the strength to bear whatever comes."

"You're just getting old . . . feeling our last one leaving."

"Ya. It might be that."

"And we will grow old — just the two of us. That's not too bad, is it?"

He allowed a smile to spread across his face. "Not with your cooking."

"You're a *shlecht* one," she said, pretending to glare at him, but bending to kiss him on the forehead.

CHAPTER TEN

Rachel Byler was cleaning the kitchen, having first made certain that Reuben was comfortably settled in the living room. Reuben had looked strangely at her, puzzled by the attention, then let it go and relaxed in his recliner. He had now found the Milroy, Indiana, section of the paper and was engrossed in the news. The scribe for the area was usually Margaret, Emery Yoder's wife. Not that it really mattered because there wasn't much room for personal expression in the writing, just a recounting of who had visited and other general happenings. Occasionally diversions were made, slight ones, only detectable if you knew what was going on under the surface. He, of course, did and always went to his home community's article first.

Tonight Reuben scanned the article, finding a listing of visitors at the Sunday service two weeks ago. It usually took that length of time to get the letter from the scribe to Ohio, then printed in the paper, and mailed back to the subscribers. Still it was an efficient way of communication between the Amish communities. Reasonably priced too — which was important.

Margaret said that Bishop Jesse Raber, his wife, and brother-in-law from Daviess County had been visiting. There followed some more names, but he just scanned those.

On Monday night Jacob Weaver had a scare, Margaret continued, when a young calf took a fright, while the youngest boy of the family was tending to it. The boy was doing his chores in the calf pen, laying down a fresh bed of straw. The family dog had entered the calf pen and was following the boy around. This frightened the calf and made it jump against the wall, causing the gasoline lantern that was set on the floor to tip over. When the lantern tipped over, the glass globe apparently absent or broken, the flame ignited the straw.

The carelessness of youth, Reuben thought, *unless maybe the Weavers made a practice of not placing globes on their lanterns, making it easier to light the lantern. Whether or not the Weavers were using lanterns in that condition doesn't matter because this was just a case of carelessness and not a church of-fense. Carelessness.* Da Hah *can handle that on His own — without my help.* With that decision made, Reuben continued to read.

He wondered whether Margaret would put things in the paper that were a church offense. He doubted it, but one never knew. It might slip out inadvertently, he supposed. Not that he wanted such a thing to happen, as many readers far and wide would read the account. The offense would then also have to be dealt with quickly, hopefully with word of the ministry's quick action trickling back around.

Anyway, the young boy yelled for help and had most of the fire stomped out by the time his father arrived. Reuben thought about fires and how they could easily — when burning out of control — take down a barn and destroy livestock in no time at all. He was sure Weaver had a long talk with his son.

Farther down, right after a mention of the snowstorm, Margaret said Nancy Yoder, wife of Amman Yoder, had been to the doctor. That was on Wednesday, more than two weeks ago. The reason for the visit was a checkup because Nancy was having some doubts about the state of her health. Nancy's worst fears were realized when the doctor found a few lumps. That Friday she received the results of the tests the doctor conducted — malignant breast cancer. Treatments at IU Simon Cancer Center in Indianapolis had already begun, according to Margaret. It also noted that Nancy might also seek more treatment in Mexico. *This, Reuben thought, isn't wise, but this too is not a church matter.* He supposed if one had cancer, things might look a little different. Mexico was a land of great suspicions to him, but one never knew until it happened what really might need to be done.

Out in the kitchen, it sounded as if Rachel was on the last of the dishes. *What has gotten into the woman tonight? Why is she being so nice? There must be something going on, but what? Is it money maybe?* Not that Rachel acted this way when she wanted some. Normally she just told him and made things miserable until he relented. The checking account was empty anyway, so it really didn't matter. He sighed. Life would be a lot easier, at least with her, if there were more of the green stuff around. Not that he knew how to get more, but it *would* be easier.

He couldn't imagine what else she would want. But then the thought of Margaret mentioning Mexico came back to him. *Is that what it is? Rachel has always wanted to go to Mexico, dropping hints about it every time someone went down there for treatments. Has she read the article already and wants to visit on pleasure?*

It could be well within the realm of possibilities. If it is that, she will soon be in and drop the hint. He stiffened in preparation. There was simply no way he was going. Not even if he was sick, would he go.

Visions of donkeys balking in the streets, stopping to bray and kick at passing visitors from the States, went through his mind. No doubt white people would stir up the worst in them. Then there were the thieves and the awful food. Returning Amish visitors from medical trips told of thieves snatching purses off the arms of women, of men not even feeling their wallets being lifted from their front pants pockets. Amish men had no back pockets, so these guys must be the real experts. He shuddered in his recliner. Rachel would not be going, and neither would he. And those awful flat pieces of flour they ate!

Even if Rachel got sick, she was not going. If she did go, it would be without him. The going would be simply beyond him — not to mention the cost. The thought occurred to him, *Perhaps she is sick. Maybe that explains her behavior.* But he soon put the thought aside. Sickness was highly unlikely.

Luke had gone upstairs to his room after supper, and Reuben supposed he would soon find out what this was all about. The dishes rattled gently again in the kitchen. It sounded, from his long experience with her habits, that Rachel was down to the last few.

True enough, Reuben had just turned to the next page of the paper, finding Leroy, Michigan, when Rachel came in and took a seat on the couch. He wasn't that interested in the Amish community in Leroy, Michigan, anyway, so he braced himself.

Rachel cleared her throat. "When's next communion?"

Reuben knew good and well Rachel knew when next communion was coming. It came in the spring around Easter, but he answered anyway, "Around Easter." There was no sense in stirring things up, in case he was wrong.

As she nodded, he noticed the bandage on her finger again. Earlier he had seen it but failed to mention anything. "You cut your finger?" he asked, trying to be friendly.

"Yes," she said.

Normally she would have commented on his lack of notice till now . . . but tonight it was just, "Yes." This only increased his nervousness. She really was after something, but there was no use imagining the worst now. He simply waited.

"I thought," she said, pausing to clear her throat, "that perhaps there were some things — church things — that maybe I needed to get done."

His blood running cold at the sound of her words, he contemplated saying nothing, but that carried its own dangers. "Yes," he managed, his lips tense.

"Some things — little things, I guess. Maybe I shouldn't be thinking about them." She almost looked apologetic. "I just want to be prepared."

He nodded. *Prepared for what?* This road looked a little less dangerous than it had a few minutes ago. *Maybe the woman is dying? Preparing for her own passing?* He felt the stirrings of sympathy, concern, and then he remembered Mexico, and the feelings left. His fingers tightened on the newspaper, the printed columns completely going out of focus. "You're not sick?" he asked as calmly as he could, turning toward her.

She smiled, her face showing a trace of amusement. "No. I'm okay. At least on the outside. It's the church that I'm concerned about."

He tilted his head, still looking at her.

She seemed to take a slow breath. "There's so much going on in the world today. You know — sin coming — pushing in when we least expect it. I've been thinking about that."

He still waited, saying nothing partly because he couldn't get any words past his astonishment. She had never been the least concerned about any of this.

"You have been working — on church matters," she continued. "I know you care about it. I've been thinking. I don't do as much as I should."

"Yes," he said cautiously. It was true, but that thought might be dangerous territory too. She didn't interfere in his deacon work, but neither was she one to be there to lend a hand either.

"I might have some dresses — you know — that are a little too . . . well, pushing things." She paused, as if waiting for his reaction.

Whether she had or hadn't, he couldn't remember no matter how much he now tried. "I don't know," he managed, hoping it covered the bases.

From the look on her face, this was apparently not the answer she was looking for. "The light blue one, for instance," she said.

"It's a little formfitting, don't you think? A little short too, for the church standard?" She was still looking intently at him.

His mind was spinning wildly, but it was simply producing no memory of a light blue dress. "I hadn't noticed," he said.

She wrinkled her brow. "I've been thinking about it. Communion is coming up. We really should be — at least I think so — be getting our house in order."

He shrugged, managing to say, "Of course — the church is always important." *Where is she going with this?*

"That's just it," she said. Her face brightening for the first time. "I want to do my part. For much too long — way too long — I haven't done enough. Before communion, I will change that dress. Luke has some socks too. Those blue ones . . ."

"But that's allowed," he said, in spite of himself.

"I don't know," she told him. "Maybe blue, but these are pretty light. It would be better not to push the line, don't you think?"

"Of course," he said. *What else is there to say when a large part of my life's work is to make sure these things do matter?*

"That needs to be changed." She nodded. "Some other things too."

"Are you okay?" he finally asked her,

relaxing a little. This could have been much worse. *Sure,* he told himself, *that was a new leaf for her but familiar ground for me.*

"I need your help," she said, ignoring his question.

He felt himself stiffen again. "You need *me?*"

"Yes — for myself, of course. If you see something — out of order — I need to be told."

"I see," he said, settling back into his chair, not seeing at all. This was a strange evening indeed.

"We have to be *pure,*" she said, getting up to go back to the kitchen. "We need all the help we can get."

He watched her go, completely puzzled, then thinking this new turn might be a benefit to him. A wife, vigorous in her defense of church rules, might even enhance his standing in church.

Relaxing, Reuben turned back to his paper and found Kalona, Iowa's column on the third page, near the top. It was only later that he noticed the uneasy feeling settling into the pit of his stomach.

CHAPTER ELEVEN

Slapping the reins, driving along the top of Wheat Ridge, John succeeded in getting extra speed out of his horse. He soon regretted it. He felt conflicted, not wanting to be seen hurrying to the Keim's home, yet wanting to get there quickly.

What if she isn't there? What if she is still in Milroy taking care of her aunt's baby? How would it look — me driving to her place? Can I climb out of this buggy and tie up with no Rebecca around to make things look appropriate? What about walking to the front door? What am I going to say when they open the door?

Bein yusht nei shtobt, he would say, feeling thoroughly stupid. *Just stopped in. How would that sound? Standing on the front porch, with my hat in my hand.*

Just stopped in. Stopped in for what? Their girl obviously. Rebecca, who might not be home, and he, John her boyfriend and supposedly the husband to be, shouldn't they know where the other is?

John almost pulled back on the reins but couldn't. He simply had to know, whatever the embarrassment would be. Tomorrow was Saturday, and he could come back then, but that would require turning back, facing his parents, and explaining his retreat.

Why is the world so complicated? Where is the simplicity of things? I had felt those feelings for Rebecca at the bridge and hope to feel them now.

There it had been just her and him, the whole world spread out at their feet to walk in it as they saw fit. *Why weren't things staying like that?* The question surprised and puzzled him.

Was this what all good things became? He had been happy then, and now he wasn't. Was this because happiness was always followed by cloudy weather? He didn't know for sure. Neither of his parents had ever mentioned anything like this, but maybe they wouldn't. They had raised him to be a faithful member of the church and to follow God. Surely with that record behind him and with the good parents he had, he would be okay.

It will have to be okay, he thought. *It just has to be.* Glancing to his right, the eighty acres on Wheat Ridge came into view. He couldn't see much in the early evening dusk, but his mind's eye could see it all clearly. The single white framed house sitting on the knoll, red barn in the background, both built twenty years ago, still in good condition for the most part. It was the place he wanted so desperately to call home — not just his home but home with Rebecca.

He had purchased the property late last year, with careful thought and knowing that he wanted to ask Rebecca the question. Waiting to buy until he asked hadn't been an option because such places sold quickly along Wheat Ridge. The place had been offered to him without a realtor, the family knowing his family.

Renters were living there now and would stay until the summer before the wedding. There was no sense in living there alone, when a little income could be realized on the side and while he was still welcome at home. Miriam and Isaac had gladly lent him the money for the purchase, at a little better than the interest rate they could get from CDs at the bank. The purchase had been a little scary, considering Rebecca had not said "yes" yet, but it was worth the purchase, he had figured, even if she turned him down. He had been so certain that they were right for each other and meant to spend their lives together, that his imagination failed him when he tried to consider any other girl. Being turned down would have been devastating, and he knew that with a certainty that sent chills up and down his spine.

He felt like pulling back on the reins again, but slapped them instead. What was wrong with him, he wondered? Why couldn't he be a little more self-confident — unafraid of losing? Was it because there really was a danger? Or was it just him and his fears making shadows out of nothing?

It must be him, he decided, and urged his horse on. Pulling past the first houses in Harshville, the sound of the horse's hooves on the pavement echoed in the trees.

Lights were on in the houses around him. He could tell most of them were English because of the brightness of the lighting. It was different in the Amish homes, which had the soft glow of lanterns. Looking at the lights, he wondered if Rebecca could ever go English. The question made its way into his consciousness and stirred up his fears again.

Surely not, he almost said out loud. She was such a decent girl, beautiful and committed to the church. He was sure it simply couldn't happen — she would never go English. Rebecca was his now, in a manner of speaking, and someday she would really be his. The thought took his breath away. The wheels of his buggy rattled across the bridge, the racket thundering in his ears.

Pulling around the sharp bends in the road, John stilled his fears and prepared for what might lie ahead. He willed himself to stop thinking, concentrating instead on searching for Rebecca's driveway. Considering how often he had been there, the task should have been easy. Yet tonight, surrounded by the familiar, he felt alienated and in uncharted territory.

Thinking that he would need to turn on his bright lights, he was thankful when it proved unnecessary. Any Amish person watching would know why he needed the extra light. *Couldn't find his way into his girlfriend's yard. Lost on the way to love, as usual . . .* The imaginary teasing chilled him.

Turning in, the gentle slope of the Keim driveway led upward. John let his horse walk, finding the familiar tying place on its own. Memories from the past were flooding his mind. He saw the times he had come here with Rebecca, certain then of what was ahead. Evenings, afternoons at times, he delighted in the anticipation of spending time with her.

John forced himself to slide open the buggy door and place his foot onto the step. Surrounded by his fears, he sensed Rebecca's presence before he could see her. Between the house and the buggy, he saw the faint form in the darkness. He tried to halt his downward movement but couldn't. Continuing toward the ground, his foot reaching, nearly stumbling, his mind and body were off balance.

John righted himself, looking in her direction. The light from the living room window found its way out to the buggy and lit up her face.

"Hi," Rebecca said. "I saw you coming. It's so good you could come over tonight."

In a rush of emotions, John wanted to reach out, to touch, but he restrained himself. He might do things that he would later regret, so he simply cleared his throat.

"How'd you know I was here?" Rebecca asked, but he couldn't see her face anymore, the weak light lost to some unseen object.

"Guessed," he got out, regretting the word because it wasn't quite the truth. "Really . . ." He tried again. "I didn't know, but I wanted to — I mean — to see . . . whether you were home."

"That's nice," she said, her face still in the

shadows. "On the way home from Milroy, I realized that I should have contacted you. But things were so busy with the baby and all, and I didn't have your address. You want to come in?"

"I have to tie the horse," he said, not directly answering her question, anger stirring in him now. *Why didn't she offer to explain more? So cheerful as if she has done nothing wrong, while I am suffering.*

"I'm glad to see you," she said, her voice sounding happy, making things worse. *How can she see me? It is so dark.* Angry voices in his head filled the places where fears had been just moments before.

Am I to demand to know? The outburst inside grew, surprising John with its strength.

"You didn't call," he said, hoping none of his anger was showing.

"I know. That was thoughtless of me, but I would have had to go to the schoolhouse. Leona doesn't have a phone shack close," she said, sounding concerned.

"I was worried," he said into the darkness, a glad perverseness running through him that she cared, but hoping those feelings didn't show either.

"You didn't have to be — I was taking care of the baby," she said. "It's hard to plan

100

things around babies."

"I know," he heard himself say, tying the rope, the lights from the house now in his eyes. "A little jumpy," he added, allowing a chuckle.

Rebecca approached. Coming close her fingers found John's in the darkness. She pulled on his hand, turning him so the light played softly on his face. "You are a dear, John," she said softly, her voice gentle. "I'm back now."

"Yes," he said, letting go of her fingers. "I just had to come and see — make sure."

"A sure maker." She now smiled, her voice vibrating against the side of his buggy and bouncing back. The sound seemed more alive than when it left her mouth.

"I think so — but not a good one," he said, trying to sound lighthearted to cover his surging feelings.

"Why don't you come in?" she asked him. "Catch up on the news. It's more comfortable on the couch."

"Your family still up?" he asked, not certain that all the things he wanted to know could be asked in front of them.

"Sure," Rebecca said. "They've heard the story. It won't bother them."

So there was nothing to do but agree. John sighed, wishing they could talk outside.

"You were worried," she said, finding his fingers again.

"You didn't see anyone else?" he blurted out, regretting the words but unable to help himself.

Her laughter sounded softly beside him. "You are silly, John. Of course I didn't see anyone — not how you mean."

"Is there someone to see?" he asked, the question bursting out.

"Not in that way," Rebecca said, after a slight pause.

Her statement caused his fears to leap forward, demanding an answer. "So there was someone?"

"Don't you trust me?" Rebecca's face was now in the shadows. "I really do love you."

John felt like stumbling, clawing the air with his hands, her question wrenching at his heart. *Trust her? Yes. But blind trust?* That's what she seemed to be asking of him. Demanding that he close his eyes to his fears and simply follow her around — whatever she chose to do.

What if she is hiding something I need to know about? The fears danced around in his head, mocking him.

"I love you too," he replied, trying to keep a lighthearted tone. "And trust you? Of course, I do."

"You sure? Another boyfriend?" Her voice didn't sound as soft as before. "You really think I would?"

"No," he said, the thought seeming to shrivel away in the light of exposure. "Just checking."

"You didn't have to check." Her voice was soft again. "I like you."

"Oh," John said quietly, standing at the door, not wanting to say more. Their words could now easily be heard inside.

Rebecca stepped in front of him, reaching to open the door. As the light from the lantern on the living room ceiling caught her face, John saw the smile of welcome. The softness warmed his heart.

"It's John!" Mattie's voice came from the couch. "Just as Rebecca thought. We heard the buggy coming up the driveway."

"Heard the news already?" Lester asked, chuckling in the recliner. "Had to get right over?"

John nodded, then corrected himself. "I didn't really know — that she was back. Just thought I'd stop by and see."

"Make yourself at home then." Lester straightened up his recliner. "This might call for popcorn, don't you think?"

Popcorn was the last thing on his mind, but John didn't feel like saying so. He wished again for time alone with Rebecca, but she was already disappearing into the kitchen. Awkwardly he stood there. "Don't want to be a bother," he finally managed.

"No bother in the least," Mattie assured him. "Rebecca just went to get a chair. I'll get the popcorn on. Just give me a minute."

"You sure?" John asked, expecting no reply.

Rebecca appeared at the kitchen door with a chair and set it beside the couch. "Best we can do," she said, smiling at him. "Not enough couches." She took a seat on the couch beside her mother.

"So you were worried about Rebecca?" Lester asked, grinning and watching John take his seat.

"Don't tease," Rebecca chided her father.

"Know how it is." Lester still had the grin on his face. "It gets better though."

John wanted to ask how Lester could be so certain but decided not to. It might sound foolish and lead to other questions. "When did Rebecca get home?" he asked, thinking that angle of conversation safe.

"She didn't tell you?"

"Dad." Rebecca's voice had a warning in it.

Lester ignored her, chuckling. "Just like a woman."

"What's like a woman?" Mattie asked, coming in from the kitchen. "Popcorn's on."

Before Lester could answer, Rebecca asked, "Yeah, what's like a woman, Dad?"

Mattie stood looking at Lester, half turned to go back toward the kitchen.

Lester was waiting. When Mattie didn't move, he grinned again, a little lopsided this time. "Oh, nothing. They just — you know — forget to mention things sometimes."

"Sounds fishy to me," Mattie said, moving toward the kitchen door.

"Don't let him get away with it," Rebecca said to her mother's retreating form. "He was insulting us."

"He means well," Mattie said before disappearing.

Lester's pleased laugh filled the room. "See? Now that's knowing your man."

"You can be glad she likes you," Rebecca retorted.

"I'm a nice person," he allowed quite confidently, stroking his chest-length beard. "I raised you."

"Don't answer him." Rebecca held her hand up in John's direction.

Lester laughed again. "He was just going to get in a good word, that's all."

"You were going to — right?" Rebecca

105

looked at John, then waited, studying his face.

John was searching wildly for words. "Ah, sure. Why not? Well, I guess so."

"You'll have to do better than that, son." Lester's grin was back in full force.

"Maybe he just needs practice — like you," Rebecca told him.

"No doubt." Lester leaned back on his recliner again. "Sounds like he'll be getting some. It's in the spring — next spring I hear."

John felt himself getting red around his collar. "That's the plan. Yes."

"Nice place you have on the ridge there." Lester nodded. "Real nice."

"I was fortunate to catch the buy. It wasn't even on the market. The folks just knew Dad and asked if he knew of anyone."

"Fair price and all?"

John rocked his head a little. "A bit high, I suppose, but there wasn't much choice. Not if you want to be on the ridge."

"Nice place up there. Good place for a business too."

"I was thinking of that," John allowed, glad that his future father-in-law was following his own thoughts. It was comforting to have his approval.

"Farming's gone by the wayside. Pretty

much over anymore."

"Nothing wrong with it," John said, not wanting to offend farming and farmers. "Just hard for young people."

"What do you have in mind?"

"Most everything's covered right now." John raised his eyebrows. "I thought maybe a cabinet and woodworking shop — specialty stuff. Make some of the things they sell at Miller's."

"Down the road sometime, I suppose?"

John nodded. "Aden pays pretty well, so I'll stay for the time being. Maybe till the place is paid off. That way there's less debt."

Lester nodded too.

"It's not just dollars and cents," Rebecca said, interrupting both their thoughts and causing John to glance at her in surprise.

Lester's grin returned. "Like love?" he asked his daughter.

"Yeah — we'll live on that," she retorted.

"You think that'll work?" Lester asked in John's direction.

John felt the red spreading and again suffered a loss of words. The thought of him living with Rebecca, sitting right there beside her, caused the color to spread even faster.

Rebecca glanced up at John. "Quit tormenting him," she said in her father's direction. "He was worried and rightly so. I should have made more effort to let him know what was going on."

"Popcorn," Mattie announced, bringing in the heaping bowls.

"Let me tell you something," Lester said, as Mattie disappeared back into the kitchen again.

"Dad." Rebecca's voice was firm, holding another warning.

Lester ignored her. "I am really thankful to the good Lord. All our children — they are turning out well."

John nodded, agreeing with the words but not certain what they meant, other than a father's general appreciation.

Lester was not done. "The two oldest — married."

John understood that to mean what it did — Amish partners at least.

Lester continued, "Money's not everything in life. The spiritual's the most important."

"Yes," John agreed again.

"We had a close call." Lester continued, looking to John and settling back into his recliner. "Especially with Rebecca."

"Dad." Rebecca's voice was now filled with alarm.

"A close call — for her?" John was suddenly quite interested.

"She had a little rough time." Lester nodded solemnly. "But the good Lord helped us through it, I guess."

"Dad." Rebecca's voice was getting a little louder.

"How was that?" John's interest was increasing, his fears hungrily reaching forward for news.

Mattie came in right then from the kitchen, catching only the drift of the conversation. "Who's worried?"

"Dad's telling him about Atlee," Rebecca informed her mother, taking the bowl of popcorn and picking at the kernels with her fingers. She desperately wanted this conversation to change.

"I was just telling John how thankful we were," Lester said.

"Oh, that," Mattie said, glancing at Rebecca. "We all have those."

Lester, his fingers in his popcorn bowl, continued. "This was pretty serious. Marrying a Mennonite wouldn't have been for the best. Rebecca, I think, would have had better sense than that."

"It wasn't that serious, Lester," Mattie said quickly. "I'm sure Rebecca already told John." Glancing over at Rebecca's face, Mattie blurted out, "Oh, you didn't."

Instead of redness now, John felt his face turn pale.

"You didn't tell him." Mattie was still looking at Rebecca.

"A little," Rebecca said, keeping her eyes on the floor. "I didn't ever date him," she added.

"Of course not," Mattie said. "It was just a schoolgirl thing."

"Pretty serious," Lester chimed in, eyeing his popcorn, munching happily away.

Mattie glared at him. "It was just a young-ster's fantasy. Nothing more."

John was all attention now, his eyes fully on Rebecca's face. She looked ready to scream, lie, say anything, he thought.

"Oh, did I say something?" Lester asked.

Mattie's eyes were daggers.

"I see I did," Lester said. "Maybe it wasn't as serious as I made it sound."

"You should have let her tell him," Mattie said, her voice low and steady.

"Sorry." Lester genuinely looked so. "I was just expressing my thanks to the good Lord."

"You should have waited till later," Mattie told him. "He didn't know."

"I can tell that now," Lester replied, see-ing John's face.

John felt embarrassment creeping all the

way through his body. Something serious was going on — or had gone on. So his feelings had been grounded in fact. Rebecca did have secrets after all.

He wanted to run, to leave this place, to never come back. But that would mean leaving Rebecca. He willed himself to calm down lest his face show his true feelings.

"She told me about something — in school," he managed to say.

"That's all it was. Lester's making a big thing out of it." Mattie was smiling, watching him.

John thought Mattie's smile was somewhat forced. A feeling of the world pressing in could be felt on his skin, yet there was simply no way he could lose this girl. *She can explain it, can she not? That is, if we could go somewhere private.*

John glanced at the stair door leading up to Rebecca's room. He saw Rebecca glance at it too. She understood, he was certain, but was not consenting to go up to her room. *Could I ask?* How stupid would that question sound to Lester and Mattie? *Ah — your daughter, I want to see her in her room. We're not married, but we need to be there.*

"More popcorn?" Mattie offered.

He glanced down at his half-empty bowl, knowing she was just attempting to relax the atmosphere. In a way he was grateful, yet he wished this could be solved now. What if he blurted out, *Tell me everything?*

"Dad didn't mean any harm." It was Rebecca's voice. "He was just concerned."

"He should have been more careful!" Mattie spoke empathetically.

"I should have," Lester said, echoing her. "If there was a real danger, see, I wouldn't have said anything. Rebecca's making a very good choice now. That's really what I was trying to say."

"We know that," Mattie joined in.

"It's okay," John told them, his voice not sounding okay, but the words were right. "A school thing is what it was."

"You got that right," Lester said.

"So have you told John about the baby yet?" Mattie asked.

"She didn't have time," John said, with a smile meant for all of them. "I really need to be going though. Maybe she can tell me all about it Sunday night."

"Of course." Mattie was beaming.

"It's just baby news," Lester said.

John was already rising to his feet, nodding his head slightly, acting as nicely as he could, and moving toward the front door. Rebecca seemed for a moment to consider staying seated. Something surely wasn't right. At the last moment, Rebecca got up to follow John out.

John held the door as Rebecca stepped outside, the late evening air chilling their lungs. "I'll get my coat," she told him, stepping back inside for a moment. John saw Mattie and Rebecca exchange glances, a reassuring smile crossing Mattie's face.

John pulled the door shut behind Rebecca, the darkness of the night wrapped itself around them, the light from the gas lantern in the living room playing on their backs.

"I could have told you about the baby tonight," she said, her voice strained.

"I have to get home," he said, but his voice was no longer nice. The soft edge from the living room was gone.

"You're upset," she stated simply.

"Of course I am." His voice rose in the darkness. "You've hidden something from me."

"Dad shouldn't have said those things," Rebecca said. "I was going to tell you. Really I was. You have nothing to be worried about."

"Oh — you were?" John asked, his voice clipped. He had never spoken to her like this before, but he couldn't stop. "Tell me what? Tell me about what you were really doing in Milroy. Baby — sure there probably was one, but what else was there? Secret meetings with some lost love? Wishing you could be with him? Hoping to hold his hands?"

John knew the words burned through Rebecca, searing her heart. Perhaps not even her father had ever spoken to her like this, but he couldn't help himself. His horse suddenly snorted behind him, the rattle of the rings on the leather bridle jingling from the sudden movement. John saw Rebecca flinch.

"Is that why you didn't write or call me?" John continued. "Wanted to break the news gently maybe? That would just be like you, tenderly and gently telling me. There's someone else, John. I just haven't gotten around to telling you before. I promised to marry you, but now I can't."

Rebecca laughed softly.

"That's all you can do? Laugh?" John's voice was getting louder in the darkness.

"It's not what you think," she stated. "I wasn't laughing at you."

"Of course not." There was bitterness now in John's voice.

"John, do you seriously think I'm sneaking around?"

"I don't know what to think. You were gone for all this time and never contacted me. Never let me know when you would be coming back. Make me come over to find out where you are. Use my concern about you to embarrass me. You think coming over here was easy? What if you hadn't been here? How would I have looked? Now, your own father tells me things I didn't know."

"I told you," she said, her voice low.

"No — you didn't." John's voice was rising again, though he was consciously trying to control it and calculate the proper volume to avoid being heard inside the house.

"I was planning to," she told him. Then she quietly said, "I love you."

"So that's what you told him too?" Sarcasm dripped.

"There is no one else."

"Is? What does this mean? How about was? Did you just see him? Talk to him? How am I supposed to trust you, Rebecca? You don't tell me everything. Is this what you were afraid of down by the bridge when I proposed to you?"

Rebecca stood there, saying nothing.

"How can you expect us to live as man and wife with secrets from each other?"

"I explained it to those who could help," she said. "I was going to tell you."

"Really — so there are others who know? Did they see you with him? Is that why you had to tell them? Is that how they know?"

"I was going to try to tell you," she said softly. "I really was."

Something in her tone must have reached him because his pause became longer, as if he was thinking it over. Then realizing how harsh he sounded, he moved toward her and said, "I'm sorry. That was unnecessary — really. I don't know what came over me."

"I'm sorry you're angry," she said and heard him sigh in the darkness.

"I'm sorry too . . . that I got angry. It's just that I care so much. I get worried about you." His arms waved in the darkness, dim shadows going up and down behind him. "Especially when things like this happen . . . When you're dad says things as he did."

"Maybe we shouldn't talk about it any-more tonight. Maybe you'll let me explain on Sunday."

He seemed to be thinking before speaking, "Maybe — yes — sure. There's a good explanation for all of this. You always . . . I mean . . . Look — let's not let this come between us. Surely, somehow this can be worked out."

"Let's talk then on Sunday."

"Okay." His hand dropped to his side. "I'm sorry. I really am. We'll have plenty of time then. I'm sure you haven't done anything wrong."

"Okay," she whispered.

"I have to go," he said, walking to the front of his horse, untying it, and climbing into the buggy.

He looked back once through the open door of his buggy as the horse took off, glad to be free from his restraint and on the way home.

A piece of gravel popped up from the narrow buggy wheel, stinging her leg, hurting her skin.

CHAPTER TWELVE

Rebecca turned to go into the house, giving one last look at John's buggy lights leaving the driveway and then disappearing as he turned left onto the main road. Pain was wrapped tightly around her heart, the tears near the surface. *Is this what love is all about? Is this what happens when a woman gives her heart to a man? Is this what happens when I tell a man I love him?* The questions burned as she walked toward the house.

Mattie took one look at Rebecca's face when she walked in the front door and quickly asked, "What's wrong? Surely not . . ."

"No, Mother," Rebecca answered, picking up on the unspoken question.

"Would you two stop speaking in riddles," Lester said from the recliner.

"Oh, it's nothing." Rebecca was biting back the tears.

"It wasn't something I said?" Lester asked.

"Not all of it," Mattie told him. "But you should have been more careful."

"I wasn't trying to make trouble," he protested. "Atlee's over with anyway."

"I think I'll go upstairs," Rebecca said, glad the tears weren't pouring down her face. There was no sense making a scene. That would only take a lot of explaining.

"It's not that late," Mattie commented.

"I'll settle down before too long," Rebecca replied, hanging her coat back in the closet, turning to go upstairs.

"Let us know if we can help," Lester said. "These things usually blow over pretty soon."

Rebecca nodded, her hand on the doorknob, wondering if she could trust her own voice. She decided she could. "He wants to talk about it more on Sunday."

"That's the way to do it," Lester said quickly. "I'm sure it won't take much."

"Was he really upset?" Mattie asked, ignoring Lester's assurances. Her eyes registered the pain on Rebecca's face.

Rebecca quickly lost all confidence in her voice and squeezed her eyes shut to keep the tears from running down her face. Numbly she nodded her head.

"Oh my," was all her mother said.

"They'll get it figured out," Lester said, assurance still in his voice. "John's a good boy."

"Well, sleep on it," Mattie said comfortingly. "Sometimes a good night's rest helps a lot."

Rebecca nodded. "I'll see you in the morning then." She opened the stair door and found the first step with her foot, her eyes not much use at the moment.

Reaching the top of the stairs, she opened her bedroom door slowly and stepped inside, wondering how the world could change so quickly. Only today she had been on her way home from Indiana, so happy to be back, certain the Lord was with her, directing and leading. How then had things gone so terribly wrong?

Things are terribly wrong, aren't they? Is this normal living and am I — Rebecca Keim — just blissfully unaware of it? Is this pain that burns in me, the usual, the expected?

She sat down on her bed. The questions crowded her mind, but the tears were now gone. *Why didn't I just tell John everything? Let it all out in a burst? Won't it all come to that on Sunday anyway?*

The question puzzled her first, then indignation started pushing into her emotions. *Why had John been so angry with me? What* had I honestly done to deserve it? Have I been the one in the wrong all along? I didn't tell John everything. That much is true. I kept something from him. But with good reason, she told herself. Look how he acts when he finds out just this little bit.

Resentment now flooded in. It just isn't right. Getting angry like that. Look at what I discovered by going to Milroy and finding out what really happened. Was that not better to do now rather than after we married? Would John like that? Finding the truth out then, wondering forever — perhaps — if I had done the right thing?

Then her anger faded away. How am I going to be a proper wife for John, if I am already questioning his judgment? She got up from the bed, looked around the dark room, and lit the kerosene lamp. The flickering flame created soothing shadows that danced across the walls and brought a calming sense of familiarity in the midst of tumult.

Rebecca dropped to her knees beside the bed, buried her head in her hands, and searched for the words to say. God was everywhere, her faith taught her. Is He here in the midst of this? Do I have a right to bother Him, with so many other things on His mind already?

She thought, lifting her head to study the light playing on the walls. Her heart hurt, but there were many who hurt worse. Of this she was sure. There were those with serious illnesses and in real trouble, living all over the world, and here she was, thinking the world was being unfair to her.

"God," she began softly, "sorry to bother You, and I'm sorry I was angry with John, but I still am, a little. I haven't done everything right, but I've tried. Not that that's an excuse, I know, but You seem to be helping me. I'm sorry if I've been wrong about that. And I'm sorry I'm so much trouble. You have a lot to do, I'm sure."

That's a stupid prayer, she thought, getting back up on her feet and feeling nothing. *That hardly got to the ceiling. Maybe I am nothing but a big mess. Maybe John has plenty of reason to be angry.*

She would tell John everything on Sunday night, and perhaps he would understand. The thought that John wouldn't understand presented itself with clarity and forcefulness, but Rebecca vowed that she would still tell him anyway and then let things go.

Life was simply getting much too complicated.

CHAPTER THIRTEEN

John urged his horse up the hill, the clattering at the covered bridge still in his ears. His anger, now gone, was replaced with the fear of losing Rebecca if he carried on like this. How could he expect a girl to stick with him — love him — if he acted like he just had?

Why did I get so angry? The question buzzed in John's ears, making him feel dizzy. Embarrassment flowed through him as he remembered what just happened. He had let Rebecca see a side of him he hadn't known was there . . . at least not to such a degree.

How stupid and idiotic could I be, to lose control like that in front of her? What all did I say anyway? John shook his head, trying to clear his thoughts. One thing he was certain, speaking in anger to Rebecca was not wise.

Then why did I carry on so? It would be a wonder if she even went home with him

Sunday night, let alone tell him about her past. What right did he have to even expect her to tell him after this?

Halfway to the top of the hill, the open fields spread out around him. He felt, more than saw, the dim shadows of the trees recede, no longer hugging the edge of the road.

She might well be hurt by my outburst. The thought pressed in on him. He felt satisfaction in the knowledge that, at least, he had cared enough to notice. *Rebecca hadn't always sounded hurt,* he remembered. *She had laughed at the start. How did she dare do that? Laugh at me, at my concerns? Was that not what she was doing?*

John felt anger rising again. He told himself that it was because he cared so much for her. Other girls might not have bothered him like this, but Rebecca he loved. He settled back into the seat of the buggy, letting the horse set its own speed on the uphill climb toward Unity.

Love will triumph despite my anger, he told himself. *It always does, doesn't it? Especially when one has such an intense, deep love like I have for Rebecca.*

John slapped the reins absentmindedly, not really meaning it. The horse didn't increase its speed but just kept its steady pace up the incline. *It will all be better come Sunday. I apologized to Rebecca. That ought to count for something. Things might still get a little sticky when she tells me everything, and it better be everything. If we have to stay past midnight, she will tell me the whole story.*

John wanted to hear it all, every little detail of this Atlee and what he meant to Rebecca. The pain cut again, giving him pause. Did he really want to know what they had felt for each other? The thought of Rebecca's fingers reaching for another boy's hand made him shiver and hunch down a little deeper on the buggy seat.

Perhaps she had done worse things. John envisioned Atlee as tall and handsome. He was confident as he reached out for Rebecca, a smile on his face, touching her gently, moving toward her. John's anger flashed at the image. This would not be easy. Come Sunday he would have to find some way of controlling his feelings.

He simply could not lose Rebecca. She meant too much to him. They would be so happy together at the farm on the hill. That was where he wanted to live his life with her, where he wanted their children to grow up, where he would love her as only he could. *Better than anyone else. I simply cannot let her past stop us.*

Deeply he breathed in the night air. Sunday would come, and he must hear her out. She would explain it so that he could understand. This keeping of secrets must come to an end.

That was how a man and wife were supposed to be. No secrets between them. It was only then that things would go the way they should. Without that, how could one trust another person?

John's father had said it many times. With his arms stretched toward heaven, he stood and preached between the kitchen and living room doors on a Sunday morning. "We are children of light. The Lord God says so Himself, thundering from heaven, from the throne of God. It is to this we are called. We must open ourselves to the light of the Word of God, to walk with open hearts, and let its light shine into every corner of our hearts. Only then can we be truly His children. In this we must walk as He Himself walked in the world.

"All that is unholy walks in darkness. Hiding in the ways of the world. Hiding in the world's excuses of why it loves its sin. We must leave sin and the excuses it brings and walk where God has called us to walk. Open before Him and each other. Those who want to hide from their brother do not walk in the light. We must not be afraid of what those of like faith see in us. To be afraid, to reject them, is to love the darkness."

Yes. Rebecca must come clean no matter how much it hurts her or me. I can take it. Somehow I will. By God's grace I will.

Ahead of him the lights of Unity were coming into view. It was late already. *That is another thing that will have to change. On Sunday nights it is okay to be out late, but these irregular evenings will have to stop. Rebecca can simply not be the cause of this much stress and trouble. It is totally unnecessary and uncalled for. We will have to find a way of working out our problems some other way.*

If it were not for her, I would already be in bed, getting the rest I need so much. I would be preparing for what would no doubt be a full and busy day tomorrow at the furniture store. Other people depend upon me, and it is simply not acceptable to be tired and exhausted on the job.

Just thinking made John even more keenly aware of how tired he was. His head ached. His muscles felt tense from the evening spent with Rebecca. He had been concerned before he left, but now he was exhausted.

The horse snorted as the buggy came up the slight incline into town. Houses became visible, mostly because they had such bright lights coming from their windows. John heard a car coming up behind him but paid it no mind. His lights were on, and he was in town. There should be no problem with being seen. Besides, home was just ahead of him, not too far down the road.

But the speed of the approaching engine startled him. *Maybe some young boys out tearing around, trying to have their English fun.*

John was turning around in his seat to get a better look, when it hit him. He heard the sound of splintering wood and he felt himself flying off into nothing. Then it all went black.

CHAPTER FOURTEEN

Mrs. Richardson — Isabelle to those around town — lived down from the corner post office at the Wheat Ridge/Unity junction. She was sure she had just heard something hit her house with a thud. At eighty years of age, Isabelle doubted her hearing at times, but this had been pretty obvious. What made the sound even more suspicious, was the loud roar of an approaching automobile from the west, just prior to the sound. The roar sounded even louder afterward. Somebody was up to no good.

Isabelle lived by herself, thankful she still could and hoping things would continue so for many years to come. She dreaded the day she would have to go to a nursing home. Her two children, Wallace and Beatrice, had tactfully brought up the subject several times, but Isabelle had told them "no" before they barely started talking.

Wallace had only recently moved to Cincinnati with his wife and two children. He had grown tired of the local options for his private law practice after graduating from Michael E. Moritz College of Law at Ohio State University. Apparently his feelings about his own abilities had been justified because Wallace had been hired on by Frost & Jacobs, which had a lot of growth potential — according to Wallace at least. Isabelle didn't know much about such things and judged Wallace's financial matters primarily by the car he drove. It was definitely larger and better looking than last time he was home.

Beatrice, a deputy sheriff, still lived in West Union. She was married to her high school sweetheart, Andy, who never did or would amount to much in Isabelle's thinking. Andy worked part-time as a mechanic at the Auto Sales place on 41. It was Beatrice who supported the family. Isabelle thought Beatrice might even make sheriff someday, but that was not a subject to bring up with Beatrice when Andy was present.

Concerned by the sound she had heard, Isabelle walked to her front window and looked out. There was nothing to see. The night was clear but not too cold for this time of the year — chilly enough, though, to require a sweater if she stepped outside.

That and the doubt that there really was something serious going on outside made Isabelle hesitate.

If whoever was in the car had actually thrown something against her house, then it could well wait till morning to be discovered. She would report it then. If they hadn't, she would be calling the sheriff's department for nothing.

Isabelle was concerned that Beatrice might be on duty tonight. Even if Beatrice wasn't, someone would tell her about the call and subsequent visit required by a deputy, how her mother had called in about nothing, imagining things being thrown against her house just because a car went by too fast.

Such a report would not bode well when the subject of the nursing home came up again. *Mom's hearing things,* Isabelle could imagine Beatrice telling Wallace. *Had to run a patrol out to satisfy her — all for nothing.*

No, Isabelle decided. It was time for bed, bump or no bump in the night. Yet stepping back from the window, the feeling of concern wouldn't go away. An impulse compelled her to simply check outside. Surely she could do that.

Hesitating, she thought the matter over carefully, finally gave in, reached for a sweater, and slipped it on. Her shoulders ached with even that slight effort. *No sense in doing this at such an hour,* she told herself, but she continued on anyway and opened the front door.

With no streetlights to help, there was little that could be seen. What light came from her living room window cast its reach only a few feet into the front lawn. Looking up and then down the dark street, Isabelle could see nothing unusual, certainly no signs of lurking pranksters or automobiles that shouldn't have been there. Checking her front yard and the sides of the house, nothing seemed to be amiss there either. Yet something had hit her house, the feeling more than the memory told her so.

Glancing up, while standing there on the front porch, she saw lights playing on the horizon, coming from the east, bouncing along Wheat Ridge, and heading into town. *This might help,* she thought. *Maybe I can see by the light.*

Waiting, she closed the front door behind her, checking the knob and making certain it was unlocked. Getting locked out of her own house wouldn't be good news either when Beatrice and Wallace had their next discussion.

The car was coming down the hill fast,

slowing only slightly as it entered the little town. *Surely not the same boys coming back to do further damage.* Standing outside on her front porch, she was a handy target. Fear filled Isabelle, but she didn't dare move now. That might only invite further trouble, if whoever this was saw her dashing into her house, perhaps falling down on her own front porch.

Isabelle held still, after moving to stand close to the wall of the house. The headlights streamed down Wheat Ridge, lighting up her front yard. Her fear made her forget why she was out on the porch. Then the car passed, its lights dimly reflecting back. Suddenly remembering, Isabelle looked to see what might have been thrown into her yard.

Little could be seen, but Isabelle was sure she saw something. A large object or at least a large bag was lying against the far wall of the house, near the corner facing Mr. Urchin's yard.

Everyone called him Bill, a nice enough fellow. He lived there with his wife, Eunice. Their children, like hers, were long grown and gone. He would see the bag come morning, Mr. Urchin would. Bill would be up early, walking over to see what the object was, knocking on her door for an explanation. An explanation she wouldn't have.

Sighing, the last of the light from the passing car's headlights disappearing down Wheat Ridge, she opened her front door, stepped back inside, and headed toward the phone. There really seemed to be no other option. Calling it in might be problematic with Beatrice, but not calling it in could cause problems at the hand of Mr. Urchin. Added to that was a feeling Isabelle couldn't quite shake. Something about the shape of the object against her house, seen so dimly in the car's light, troubled her.

She reached for the phone on the wall. Wallace had wanted to have a cordless model installed the last time the nursing home subject came up, but she would have nothing of that either. It smelled of coming doom, especially when Wallace had told her, "What if you fall down — the stairs maybe — a cordless phone might be closer. Now you have to reach all the way up the wall. That might be hard to do depending what happens."

"No," she had said. And "no," it would remain. *Anything to stave off this approaching dread in whatever manner possible.*

Holding up the phone, its large numbers lighted, she dialed the number by heart. Sally, the night receptionist, answered, "Adams County Sheriff."

Isabelle cleared her throat, wishing all this wasn't necessary. "Ah, Sally," she half whispered, "I think something — a little bit ago — was thrown against my house. Sorry to bother you, but could you have someone drive by?"

"Any idea who it was?" Sally's voice sounded clipped.

"No," Isabelle replied, wishing again she was not making this phone call. Sally sounded just like Isabelle figured she would when a call came in from an old woman. So Isabelle added quickly, "Could you keep this from Beatrice? Maybe it's nothing . . . But it made a loud noise."

"Have you checked outside?" Sally asked, ignoring the question about Beatrice.

"Yes — I stepped outside the front door. There's something there."

"I'll send someone out, okay?" Sally responded, her voice not as clipped anymore. "We'll see what it is."

"Could you keep this from Beatrice?" Isabelle asked again, her voice strained.

"I can't promise, Isabelle," Sally said. "Beatrice's on call tonight, and the deputy nearest you is the one that stops by."

"Okay," Isabelle said in resignation. The world tonight seemed to be working against her. The walls of the nursing home were moving in closer. She could feel it all for sure.

"Lord, help me," she whispered, hanging the phone on the wall, reaching for her childhood faith in God. "You will have to help me. This may be a bigger cross than I can carry. Maybe You can take me home before they carry me to that place."

Struggling with her emotions, she walked into the living room to wait.

In town Sally pressed the mike down. "Base one to mobile units. Possible disturbance reported in Unity. Anyone in the area?"

"I'm near Manchester, down by the river." The voice of young Tad Johnson, only on the force for a year, came back quickly.

"Beatrice, where're you at?" Sally asked into the mike, waiting for a response.

When there was silence, Tad asked, "You want me to run up?"

"Just a minute," Sally told him. "It's her mom. Might be best if she goes in."

"The old woman in trouble?" Tad asked, concern in his voice.

"Sounded fine, but thinks someone threw something against her house."

"Any other reports from the area?" Tad asked the logical question.

Sally didn't answer him, broadcasting

more specifically this time, "Base one to mobile three. Base one to mobile three. Respond please."

"Yes, Sally." Beatrice's voice came through faintly, the static buzzing.

"Where're you at?" Sally asked. "You're not coming through clearly."

"South of Cherry Fork," Beatrice replied, her voice clearer this time. "Radio might be making trouble."

"Your mom called. Can you check it out? Thinks someone threw something against the house."

"Sure. You don't think she's imagining things?"

"That's why you'd better go," Sally said. "Tad's not as close either."

"On my way."

"Have Charley check the radio tomorrow." Sally clicked her mike off.

"Will leave a note on the dash when I come back in." The transmission sounded weaker again.

"You have your cell if it gives out?" Sally asked.

"I do. I'm on 247 right now. Will let you know."

There was silence from the station as Beatrice drove north on the state road, wondering whether the radio had given out but deciding it likely had not. Sally kept her words to a minimum, calling only when necessary.

So what is Mother up to? Beatrice wondered. *Is she seeing things?* It appeared as if she and Wallace might be right about the nursing home. Having an eighty-year-old woman living by herself, even in town, was no longer acceptable, if she was acting like this.

This will certainly make the case easier with Wallace. If Mother is seeing things, imagining objects being thrown against her house in the night, then it is time Wallace and I take action. Now we will have solid reasons to back up our feelings. The sheriff department's time can simply not be spent on imaginary things.

Beatrice rattled across the Harshville Bridge, the clatter irritating her.

CHAPTER FIFTEEN

Isaac Miller had retired to the living room already, studying the Scripture texts the bishop supplied at last preaching Sunday. This weekend might well be his turn to preach, although one could never be quite sure. There was a normal rotation for preaching, but it could easily be changed with a visiting preacher who always got priority.

Not that Isaac cared one way or the other. Preaching was a light burden to him, but one was not wise to mention such things. Common Amish belief required preachers to walk in humility, suppressing natural talent lest it spoil the man. Everyone knew in theory that God could work just as well through the most stumbling sermon as through the well-delivered one. But in practice the people enjoyed the latter ones better — but that too was not something to dwell on. One's soul, it was widely believed, could quickly be damaged with such prideful thoughts.

So Isaac studied the texts to be used that Sunday. They came from Mark, chapter eleven and Luke, chapter eighteen. His eyes caught on verses twenty-five and twenty-six in the book of Mark. He read them in German to get the full meaning and to memorize them, should they need quoting and if preaching fell to him.

"And when ye stand praying, forgive, if ye have ought against any: that your Father also which is in heaven may forgive you your trespasses.

"But if ye do not forgive, neither will your Father which is in heaven forgive your trespasses."

Isaac pondered the verses, trying to fully grasp their intent. He let the familiar words roll off his tongue again.

Miriam interrupted him, as he was turning the pages to Luke. "John's not home yet," she said, concern in her voice.

"He's probably catching up on all the news — you know — Rebecca's been away for a long time." Isaac chuckled at his own humor, thinking that time was considered to be of greater length by young people, although it consisted of the same twenty-four hours everyone else had.

"I just heard a horse run in the driveway," Miriam said, still concerned.

"Then he'll be right in." Isaac had found Luke, chapter eighteen and dropped his eyes to the page.

"It sounded like just his horse," Miriam insisted. "No buggy wheels."

Isaac raised his eyes skeptically. "You're probably hearing things."

"It's time for him to be home. He doesn't like being out late . . . except on youth nights."

"He'll be in." Isaac was on the first verse of the chapter, anxious to continue.

"I think you ought to look," she insisted.

"What could be wrong?" Isaac tried to keep the irritation out of his voice.

"It just sounded strange. You should go look. It's not normal for him. I just — I don't know." She stood still in the living room doorway.

"Just wait a minute — he'll be in."

"Where's your flashlight?" she asked.

"In the mudroom — left it there last night."

A minute later Isaac heard Miriam open the door. *She just has to worry. Must be the mother in her.* He let the German words of the Scriptures from Luke form on his tongue. It helped with the memorization. At least it did for him. How the others ministers prepared, they never discussed.

Only seconds had passed before Miriam's hurried footsteps were heard from the mudroom, causing a brief stab of worry in Isaac. *What can be her rush?* Simple worrying would not explain this. He rose from the recliner as she opened the outside kitchen door.

Her face was white. In a blur of motion, Isaac saw Miriam standing there, her lips open, but no sound was coming out. She held out a trembling hand to him as if beseeching him for something she was unable to ask for. Her other hand was still on the doorknob, holding her body steady.

"What's wrong?" he asked, moving toward her.

She worked her mouth, but still no sound came out.

Isaac was now close to Miriam, reaching for her upraised hand, his other going to her shoulder, his eyes finding hers. "What is it?" he asked, insistence in his voice.

"John — John," she managed, making a smothering sound. "Something's wrong. Oh Isaac! What if he's dead?"

"Dead?" Isaac repeated numbly, a cold fear sweeping through his body.

"The buggy. It's not here. Just the horse

— it's still — things are hanging on him. Something terrible has happened."

Isaac shook his head, trying to absorb the news but not succeeding. It made no sense. "Show me," he said, moving toward the door, his hand still holding hers.

"I can't," she said, reaching for a chair from the kitchen table and seating herself slowly. "I just know he's gone. John — the only son of our love. *Da Hah* has taken him."

Gently Isaac took the flashlight from her fingers, having to apply force to loosen it. Miriam seemed not to notice. He went out the door.

Using the flashlight, Isaac ran across the front lawn, quickly finding John's horse standing in front of the barn door, pieces of harness hanging on him, his front quarters shivering violently, the muscles jerking in reaction to some recent trauma.

Isaac's mind reeled as he forced himself to think what must be done. First, he walked to the end of their driveway but heard no sound of sirens in the distance, nor could he see any police cruiser lights. What happened must have just happened, or perhaps no one had discovered it yet.

Images of John lying beside the road ran through Isaac's mind, and he almost took off running down Wheat Ridge toward the west, with only his flashlight to guide him. No sooner did the thought come than the foolishness of that course of action became apparent. Miriam was in the house in shock and needed attention first.

Running back to the house, he opened the door to find Miriam still on the kitchen chair staring into space. "*Da Hah* must have wanted him," she said numbly, when he came up close.

"We don't know that," he said a little too loudly, but he wanted to be sure she heard. "Get your coat. We're going to look."

"I don't want to see him now," Miriam said. "There will be time later."

"I'm not leaving you," he told her.

Isaac saw Miriam's eyes show the first signs of life since she had returned with the news. "You must go. I'll be okay." She lay her hand on her heart. "*Da Hah* will be with me."

"You sure?"

She nodded. He looked sharply at her, not certain, but when the first tear came down her face he said, "I will go then."

After walking rapidly to the barn, Isaac first unharnessed John's horse, taking care that none of the pieces of shafts stuck it. He then put the horse up in its own stall. Quickly getting their driving horse, he threw the harness on, buckled it up, and led the startled horse outside and into the shafts of his own buggy. Urging it on, Isaac drove out the driveway and turned west.

After rattling across the Harshville Bridge, Beatrice drove the speed limit, her lights and siren off. Mother would be fine when she got there, maybe a little scared but fine. Beatrice figured there was no sense in causing an unnecessary scene by driving fast and using the lights. With any luck she could pull the cruiser up short of her mother's house, get out, walk to the house, calm her mother down, and then leave.

No one would be the wiser, especially that Mr. Urchin from next door. He would gladly have the news of this visit spread all over town, making things uncomfortable for her mother's remaining days in Unity. Those days would be short, Beatrice now had no doubt. Her mother belonged in a home where she could be looked after.

As her headlights cut through the dark, Beatrice kept her eyes open for any other signs of trouble. The training in the academy, amplified by experience, kept her alert in the squad car in ways she wasn't when off duty.

Beatrice slowed down. Mother's house

was on the right. The street in front was wide enough to park along. That would be the best and less conspicuous way of making this visit. *A bummer, being a police officer and having to deal with my own family. Why wasn't Tad closer?*

As her headlights hit her mother's lawn, Beatrice noticed something wasn't right. Stray pieces of wood debris and black cloth were draping the ditch. Something resembling a couch was lying in the ditch. A passerby might readily assume the homeowner had put stuff out for a garbage service.

Only Beatrice knew her mother did not use a garbage service.

CHAPTER SIXTEEN

"Mobile three to base. I'm at the site."

"Yes, Beatrice. Your mother okay?" the answer came back clearly.

"I just got here. Still outside. There's debris in her yard. It looks like more than just a prank."

"Okay — advise."

"It looks like parts of a buggy."

"You sure?"

"Affirmative. Quite sure. Some large pieces too. You had best advise the highway patrol. They may want a look."

"An accident? You need medical?"

"I'm checking. I see no vehicle around," Beatrice said into her radio. "Will get right back."

Pulling her flashlight from behind the seat, she stepped out of the cruiser, the darkness deep where the headlights did not reach. Stepping across the piercing lights, she swept the flashlight beam and found nothing.

Pieces of splintered wood lay halfway across the yard, but most of the mangled pieces, which she now knew came from a buggy, lay along the ditch. No sign of any human beings could be seen.

On the point of turning back, Beatrice remembered her mother's complaint of someone throwing an object against her house. Maybe a large piece had flown that far. Bringing her flashlight beam up, she ran it along the front of the house, halting when the beam landed on a crumpled form at the far edge of the building.

Beatrice held the light to the side and ran toward the sprawled figure. It was a man. An Amish man. His hat, as she was used to seeing on Amish men, was nowhere near. It could well have been lost in the mangled debris by the road. The young man lay as he had fallen, his face toward the road, unmoving.

Beatrice's first reaction was to check for signs of life. Searching, her fingers pushed his collar back and found the faint pulsing of a beat. She looked for blood but found none, either on him or on the nearby ground. Beatrice noticed the shallow breathing and moved his head back slightly for better air movement. Checking his front pants pockets, she found a billfold. Holding her flashlight under her arm, she flipped through its contents but found no ID. The strangeness of that struck her, but these were the Amish, and she remembered that they don't own driver's licenses.

Because she couldn't do anything more, even with her basic first responder's training, she stood to run back to the cruiser. The sound of her mother at the front door stopped her. "Is that you, Beatrice?"

"Yes."

"What's out there?" Isabelle asked, half in and half out of the doorway.

"I'll tell you later, Mother. Can you just stay inside? I'll be in after a bit."

"So they did throw something against my house? They were young boys, I think. You don't know how glad I am. I thought I might be imagining things."

"Mom, please go inside. I'll be in." Beatrice couldn't keep the tension out of her voice.

"Oh, it's something serious." Isabelle glanced down the side of her house, searching now, pulling in her breath when her eyes locked on the sprawled body at the corner. "It's a man," she said, stepping fully onto the porch. "We have to bring him inside —

right away."

"No, Mother." Beatrice's voice was firm. "He can't be moved until the medics get here. I have to go call it in."

"Then I'll just stay with him," Isabelle said, taking firm steps toward the sidewalk, her hand finding the familiar handrail even in the darkness.

"Don't move him — I mean it." Beatrice was already halfway across the yard.

"Of course not," Isabelle said. "He just shouldn't be left out here alone."

Reaching John she knelt down beside him, brushing the hair back from his face, listening to his breathing. "The good Lord will take care of you," she whispered. "He always does — for his own — that is. You are His own, aren't you?"

She looked at him in the dim light of the cruiser's headlights. "Of course you are." She took his hand in hers, their touch warm. "You'll be okay, young man. Many are the troubles of the righteous, but the Lord delivers from them all. Yes, that's what David said, and I can testify it's true. Eighty years of my life, and it's still true. The Lord, He will take care of you."

Out at the car, Beatrice pressed down the mike. "Unit three to base, advise the need for medics. Injured — male — early twenties."

"It's already on the way," Sally replied.

"How'd you know that?"

"Buggy wreck with pieces lying around. Just figures, I suppose. See anything of the horse?"

"No," Beatrice said, not really having thought of that.

"Must have gotten away then. You'd see it . . . if it was there."

"Really," was all Beatrice could manage, the images going through her head of what an automobile could do to such a large animal.

"If it ran off, you'll have some visitors soon." Sally added. "Thought you might want to know."

"How do you know who this is?" Beatrice asked because Sally seemed to know so much. "He has no ID, and he's unconscious."

"Ask whoever shows up. They all know each other."

"Really," Beatrice said again.

"Any sign of the medics?"

Beatrice listened before responding, "Hear them in the distance."

"Good."

"I'll keep you advised." Beatrice placed

the radio back in the holder, closed the cruiser door, and stood with her back to the piercing colored lights.

The distant wail of sirens filled the air, as Beatrice walked back to her mother, who was still bent over the sprawled form. "You haven't moved him, have you?" she asked, a touch of anger in her voice. "You should be inside, Mother."

"The Lord will take care of him." Isabelle got to her feet, ignoring her daughter's tone. "He's such a sweet boy."

The approaching wail of the ambulance siren reached a crescendo and then stopped. The flashing lights came around the first house, going south on Unity Road. "The medics are here," Beatrice said to no one in particular.

"Yes, but the Lord will take care of him."

"I'm sure He will." Beatrice took her mother's hand and led her toward the house. "Let the medics take care of him now."

"He's still breathing. I could hear it."

"Did you by chance see who hit him?" Beatrice asked, her mind already going to prosecution and finding who the hit-and-run driver was.

"No, just a loud car. Then the bang on the house."

"You didn't look outside?"

"After the car had roared away, I wasn't sure if I was hearing things. You know how it is. I wanted to be sure."

"It's good you called it in," Beatrice told her mother.

"The Lord must have helped me," Isabelle replied. "I wasn't sure. That young man could have died."

"That's right."

"Lord," Isabelle looked heavenward and prayed, "this world is getting too much for me."

"You'll stay inside now until we're done?" Beatrice held the front door open, waiting.

"Yes. You'll stop in then?"

"When it's done." Beatrice gently shut the door, already seeing her mother heading toward the front window. Isabelle would be watching till it was over.

Already the medics were rolling their stretcher across the front yard, moving fast. Reaching the prostrate form, they checked for vitals, not taking as long as Beatrice expected they would. Dropping the stretcher down and off the wheels, they gently lifted the body onto the platform, one attendant at each end. They placed the stretcher back onto the wheels and rolled it out toward the road.

"Any ID?" the lead attendant shouted across the yard.

"Not that I could find."

"He's Amish?"

"Looks so to me."

"Figures then."

"State's on its way. Can you wait until someone that knows him shows up?"

"No."

Beatrice glanced at the form strapped to the stretcher, his breathing still shallow. Feeling the need to stall, she asked, "Injuries extensive?"

"Seems stable." The attendant shrugged his shoulders. "Unconscious."

"Life flight?"

"No. Doesn't fit."

"There might be someone along soon — like his kin."

"You know his kin?"

"Dispatcher thinks that because the horse isn't here, word will spread."

"What? Horses talk? Strange ways, these Amish. Might work — might not. If anyone shows up to ask, we're at Adams County Medical."

"Okay."

"Did you see who did this?" the attendant asked.

Beatrice noted that they were curious

enough to take time to ask that. "No. My mother lives here. She called it in. Saw nothing though. Just heard the noise."

"Nasty piece of work."

"Yeah. Looks like it hit him from behind. Swerved at the last minute. State will investigate. This will be their case, not mine. Didn't see any skid marks." Beatrice was playing for time, hoping for what, she wasn't quite sure. She stepped away from the ambulance and then stopped at the sound of horse's hooves on the blacktop coming fast from the east.

The attendant heard it too. "Kin coming?"

"I would guess so. Surely you can wait a minute. It's the Amish."

The attendant shrugged, his hand on the door handle. "A minute."

Stepping off the blacktop to wait, Beatrice watched the buggy come up, its horse panting, nostrils flared from the fast run. An older, bearded man, his hair white in the flashing ambulance lights, came out of the buggy in a rush, leaving his horse standing in the middle of the road, its sides heaving.

"I'm looking for my son," the man said.

"You just had a horse come home unattended?" Beatrice asked him, moved by the intensity in his eyes.

"Yes — you know that?"

155

"There's been an accident. Don't know who was involved. He has no ID on him."

"Is he a young man?"

Beatrice nodded. "And your name, sir?"

"Isaac. Isaac Miller. Is he . . . dead?" Isaac's eyes went toward the closed ambulance door.

"No, Mr. Miller. He's alive. Let's see if this is your son."

The attendant was already swinging the door open, motioning for Isaac to climb up. He did so, slowly, almost cautiously, Beatrice thought. The dome light shone on the uncovered man strapped to the stretcher, the oxygen mask in place.

"It's John," Isaac said softly, his back bent in the ambulance's tight space. "How serious are his injuries?"

"No broken legs and arms. Don't know beyond that," the attendant told him. "Seems to be in a coma. Probably from a head injury. We're taking him to Adams County Medical."

"You can't take him to Cincinnati? Bethesda North?" he asked. "Good people there."

"No, too far," the attendant said. "You can transfer him, if you want."

"You can ride along," Beatrice interjected, trying to make things easier for Isaac. "I'll see that your horse is taken care of."

"No." Isaac shook his head, slowly climbing back down the ambulance steps. "I will get my wife. We will come as soon as we can."

"Sorry this happened," the attendant told him. "We have to be going."

"The Lord will do as He pleases," Isaac said, taking off his hat, stepping back toward his buggy. Standing there, Isaac watched as the ambulance slowly took off and then picked up speed.

Beatrice cleared her throat to get his attention. "If you could give me some information, Mr. Miller, it would be appreciated."

"Oh, yes," he said, pulling his eyes away from the fading ambulance lights. "His name's John. John Miller."

CHAPTER SEVENTEEN

Isaac got back into his buggy. His horse, still standing patiently in the middle of the road, was breathing normal now. Isaac groaned wearily and slapped the reins to gently get the horse moving. His mind, though, was with the ambulance speeding toward the hospital in West Union. His son was not dead, but he was surely seriously injured.

The ride home was much slower. When Isaac finally reached the driveway, he wondered what he would say to Miriam. She would need a few minutes to gather some things together because she might want to stay at the hospital.

When he entered the house, Miriam was on the couch. She looked up, her face composed.

"Is he . . . ?"

Isaac shook his head, not sure how to proceed. "They took him to the hospital —

in West Union."

Her face was unbelieving, processing the implications. "*Da Hah* didn't take him?"

"No," he said softy, "they just took him in the ambulance."

"We're going to him, of course." Miriam rose quickly from the couch, gladness in her face, her hands reaching out to Isaac.

Isaac nodded. "I left the horse tied to the barn. Get something — you might want to stay for the night."

Miriam understood, moving quickly into their bedroom. She soon returned with a small pouch. "Will you stay too?"

"I don't think so. One is enough."

"We have to tell Aden."

Isaac hadn't thought of that, but it made sense. "We can stop in on the way. They'll be in bed though."

"We should tell them. They'll want to know. Rebecca too, but maybe not tonight."

Isaac nodded. "I suppose so."

"Someone needs to know," Miriam stated.

Isaac knew she was right. Life was a community matter to them, deeply rooted in the conviction that major events were not to be lived alone. "Let's go then. We have a ways to travel."

"Should we call for a driver?" Miriam asked, hesitating.

"It will take longer. The horse is able to make the trip quite well. I'd hate to call for someone at this time of the night."

"Mrs. Coldwell might do it."

Isaac waited, knowing Miriam well enough to know she needed time to think without pressure or persuasion. Then he said what she already knew. "No, let's go with the buggy. We'll get there quicker. It might take an hour for her just to get here."

After the short drive to Aden's, Isaac handed the reins to Miriam and walked toward the darkened house. Wishing he had a flashlight, Isaac found his way up the walk with the light coming from the stars. After knocking, Isaac received no answer. And so he repeated the motion, louder this time.

Isaac was about to knock again, when a kerosene lamp light flickered in the front window. A drowsy Aden slowly opened the door, holding the kerosene lamp. His shirt was hanging over his pants, his suspenders limply swinging down the sides of his legs. Before Aden could speak, Isaac said, "John's been hurt in an accident."

"Seriously?" Aden seemed to be fast waking up.

"Don't know. He was unconscious and in the ambulance when I got there. They took him to Adams Medical."

"What happened?"

"No one seems to know. Got hit from behind, coming back from seeing Rebecca."

"You need anything tonight?"

"Don't think so. Miriam will probably stay at the hospital. I'll come back home — I think."

"Let me know then if you need anything. And let me know when you find out how he is."

Isaac nodded in the starlight, moved off the front porch, and headed back down the walk, hearing the door shut behind him. *It is good that someone knows.* A feeling of safety filled him. *Da Hah does indeed not want for anyone to be alone, especially in times like this.*

In the silence of the night, they drove down toward Dunkinsville and then south on 41, each lost in their own thoughts. Isaac turned on the rear flashers of the buggy once he was on the state road, their piercing light clearly visible behind him.

Isaac grimaced, thinking of the battery power being used. Hopefully the charge would last for the night's work. There was just no way he was turning them off on the state road.

Some of the younger boys were going to solar power to recharge their batteries, but

Isaac still lugged his out from under the seat of the buggy the old-fashioned way. Only last week had he completed the routine. To reach full battery charge, he had to run the generator in the barn for an hour. The battery ought to be in good shape.

"How bad was he hurt?" Miriam asked, returning to the more urgent matter at hand.

"I couldn't tell," Isaac said, hoping his fears would not reveal themselves.

"Did you get to talk to the ambulance attendants?"

"Yes," Isaac said, knowing Miriam wanted to know more, "one of them said there were no broken legs or arms."

"He didn't say why John was unconscious?"

"Likely a head injury," he said, as calmly as he could.

She said nothing more as the horse's hooves pounded the pavement. The darkness of the night lit up periodically by passing automobiles. Isaac could see them slowing down and dimming their lights until they figured out what was ahead. Once they identified the horse and buggy, they passed them and sped on their way.

CHAPTER EIGHTEEN

At the crash site, Beatrice was still looking around, having given the state cop, Mike Richards, the information she had obtained from the Amish man, Isaac Miller. Beatrice could have left some time ago because Mike was now in charge, but she was still curious. It was her mother's house where the accident had happened . . . and it was in her county too.

Mike might solve this case and find the one who had hit the buggy. Then again he might not. The fact that there was no one around to claim responsibility pointed quite distinctly to guilt. Why else would the person run? And was it done intentionally, or was it an accident?

Was it possible the buggy didn't have lights, or perhaps they were malfunctioning? From Beatrice's experience with the Amish, that was unlikely. She had always noted how careful the Amish were to keep their lights in working condition. Then there was the rectangular slow-moving vehicle sign posted on the back of each buggy as a backup.

Beatrice knew from driving up behind buggies at night in her squad car, that the signs lighted up well even without lights. There could then be no reason to hit this buggy in town, unless someone was impaired or careless.

"Any ideas?" she asked Mike.

"Some tracks in the ditch — so the guy didn't stay on the road."

"No skid marks either," Beatrice said, having noted that earlier.

"Must not have slowed down much, or very little," Mike agreed. "Swerved though. That's what threw the boy against the house. Saved the horse too."

"You want to ask the neighbors?" Beatrice was thinking of Mr. Urchin, now seated in front of his house, his porch light on. He usually knew everything that went on around the neighborhood, and she had seen him out on his porch minutes after the ambulance arrived.

"No — go ahead," Mike told her, busy with his report.

Beatrice made her way to the Urchin yard. When she got within earshot, she called out

"Good evening" to the neighbor who looked cold despite wearing a bathrobe over dark blue flannel night clothes.

"Evening," he said. "Buggy got it good."

"Yes," she agreed, "you see anything?"

"Young Amish man." Mr. Urchin ignored her question.

"Yes. John Miller. You know him?"

Mr. Urchin nodded, his brown bathrobe soaking up the beams from the porch light, deepening the sense of night. "Lives on top of the Ridge. Good people — his parents. Those are the ones to go young — the good ones."

"He didn't die," Beatrice told him.

"Oh." Mr. Urchin was nonplussed. "Just told the missus he was dead. Looked that way on the stretcher."

"He was unconscious." Beatrice wanted to get on with the conversation but knew better than to rush the man. If she wanted information, it would have to come out in Mr. Urchin's own good time.

"Didn't look so to me," Mr. Urchin retorted. "He wasn't moving when they took him away."

"He was just unconscious," Beatrice repeated. "You didn't happen to see or hear what hit him?"

"Mighty strange. He looked dead." Apparently Mr. Urchin was not about to be convinced just yet. "Who says he was unconscious?"

"Paramedics."

"Young people — all of 'em." Mr. Urchin snorted through his nose, his brown robe separating a little more at the collar. "They know nothing nowadays. Think they do, but they're dumber than rocks. Don't teach 'em nothing at school anymore. Drawing pictures and talking about their feelings. Ought to teach 'em read'n and write'n."

"The paramedics are usually right," Beatrice told him, hoping not to anger the old man too much. "They know what they're doing."

"Looked dead to me." Mr. Urchin settled back into his chair.

"Did you see anything of the accident?" Beatrice probed again.

"Been out here on my chair the whole time." Mr. Urchin snorted again, scorn in the sound, apparently directed at the implication that he would have missed anything this important.

"I mean before it happened?"

Mr. Urchin seemed to be thinking, so Beatrice waited. "It was that young boy from down the hill." His head tilted toward the north of town. "Jeremy — wild one he is. Hate to see him in trouble like this, but he always is. Roars through here all the time."

"You saw him?" Beatrice asked.

"Yep — right after that awful crash. I saw the red pickup truck when I looked out the window."

"You were up then and saw it?"

"Got up." Mr. Urchin shifted uncomfortably in his chair. "Night troubles — bathroom you know."

"And you saw Jeremy's truck?"

"Saw it with my own eyes. Right after the crash." Mr. Urchin seemed to be getting more certain by the second. "Always knew that young fellow would end up to no good. Rough upbringing — that's what he's had. Running wild like he does. No discipline — that's what's wrong with kids nowadays. No one takes control or makes them own up to what they do. Sorry to see him come to this end. Really sorry."

"You sure about this?" Beatrice eyed the old man skeptically.

"Now, lookie here," Mr. Urchin replied, getting up from his chair. "Do I look like I's lying. I told you what I saw and that's just the way it is. That's another trouble this world is in. No one believes the ones who really know. Takes the word of the smart alecks from the universities over the ones with sense. Common sense and decency's being lost, that's what I say. Of course I saw him. As plain as day."

"I see." Beatrice tried to keep the skepticism out of her voice. "Well, you have a good night, Mr. Urchin." There was really no sense in asking anymore questions. It would just get the old man's dander up more.

"A good night to you." Mr. Urchin settled back into his chair, apparently planning on staying there until this show was completely over.

"Know anything?" Mike asked Beatrice, when she got back to the street.

"Said it was the boy from the other end of town." Beatrice shrugged her shoulders.

"Worth checking out?"

"I suppose," Beatrice told him, seeing her chance. "Ask and ask again."

"That's what I say," Mike grinned, recognizing his own words. "You'll take care of that?"

"I've got the time, yes."

"Good — I just got a call. Another accident out on 32. You'll get the county to clean up in the morning?"

"I'll take care of it. It's my mother's house."

Mike grinned again. "The report will be at the office, if you need it."

"Thanks. I'll get a copy."

Beatrice felt her anger rise as she recalled the sight of the comatose young Amish boy, his unmoving form strapped to the stretcher. It would not go well for whoever did this. She was determined to see to that.

Walking quickly to the front door, she entered her mother's house without knocking. Isabelle was in the kitchen, seated, a cup of freshly brewed tea in her hand, its steam still rising. "Want some?" Isabelle asked. "Just made it."

"Mom, you should be in bed." Beatrice couldn't help from saying it.

"Old people don't sleep anyway," Isabelle said, without much emotion. "Sleep was all a long time ago."

"That's why you should have someone looking after you." Beatrice went to the subject automatically, without thinking.

Her mother looked up, shrugging her shoulders, "You and Wallace can forget the nursing home for a while yet. I thought for a minute there I was hearing things, but it really was something serious. God will take care of the young man. Me too," she added.

Beatrice decided to leave the subject alone for now. It would all come in its own good time, she hoped.

"Mom, did you see anything before the crash?" Beatrice asked.

"Nope — just heard it. I told you before. Didn't see anything."

"Mr. Urchin claims he saw Jeremy's truck."

Isabelle glared at the mention of that name. "Like *he* knows anything. Thinks he does. Meddlesome body, he can be."

"Seems pretty certain." Beatrice smiled at her mother's reaction.

"Certain about a lot of things," Isabelle said. "Take it with a grain of salt. That's what I say."

"I'll need to check it out."

"A nice young man fell against my house." Isabelle returned to the other subject.

"You shouldn't have been praying for him," Beatrice told her, knowing what her mother had been doing. "He's Amish."

"So what?" Isabelle's eyes flashed now. "They're people too."

"But — it just doesn't seem right."

"I'll pray for whomever I want," Isabelle told her, sipping on her tea. "Sure you don't want some? Everyone can use the Lord's help. Even you can, Beatrice, especially with that shiftless husband of yours."

"Mother." Beatrice's voice had a warning in it.

"Well, he is. You married him, so now you live with him."

"He's got his good points."

"So does a skunk," Isabelle retorted.

Beatrice rolled her eyes. "He's good to me, Mom. You should be thankful. At least I don't come home beaten."

"A low standard to live by."

"I'll see you then, Mom." Beatrice reached for the doorknob. "You get some sleep."

"I'm *not* going to the nursing home," Isabelle said quietly.

"I know, Mom, I know." Beatrice stepped out into the night again. *Getting old must be hard. No sense in making it harder than it already is. But the thought of Mom living here alone is still unnerving.*

Beatrice knew her mother would say she wasn't alone. She had the Lord with her. But she didn't quite have the faith her mother did. That had gone by the wayside years ago, eroded by living with the world's trouble and evil.

She sighed as she turned her thoughts to checking out Jeremy. No doubt her mother would be praying for him too.

She got in her cruiser and drove the distance to Jeremy's house. Pulling into the

171

driveway, her headlights lit up the red truck in question, holding it like prey in two giant claws. Playing her flashlight along the sides of the truck as she got out of the cruiser, she looked for signs of damage or paint scratches. Fully expecting to find them readily there, she was a little surprised when she found none. Going around the truck a second time, she had to admit there simply was no damage. It was impossible for this vehicle to have hit a buggy an hour before. Apparently old man Urchin had been too certain.

Behind her a door opened and Jeremy's father, Alex, whom she knew well, stood in the doorway. "Anything wrong, Beatrice?" he asked.

"Just checking. Jeremy home all evening?"

"Since nine or so. Got in early." His voice was not too friendly. "Something wrong?"

"Just checking," she repeated. "Sorry to disturb you."

"Quite all right," he said sounding relieved.

She got back in the cruiser as he shut the front door. "Mr. Urchin, next time I'll ask someone else too," she said in frustration, backing out on the blacktop road.

CHAPTER NINETEEN

Isaac found the correct street once he was in town. The bright streetlights blinded his eyes until they adjusted. His horse looked like it had the same problem by the way it shook its head as they drove under the lights. A carful of young people, driving slowly around them from behind, gave the buggy a good looking over.

"Must think us strange," Miriam said, watching the driver pull his sunglasses down for a better look.

"It's just the late time of night. Buggies coming in during the day look more normal."

"Why's he wearing sunglasses in the dark then?" Miriam asked.

"Just the world's way," Isaac told her. "It doesn't have to make sense."

"Lots of things don't make sense. Does *this* make sense to you?" she asked.

He thought about it for a moment. "You

mean John?"

Miriam nodded as they drove under another streetlight.

"Don't know. Haven't thought much about it."

"He's our son. The child of our old age. Bethany was born soon after we were married. I thought we would never have another child."

"Then we should consider ourselves blessed to have had him."

"You know I do — always have." Her tone seemed to rebuke him. "Why would God take away such a blessing?"

"He hasn't."

"No," she allowed. "But what if God takes him — in another way."

"What do you mean?"

Miriam was slow to speak. "What if . . . if . . ."

"What if he's paralyzed?" Isaac finally said the dreaded words, feeling glad they were now out.

"That's what I mean. What if God takes him — in that way."

"Then we must bear the burden. *Da Hah gebt un Da Hah nemt.*"

"I know," she said softly. "The Lord gives and the Lord takes. That's what you say on Sunday. Do you still say it now?"

"I just did." He pulled on the reins to make another turn.

"I know," Miriam said patiently. "I know you well enough for that, Isaac. Do you feel that way — really?"

Isaac found himself lost in thought, looking out at the passing streets. "No — not really," he allowed. "But that doesn't change anything. I still believe it. Our feelings must follow our faith, Miriam. Not the other way around. You know that. That is how we live our lives. We couldn't go on for very long if we doubted everything when the feelings weren't right."

"Do you think God actually means that?" she asked gently, as if she were treading on thin ice. "I know Job said it, but . . ."

"Yes, He does really mean it," Isaac said without hesitation. "It's the Word of God."

"Ya, I suppose," she allowed.

Isaac said nothing, allowing Miriam to feel what she was feeling. It was better that way. She would come back sooner than if he tried to convince her that everything would be well. Everything might *not* be well, at least from their point of view, and that hurt him too. At the moment, any words he might speak of John's eventual wellness would not be genuine. It was better to let the pain hurt. God would understand, Isaac was sure. He should, after all, be big enough to handle some doubts.

"If he's crippled," Isaac finally said, "there will be *gnawdi.* Others have found it so before us, and we too can carry the load."

Isaac was sure he saw tears in Miriam's eyes, as he found something he could use as a hitching post. Obviously none of the hospital designers thought about buggies using the parking lot. One of the bright streetlights would have to do, its light buzzing above them, attracting the night insects. Isaac tied his horse to the pole, making sure the rope was secure.

They entered by the front doors, finding the information desk unattended.

"There's no one around," Isaac said, looking up and down the hall.

"There's someone coming now," Miriam whispered, pulling gently on Isaac's arm to make him stop craning his neck.

The side door opened, and a white-clad nurse approached. "May I help you?"

"We are the Millers. John's parents," Isaac told her.

"John Miller . . . oh, yes." She nodded her head. "I believe he's out of ER and in a room. Let me check." She sat at the desk and logged in on a computer. Within seconds she said, "Yes, he's in room 201 —

down the hall."

They followed her silently, feeling out of place with the antiseptic off-white walls surrounding them. The nurse stopped in front of a closed door, opened it, then stood aside for them to enter. "I'll tell the doctor you're here."

Miriam had eyes only for the still form lying on the bed, a single tube running into his arm, his head appearing swollen on one side but with no other visible signs of injury. She approached the bed, while Isaac lagged behind, self-consciousness sweeping over him.

Isaac brought his hands together in front of him, but they too felt unfamiliar, rough, foreign, as if they weren't even his own. Miriam seemed to be having no such problems moving closer to John.

"John," she whispered, receiving no response. "We've come." She reached out to touch his hand and held it between both of hers. "Can you hear me?" she asked, still in a whisper.

When there was no answer, Miriam gently laid John's hand by his side again. "John," she whispered, reaching out to brush his forehead, in a gesture from his childhood.

"He's still unconscious," Isaac said, know-

177

ing Miriam knew, but needing to say it anyway.

Miriam nodded. "John, *Da Hah* will help you," she said softly. "*Da Dat* — your father is here too. We came as soon as we could."

"He can't hear you," Isaac felt the need to say.

She nodded but continued, "We don't know yet what's wrong with you, but they have good doctors here. You're in Adams County Hospital. They brought you here in the ambulance, *Dat* said."

Behind them the door opened, letting in a young man.

"I'm Dr. Wine," he said. "Mr. and Mrs. Miller?"

They nodded.

"Let me look at John's chart again," he said, walking over to the bed. A moment later, he motioned to them to be seated. Across the room, he took one of the chairs from against the wall.

"We only have X-rays to go by at this time. We can find no internal injuries. Breathing, vitals, in good shape. That was quite a distance to be thrown, from what the medics on the scene told me."

"What is wrong with him?" Isaac asked, dreading the all-important question.

"He suffered a skull fracture — a *linear*

fracture. It means that a portion of the skull is broken and there is the possibility of further complications. Quite a severe blow, as you can tell from the swelling. That's what's causing the unconsciousness at this point. We will do a CT scan in the morning to see if there is anything else."

Isaac waited.

Dr. Wine sensed their fear. "Your son's condition will be monitored closely. With the care that we have here at Adams, he should be okay."

"What do you expect to find on the scan?"

"We're not sure." Dr. Wine wrinkled his brow. "Hopefully there is nothing else, but there could be bleeding into the brain."

"Did he break his neck?" Isaac asked another dreaded question.

"No — thankfully not."

Isaac drew a relieved breath.

Dr. Wine noted Isaac's relief and said, "That's always a concern, but no broken neck this time."

"The Lord was taking care of him," Miriam offered.

"I'm sure it helped," Dr. Wine agreed. "Now if one of you wants to stay the night, the nurse will help you. It's not too comfortable, but it will do. You can come and go in this room as you please. I'll see you in the morning."

They nodded again as he left the room, the door clicking shut behind him.

Miriam got up, leaving Isaac seated. Walking over to take John's hand again, she asked Isaac, "You think he knows what he's talking about?"

"The doctor?"

"Yes."

"Seems knowledgeable, like all of them."

"They're taught that — in the schools."

"At least his neck isn't broken."

"You don't get this without something being the matter." Miriam ran her hand lightly over John's swollen skull.

"Doctor was talking about a scan in the morning. That's sounds good to me." Isaac shifted on his chair.

"They don't do scans unless something's wrong. I'll feel a whole lot better once we know for sure."

Isaac nodded, wanting to leave it there. "You staying for the night?"

"Yes. Can you bring in my bag?"

He nodded. "I'll go out and get it."

Stepping outside the room, Isaac wasn't sure which way was out. The walls all looked the same. Taking a guess, he turned right and found the front desk they had passed on the way in. There was still no one there, nor when he returned with the small bag for Miriam.

As he walked into the room, he saw Miriam silently staring into space. "I'll be going now," Isaac told her quietly, setting the bag on the floor.

When there was no response, Isaac slipped away, leaving Miriam alone. This was for the best, he figured. In the days ahead, they would all pull their lives back together, as the Lord supplied them strength. Now it was important that each of them was allowed to grieve fully, and Miriam wanted to be alone with John. Isaac knew her well enough to know that.

Back on the highway, Isaac used his flashers only when a car was coming, conserving battery power. The horse pulled the buggy at a slower speed than coming into town. The miles were adding up, and so Isaac let the horse have its time.

Thoughts from earlier in the evening returned to him in the midst of a great wave of sleepiness. Shaking his head to stay awake, Isaac knew it would simply not do to fall asleep on the state road. His horse would no doubt be able to find the way home even with Isaac asleep at the reins, but it was dangerous to take the chance.

Adding another accident to the night would not be worth the few winks of sleep he would gain.

It was his memory from the scene of the accident, those pieces of buggy scattered around the yard, that woke him out of his stupor. He felt a surge of anger at whoever had done it. He hoped the police had caught the person by now, letting his mind imagine who that person might have been.

It was likely some young person. Perhaps from Unity, someone he might know, wild, reckless, and evil. Who would be capable of doing such a thing to his son? No sooner was Isaac fully aware of where his thoughts were going, than guilt for thinking them followed.

Had he not earlier in the evening been reading the words of the Lord Himself? One must forgive. Did he not know he would have to live by those words? Live them because he wanted to, yes, but also because this was what the Lord said.

Isaac breathed deeply, realizing he must let the anger go. Must do it even for someone he knew or didn't know. Must do it even if John was paralyzed. *Yes, regardless,* he told himself.

The words had been words to not only preach but words to live by. It was the will of God, sovereign in all His ways, who had brought those words to his attention, even for this very purpose.

Isaac sighed, not sure he liked this. He thought of John lying on the hospital bed, a tube running into his arm. But barely thirty minutes later, he made the turn up Wheat Ridge and soon into his own driveway. And in the wee hours of the morning, he dropped into bed and fell instantly asleep.

CHAPTER TWENTY

Beatrice had no other calls that night but drove to the other end of the county anyway, to the Shawnee State Forest. She pulled into the state park and did a drive-through, looking for what, she wasn't certain. All appeared normal, the cabins mostly unoccupied for the winter. She reported her findings to Sally and received a sleepy acknowledgement on the radio.

Beatrice then called it a day and drove back to the station, where she parked her cruiser, said goodnight to Sally, found her keys to her 99 Volvo, and headed for home.

Home was on Heidi Ridge Road, in a small house purchased just after she and Andy got married. *Andy.* Sometimes she wondered if her mother had been right about him. Isabelle had never wanted her to marry Andy, but she had thought she knew better. Like many a girl who wished to try different roads from those chosen by her mother, she married him despite any and all objections.

Have I been wrong? The question was fresh in her mind tonight as she pulled in the driveway. She gathered her purse and reached to turn out the headlights when she saw Andy's red Ford truck parked in its usual place in the driveway. There was nothing wrong with the parking. But it was the dent that caught her eye. The metal was bent as if a large object had been hit with brute force. Beatrice felt a wave of weariness and anger engulf her as she considered the obvious cause.

She took a closer look. The brief inspection produced a firm conclusion. Andy had hit something large and hit it hard. Beatrice stood there in the night air, the red Ford lit up by her Volvo's headlights, her deep tiredness cruelly pushed aside by a now rushing anger.

How could he do this?

With purpose in her step, she turned her headlights off, slammed the car door, and went inside. She expected to find Andy in the bedroom, sound asleep. Instead he was seated at the kitchen table, his back turned toward her, a cup of coffee between his hands.

The unusualness of this only served to cement her conclusions. "So, what have you been up to tonight?" she asked, wondering if he would admit his guilt.

He didn't move or flinch, his arms on the table, his shoulders stooped forward.

"I asked you, what have you been up to tonight?" she asked louder.

Still nothing.

So much for subtlety. "You had an accident tonight, didn't you?" she demanded, marching around in front of him. "Hit an Amish buggy."

He kept his eyes on the cup of coffee. "What are you talking about?"

"You hit a buggy," she said firmly. "Don't try denying it. I was at the scene."

"I just went out for a ride. What harm is there in that?"

"Like hitting a buggy? Like leaving the scene of an accident? Do you know how much trouble you're in? In trouble with *me?*"

He shrugged his shoulders. "I didn't hit a buggy."

She glared at him, her anger flaring fresh and vigorous. "Then what are you doing up at this hour of the night? And why is that fresh dent in your truck?"

"I hit a deer," he muttered, his eyes still on the cup of coffee. "I was out for a drive.

I needed some air."

"And I'm supposed to believe that?"

His eyes refused to raise or meet hers.

"Look at me, Andy," she demanded. "Tell me the truth."

"I hit a *deer*," he repeated, cautiously looking up. His blue eyes looked glazed, and he dropped them again.

She thought for a moment and came to a conclusion. "Andy, I want you out of the house. I want you to leave now."

There was fear in his eyes now. "For hitting a deer?"

"For hitting a buggy . . . For leaving the scene of the accident like the coward you are . . . and for whatever other reasons I don't know about. Another woman, perhaps?"

He flinched, and she saw it.

"Thought you could get away with it?" she continued, slamming her purse down on the kitchen table. "Start packing — now." Leaving him sitting there, she headed for the bedroom. Then it occurred to her that Andy would need access to the bedroom to pack. And sure enough, she heard the bedroom door open slowly.

"You have ten minutes," she said.

"I don't need that long," he said resolutely.

"You have ten minutes," she repeated.

"Pack and then go. I'll be in the bathroom. Be gone by the time I'm out."

He cleared his throat. "I'm guilty of what you said. Everything but one. I wasn't with a woman."

"So you hit the buggy?"

"I hit one of the holy people," he said, his hands trembling.

"You hit one of them."

"Did he die?" he asked, his lips barely moving.

There was no doubting the sincerity of his concern, and it kept her from moving toward the bathroom door. "No. He'll live. What happened?"

He clasped his hands, relief evident on his face that she was still listening. "I wasn't paying attention, I guess. Saw some lights. It happened so fast. Just a loud bang and the horse running in my headlights. I couldn't stay there. I just couldn't. I was sure he was dead, and God was going to judge me with fire from heaven. If not, your mother would. It was in front of her house."

"You saw the injured man?"

He shook his head. "But he had to be around somewhere. Someone had to be — it was a buggy."

"I see." She felt her resolve leaking away, compassion for Andy stirring. "There was

188

no woman?" She hoped the desperation wasn't showing in her voice.

He shook his head, not seeming to notice. "No. Just a very stupid thing to do."

Beatrice took a deep breath, uncertain what to do with the emotions she was feeling. "I'll tell you what," she finally concluded, "go down to the station. Sally's still there, I'm sure. Give her your statement. Be sure it's a full and detailed one. Don't try lying."

His hands were trembling again, but his eyes were raised to her face.

She continued, "Tell Sally that Mike Richards from state handled the scene. She'll know how to get the information to him."

He nodded his head, then left. As simple as that, she thought. But was he going to the station? She heard his truck starting up.

Pacing the bedroom floor, she realized she had to know. Picking up the phone, she dialed the number and waited for someone to answer it. "Sally," she said.

"Yes . . . Beatrice."

"Andy's supposed to be on his way there. Call me and tell me what he told you when he's done. Right away. It's about the accident tonight."

"Oh, Beatrice," Sally gasped, "not Andy?"

"Yes, I'm afraid so."

"Want to tell me more?"

"No. Let's see what he says."

"Okay. Will let you know."

"Call me in ten minutes if he's not there."

"Nasty deal, huh?"

"You could say so."

Beatrice paced the floor to calm down, then got ready for what was left of the night's sleep. Still there was no return phone call. So far, so good. She was wondering why she hadn't stuck to her plans of forcing Andy to leave when the phone rang.

"Yes," she said, lifting the receiver.

"He told me everything," Sally said, without saying hello.

"Read it to me."

Sally sighed and said, "You should trust him a bit. He's a nice man."

"Just read it," Beatrice snapped.

The reading of Andy's statement took five minutes, and when Sally was done, she asked, "Was that what he told you?"

"Yes."

"So he's not lying."

"No."

"Then you have a good night's sleep. Take care of that man — will you?"

"I'll try," she said.

A few minutes later, she heard the sound of Andy's Ford in the driveway. The bedroom door opened soon afterwards.

Andy stopped halfway across the floor. "Can I stay?"

"I suppose," she said, still not certain why. The confession had taken courage, something Andy hadn't displayed too often in his life.

Andy cemented her decision by saying, "I want to talk to the holy people in the morning. The one I hit. I want to apologize and pay for the damage."

"He's in the hospital," she said. "The state will charge you."

"I know," he said quietly, but his hands weren't trembling anymore. "I want to make it right. The insurance will cover the damage — the hospital bill."

"You have it paid up?" she asked, knowing his weakness.

"Yes."

"Andy, you can't talk to the victim. It doesn't usually turn out well. And it's against department policy."

"But I need to do this, Bea. Help me make things right."

Beatrice looked at Andy. In some ways he was like a child. But his desire to make this right was a step toward being a man. "I could lose my job for this, but I'll talk to the father of the victim and see what I can do. But I can't promise anything. If he doesn't want to talk to you, there's nothing I can do."

"That's all I ask," Andy said. He then approached Beatrice and offered himself for an embrace.

She slowly extended her arms and wrapped them around him and repeated, "I'll do what I can."

CHAPTER
TWENTY-ONE

Rebecca woke with the alarm clock, a sleepy fog on her brain. She reached out to shut off the racket, frustrated that it had taken such a noise to awaken her on her first full day home. She ought to be fresh and enthused to be here, not needing help to get up.

All night she had tossed and turned, trying to sleep. John's anger had left her in a turmoil. The talk with her parents afterward had done little to resolve the situation. She was still surprised that last night had been so upsetting.

Rebecca had thought that when she arrived home, she'd have a fresh start, a new capacity to love John and to leave the memory of Atlee behind.

The memory of how John had acted rose before her. It was simply not right, the way he had talked to her. She had hoped by this morning things would be looking different, but now, if anything, it was looking worse.

Rebecca stared at the dark ceiling, wondering how things could have gotten so bad, so quickly. *Has John been like this all along? Have I just not noticed, or have I pushed him into something by my actions?*

Guilt and worry played with Rebecca's mind until she resolutely pushed them away. There was simply no way she was completely at fault. Maybe she had not done everything right, but she was trying, and such an outburst from John was simply over the edge.

Rebecca got up and lit the kerosene lamp. The glass chimney warmed in her hand once the wick was burning. The flame danced wildly, then calmed down within the safety of the glass. A last puff of black smoke rose from the top before the wick burned steady.

What about the upcoming Sunday evening? That was the evening she had promised to go into the details about Atlee. *Why did I promise John I would tell him everything?*

From across the hall, she heard Matthew's door open and his footsteps going down the stairs. He was doing real well, getting up on time, developing into a right good young man. She wished with all her heart she could say the same things about her own life.

Well, *Da Hah* would just have to help her. That was all there was to it. She certainly was in deeper than she could handle.

Sunday would come, and then she would have to face John. If John made too big a fuss, she would simply tell him the engagement was off, her heart missing a beat at the thought, sorrow filling her.

What would John do if she dared to take such a bold step? Declare her damaged material, spread word around the young people's circle she had a Mennonite boyfriend hidden away somewhere?

That could be quite damaging. It could make her prospects of finding another boyfriend among the Amish slim. Not that she wanted to, she quickly told herself. Although she was filled with shame at the thought, she also took comfort remembering Emma's happiness as a single Amish woman.

It was strange. Did John know that the very thing he feared, he was causing by his actions toward her? Hardly would he believe it.

Yet with all the emotions spinning in her heart, life must go on, and the chores were calling. She must not let Matthew do them all himself. He would think she was shirking her duty if she waited much longer, and this her first morning home.

The sounds of her mother stirring in the kitchen came up through the heat register as she slid it open. She smiled at the familiar sounds, letting the feelings of home soak in. How good it was to be home — so safe and secure, a place where things were as they should be, where others had made so many decisions for her, deciding what was right and wrong.

But she was grown up now. She would leave one day soon. Either as John's wife . . . or not. The time was coming, no matter what she did to stop it. Marrying or not marrying John would involve entering another world, a world where responsibilities would rest squarely on her shoulders. Having been in Milroy with Stephen and Leona, she felt with acute freshness what that might all include. Feeling a recoiling against it, she paused before leaving her room, drinking up the sounds coming through her register.

"Home," she whispered. "I don't want to leave you. But I must. We can't be children forever."

Glad no one was around to hear her talking to herself, Rebecca found her way down the dark stairs, taking care not to trip.

She stuck her head in the kitchen, taking in a deep breath.

Mattie noticed her daughter, still disheveled from sleep, and asked, "Good to be home?"

"Yes."

"Matthew will be glad for the help."

"You need any help in here?"

"No." her mother said.

"Don't go all out on breakfast on account of me," Rebecca said, suspecting her mother would anyway.

"It's your first morning home."

"I know, but you don't have to."

"Lester will love it," Mattie said, shifting the blame as if that would help.

Rebecca smiled, knowing there was no persuading her mother. "Matthew's wondering where I'm at," she said, as she tugged on her coat and went out the door.

True to her suspicions, Matthew spoke up before she had even shut the barn door behind her. "Where've you been, sleepyhead? Did you get spoiled, sleeping in late in Milroy?"

"Oh, be quiet," Rebecca said. What would he understand about the night she had just spent tossing in bed?

"Troubles, have we?" Matthew looked in

197

Rebecca's direction, his nearly twelve-year-old forehead wrinkled. He hardly paused to ask the question while shoveling feed for the soon incoming cows.

The thought that Matthew might have heard what was going on last night crossed Rebecca's mind, along with a stab of fear. In that case there would be nothing like talking about dating troubles with a young brother. Matthew would never understand, nor was it any of his business. Rebecca wished she knew how much he knew before she said anything. Walking toward the milk house, Rebecca hoped that ignoring Matthew would work.

Seeing his sister return, Matthew spoke up knowingly, "Baby troubles in Milroy."

His statement gave her relief and a new venue for conversation. Rebecca replied, "They always are."

"That's why I'm never having any," he pronounced, swelling out his chest and acting like he might thump it. "That avoids all the troubles."

"Huh! Babies aren't the only cause of troubles."

Matthew stated firmly, "But most of them happen because of babies."

"I thought girls caused all the trouble," Rebecca reminded him.

Matthew snorted in disgust. "They start it, but babies are the end."

"So who told you that, wise guy?"

"Boys at school. We figured it out "

Rebecca laughed. "Don't you think it's a little too soon?"

"Soon for what?" he asked confidently.

But she heard the edge of uncertainty in his voice. "You'll get over it. All boys do," she said in her best sisterly voice, while hanging the milkers on the wire.

"Good morning." The cheerful voice of their father came through the barnyard door, cows crowding in as he opened it.

"Good morning," she returned, not as cheerfully.

"It's good to have you home," Lester replied, whacking a slow cow on the behind with his hand.

The cow paid him no mind. Spotting the pile of feed Matthew had just shoveled out, the cow let out a low bellow, lurched forward, and stuck its head through the neck rods, tongue reaching out hungrily.

"Mom got a big breakfast going?" Lester asked.

"Of course. Because I'm home," Rebecca said.

"I thought so." Lester grinned. "Good for all of us."

"Why don't I get big breakfasts?" Matthew protested.

"You will," Lester told him. "Your turn is coming."

"Why does everyone keep saying that?" Matthew protested again.

"Because it's true," Rebecca said.

"Let's get these cows milked," Matthew said quickly, "so we can get to that breakfast."

"Sounds like a good idea," Lester said, shutting the barnyard door and reaching for the water bucket to wash the cows' udders.

Noting his dad's agreement, Matthew grinned triumphantly.

Rebecca figured Matthew deserved these few moments of satisfaction. *Males need moral support too,* she thought wryly, remembering John's actions last night.

CHAPTER
TWENTY-TWO

Despite his late night, Isaac was up with the rising of the sun, needing no alarm clock to awaken him. There was plenty on his mind to disturb his sleep. Even in the light of day, things were still a little hazy. *Is John really in the hospital, or did I just imagine it?*

The empty place in the bed beside him confirmed his memory. The whole house was empty and quiet. *Yes, John really is hurt and in the hospital.*

The silence pressed in on Isaac. It dampened his spirits, and he tried to shake the sense of something missing. He reminded himself that life was in the hands of God and that in such faith he could rest secure. Feeling somewhat better, he got dressed and went to the kitchen, hungry for breakfast. It was there he missed Miriam again, the emotion striking him hard.

There was no hot meal waiting, so Isaac reached for the cold cereal that Miriam kept for occasional use. Bringing it out, he thumped the cereal down disgustedly on the table. From the picture on the box, the cereal looked edible, but he knew from past experiences how such prepared food tasted.

Isaac halfheartedly poured the cornflakes into the bowl, the dry flakes rustling as they tumbled from the box, sounding like his bones trying to get going in the morning. Adding milk and sugar, he ate, but his spirits were sinking again.

Aden would be over soon, checking for news before opening his store. Isaac really didn't want to be caught eating this stuff, so he kept glancing out the kitchen window.

In the old days, the folks didn't even know what cornflakes were. Well, the real old folks, he amended his thoughts. He ate faster than he should have, the cold milk hurting his teeth and forcing him to slow down. He finished just in time to see Aden walking across the front yard, frosty mist rising with each breath.

Opening the front door, Isaac let him in.

"Any news?" Aden asked, standing just inside the front door, rubbing his hands together.

"Left Miriam at the hospital for the night," Isaac said. "John was still in a coma then, and the doctor didn't really know anything beyond a severe skull facture."

"They doing more tests?"

"A scan this morning. He got hit in the head pretty hard."

"Figure it's serious?"

A worried look crossed Isaac's face. "*Da Hah* knows, I guess."

"Whose fault was the accident?"

"Officer was sure it wasn't John's. I talked to one of them at the scene."

"Has Rebecca been told?"

"No. Miriam thought we'd better wait."

"Engaged — aren't they?"

Isaac nodded. "John just told us. Someone needs to tell her soon, I suppose."

"I'll send Sharon down right away."

Isaac wrinkled his brow. "It could be quite a shock. Maybe someone else should go. Someone older."

"Well," Aden allowed, "you're probably right. Sharon's a little young to deliver such news. I'll send my wife."

"Esther would be better." Isaac looked relieved. "Tell her everything we know."

"You think that's wise?" Aden didn't look too certain.

"It's best," Isaac assured him. "She'll find out anyway. Better that she hear it as soon as possible."

"I'll tell Esther then. You want to call the

hospital?"

"Yah." Isaac didn't have to think long on that. "I'll be down in a little while. Probably visit later — depending."

"You need a fresh horse? Yours is probably worn out from last night."

"I could." Isaac nodded his appreciation.

"You can use ours then — after you call. Let us know if you need anything else."

"I will," Isaac assured him, as he watched Aden open and go out the door. Glumly Isaac returned to the kitchen and rinsed out his cereal bowl. This day looked long and weary, stretching out in front of him as one long hard road.

The thought of hospital bills came to Isaac suddenly and forcefully, even as he noticed a police cruiser pull up the driveway. No doubt they were coming to ask questions about the accident. But neither John nor he had money for large hospital bills. Yet *Da Hah* would surely see to the need, perhaps through help from the church. Still the load felt heavy on his shoulders.

He recognized the female officer climbing out of the cruiser. A man accompanied her, which was puzzling, but maybe he was a detective, come to find the man who had done this to John. Hoping the questions for him wouldn't go there, Isaac walked to the front door. Last night he had found a peace about the accident. *Da Hah* had allowed it, and there would be no prosecution effort from him or John even if the officers knew who had done this. Isaac believed that vengeance was in the hand of God and so was the seeking of justice.

Isaac opened the door before his visitors knocked.

"Good morning, Mr. Miller," Beatrice said, greeting him. "I was the officer you spoke to last night."

"I remember," Isaac told Beatrice, adding nothing else. It would be best, he figured, to see what the law wanted before answering any questions.

"This is my husband, Andy," Beatrice said rather uneasily. "Mr. Miller, my husband has something he'd like to tell you." And then she stepped back slightly so that Andy was in front of her.

"Yes?" Isaac looked at the man.

Andy fidgeted a little, glancing quickly up at Isaac and then back to the ground. Isaac figured he must look strange to the man, his white beard still a little unkempt, his shirttails half-tucked in, one suspender up on a shoulder, the other hanging to the side.

"Mr. Miller, I was the one who hit your

son last night," Andy stammered. He quickly added, "I'm very sorry."

There was silence as Isaac processed the information. "You must come in then," he stated simply. "It's more comfortable in the living room."

"But . . ." Andy was clearly flustered.

Isaac held open the door. Beatrice shrugged her shoulders but led the way in.

"I would serve you coffee," Isaac said, motioning them farther inside, "but the wife's not home."

Andy took the couch, cleared his throat, and said, "I'm not sure you understood me, Mr. Miller. I really shouldn't be in your house."

"I understood you," Isaac told him in a patient tone. "You hit my son. The Lord has allowed it."

"I got scared and ran," Andy added, a look on his face implying he wanted to tell it all.

Isaac saw Beatrice's face out of the corner of his eye. She kept silent but looked intent, very interested in this exchange. He ran his hand down his long beard, lifting his eyes to Andy's face. "You have done a great wrong to John and . . . to us."

Andy was keeping his eyes on Isaac's face, not flinching from the stern words.

Isaac continued, "It is in God's hands as

to what His judgment will be. It is in our hands to forgive."

"You . . ." Andy still had his eyes on Isaac's face. "I just hit your son — one of the holy people."

A gentle smile softened Isaac's face. "No, son," he said, "we are just like other men and woman. It is but the Lord's grace that any of us make it." Isaac pointed toward the sky. "Are you at peace with God?"

Andy looked startled. "I — I don't know."

"Then you have a much greater problem than hitting someone's buggy," Isaac said slowly, "even if he is in the hospital and is my son. You must think on the coming judgment, Andy, when the Lord judges all sin and unrighteousness."

"I — I'm sorry, Mr. Miller," Andy stammered, at last finding his voice.

"We can forgive you for what happened last night," Isaac said, "but only the Lord can forgive all your sins. All of us must repent from our sins, do works worthy of the Lord's grace. It is the Lord's blood that cleanses us — shed that day when He died."

Andy said nothing, but listened. "I'll think about it," he finally said.

Isaac nodded, lost in sober thought.

"My insurance company will pay for your hospital bills," Andy spoke up.

"Oh, yes, the bills." Isaac seemed to see Andy again. "If it is the Lord's will, that's good," he finally said. "It wasn't John's fault, but the hospital bill is all that will be paid."

"I see," Andy said meekly. "I'm being charged too — with a criminal offense."

"That is in the law's hands," Isaac said thoughtfully. "You must take it as instruction from the hand of God, needed for your benefit. Do not fight it, but we will not press charges."

"I see," Andy said, glancing toward Beatrice for the first time.

Beatrice shrugged her shoulders.

Isaac thought she looked pleased. "It's for your best," Isaac said, rising from his seat, the discussion obviously over. "I need to be calling my wife." With that he ushered them out with the same quiet manner he had asked them in.

"Well! He told you good," Beatrice said, once they got back in the cruiser.

"Yeah," Andy said, letting his breath out slowly.

"You'd better listen," she said, giving him a stern look.

"I will," he said meekly, a strange tone in his voice.

"I'll be watching you," she said, putting the cruiser in drive and pulling onto Wheat Ridge Road.

But Andy wasn't paying attention. He seemed to be thinking — and thinking hard.

Chapter
Twenty-Three

Rachel Byler's morning had not been going well. Getting up early, she lit the gas lantern, hung it on the nail in the kitchen ceiling, and began fixing Reuben's favorite breakfast. She was feeling a bit off. Nothing she could quite put her finger on, but something was wrong.

Stirring the pancake batter, she noticed, to her horror, little black crusty bugs on the spoon.

The flour was bug-infested. There simply could be no other explanation. How this had happened was beyond her understanding. She took great care to keep a lid on the flour box. Although this reflected poorly on her abilities as a housewife, the situation was made worse because she had used the flour yesterday to bake bread. Bugs did not grow overnight.

She flushed with anger. Was this why she felt sick this morning? Was it the bread from last night's dinner? Did Reuben and Luke awake with a sick feeling? Was this not just a little more than any human being should be asked to bear? Grimly she took a loaf of yesterday's bread out of its plastic bag and prepared to check for bugs.

Hearing Reuben's steps coming from the bedroom, she quickly slid the loaf back into the bag. Normally she wouldn't have cared if he walked through the kitchen. For a man who couldn't notice much of anything when it was important to her, Reuben *would* notice this. If there was bread out of the bag and pancake mix in the bowl, he would, no doubt, question how they were to eat the two together. A question she did not wish to answer.

"Pancakes," he said, stopping at the kitchen opening, a smile in his sleepy voice. "We haven't had those in a long time."

"Thought you might like them," she replied, not looking in his direction, hoping against hope he would continue on to his chores in the barn.

"I will," he said, as he headed out the door.

She breathed a sigh of relief.

Horror overwhelmed Rachel once again as she thought about what this meant. It was the prevailing opinion among the Amish, that only the most careless housekeepers found bugs in their flour. Poverty was no disgrace among the Amish, but poor housekeeping was. It ranked among the sins mentioned with lowered voice and raised eyebrows.

Bugs in one's flour had a way of sweeping away any admiration anyone felt for such a woman. This she was certain of. If it be found out, she would be the one to receive those disdainful looks from the women at monthly sewing.

Rachel slid the loaf out of the bag for the second time, stiffening as footsteps came down the stairs. This would be Luke, following his father to the barn. The chances of him stopping or seeing anything amiss in the kitchen were slim, so she simply waited as the stair door opened.

True to her expectation, Luke continued past the kitchen without so much as a pause or glance in. Poor boy. He deserved so much better than what he was getting from his family. Born by right into a well-to-do Amish family, he was being subjected to a bare existence, not just by his father's lack of ambition, but by her late father's eccentric will. An entire family's rightful heritage was being held hostage by forces Rachel could not understand.

The injustice of it all returned with force

as she listened to Luke's footsteps pause at the front door. He was putting on his threadbare coat, the best they could afford, but not nearly what it should be. She had intended on making him a new one this fall, but the money had simply not been there.

Reuben had seemed to have some sympathies when she told him, but his only solution had been to state that, "*Da Hah* will help us. Life's not supposed to be easy," he had added. "Heaven's our real home."

That it was, Rachel had no doubt, and so she had not said anything back to Reuben, though she had wanted to. It just seemed to her that with so much treasure stored up with *Da Hah,* like the preachers said there was, He might be willing to share some of the abundance this side of the pearly gates.

But what did she know about theology? Reuben would hardly be taking anything from his wife when it came to such matters.

What he would listen to, though, were her comments on keeping and strengthening the *Ordnungs Brief,* the church rules and other people's infractions of it. Today was Saturday, the day Reuben would go on his rounds. He would be bringing correction and seeking repentance from the rule breakers who had been reported to him.

Rachel had planned during the night to

become involved in Reuben's work. Last night Reuben had seemed open to the few things she had told him. She had decided what the next step should be on this, her mission to cleanse the sin that must be in her own family.

Rachel had remembered an infraction her brother committed a few months ago. Normally Rachel would never have mentioned it, but now things were different. Finding strength from just thinking about it, the loaf of bread now completely out of the bag, Rachel paused, glad for the good feelings coming her way. Depending on what she found in the bread, she would need all the help she could get.

The brilliance of her deduction from last night swept through her, giving her courage to examine the loaf of bread in her hands. She — Rachel, a woman — had discerned the mind of the mighty God of heaven and figured out His ways. She was sure of it. The joy of this knowledge rose in her.

She broke open the loaf and discovered many black-shelled bugs, dead, but very much in the bread. *"Dei aldi aysel,"* she told them out loud because no one was in the house and because she was angry again.

How in the world had the bugs gotten in the flour? Perhaps it was just one of those mysteries of life for which there was no conclusion. She knew though — with a certainty — that this must never be known by anyone. If Reuben found out, it might very well destroy her credibility for the task ahead. He might even refuse to take her comments about the *ordnung* infractions.

Her options ran rapidly through her mind. *Shall I throw away the bread at once?* That might be too obvious. The bread was almost impossible to dispose of without taking the loaf so far outside that Reuben would see her. And what was to be done with the pancake batter?

Better to wait until Reuben had gone somewhere during the day. Then she would bake fresh bread and feed the current bug-infested loaves to the pigs. They would enjoy the meal and make short shift of the evidence, leaving nothing to be found of the deed.

For now she could get rid of the pancake batter, stir up some fresh flour, and Reuben would never know. Sliding the loaf of bread back into the plastic bag, Rachel turned the twisty tight. Grabbing the bowl of batter, she went outside into the darkness to dispose of the matter into the chicken yard. She would dump it where the chickens could feed on it when they woke up. Thankfully they were not awake yet and didn't make their usual racket at the sound of food being poured into their yard.

She looked carefully at the pile the batter made just inside the fenced yard. It looked ordinary enough. Reuben would surely notice nothing. If he did see anything in the chicken yard, it would be a first, she thought ruefully. The chickens could die from starvation, their bodies stretched out cold, their feathers blowing away in the wind, and the man wouldn't see it.

It was on the short walk back to the house that she felt suddenly sick. Before she made it back to the house, she vomited. She bent over, retching on the ground with a force that pounded in her head.

The smell from the pancake batter rose to her face, provoking another bout. Her stomach strained from the effort. Holding the bowl away, as far as her arm could reach, she made her way to the concrete steps and sat down. A sense of deep weariness and hopelessness swept over her.

Thoughts spun in Rachel's head as she questioned what was going on. It had been many years ago, but the memory came back with force. She placed her free hand on her stomach, feeling nothing, but wondering.

Could it possibly be that she was with child again?

After all these years, how had this happened? She knew the how, but it was the why she couldn't understand. After Luke was born, she had been expecting more children, but none had come. Rachel had been secretly thankful because she carried the weight of their poverty on her shoulders. She considered it the mercy of heaven on her condition.

Even when the women at the sewing had raised their eyebrows at her childlessness, Rachel had been able to wrinkle her brow as if in sorrow, saying with absolute truthfulness that she didn't know why there were no more children.

If there had been the least doubt in her eyes, they would have known, and there would have been trouble. Intentional childlessness that stretched into years, even by the most natural of means, was not only frowned upon but a matter to be referred to the deacon for discipline.

That Rachel was the deacon's wife would not have shielded her, but it had been none of her doings. She had assured the questions in the women's eyes. "Not even natural," she had whispered once, as if that were even possible. So the childless years had rolled by.

Now though, Rachel remembered the feeling she had known with Luke's pregnancy. This was the same. Just the same. She sat on the concrete steps by her backdoor and unashamedly wept in the early morning darkness. She wept for her poverty, for her age at which she must bear this, and for the doings of the Almighty she couldn't make sense of.

CHAPTER
TWENTY-FOUR

Rachel finally roused herself, her duties of the moment returning with enough force to make her move. She would go on about her day but with the knowledge that her life was different now. She was with child. The suddenness of it left her numb.

The day had started with such hope but now was full of bugs. The thought of the child should make her feel thankful and glad, but it didn't. It filled her with a sudden and stabbing guilt.

"It's the money, always the money," she told herself bitterly, standing up. The hardness of life pressed in from all sides, matching the hardness from where she had just risen. "It's not fair," she told the heavens, knowing no one would hear in this world, hoping someone would in the other.

When nothing happened, a sense of urgency returned and propelled her back into the house. Now, more than ever, she *must* succeed. If there was another child involved — a child to carry to birth and to rear — then she must not fail in her mission. God must be appeased — and right quickly.

Failing to provide Reuben with pancakes, now that he knew she was making them, wouldn't help. Certainly she couldn't use the bugs as an excuse for failing to produce pancakes. The news of the coming child might help, but Rachel doubted whether Reuben would think that much of a reason either.

Even if she told him about the weeping spell on the back steps, he would think her sinful for being sorrowful. To Reuben such an attitude was not only against *Gottes villa,* but against His favor and that of the church. Rachel needed Reuben to continue seeing her in as good a light as possible.

Rushing in, she opened a new bag of flour, ran her fingers through it, and checked for bugs. Breathing a sigh of relief when none appeared, she mixed the new batch of pancake batter, careful not to breathe in the smell too deeply lest the nausea return. Even then, with all the rushing, she barely got the pancakes and eggs done by the time Reuben came in from the chores.

A stack of steaming hot pancakes and a full plate of eggs greeted Reuben's hungry eyes when he walked into the kitchen and sat himself. "Let's eat," Rachel told him to cover up her feelings and shortness of breath. "Things will get cold."

This efficiency he understood — appreciating the practical side of her.

"You do make good pancakes," he said, a smile spreading across his face.

"I try," she said, knowing enough to be modest. Any signs of pride would fast change his mind about her, even with pancakes and eggs on the table.

"Maple syrup?" he asked.

"Of course," she said because there was some — enough she hoped — purchased with precious money that never seemed to stretch for such luxuries as maple syrup.

"That's good," Reuben said, his smile even wider, his chair scraping the floor as he pulled the seat in closer.

Luke came in and sat down on the opposite side of the table.

Bitterness ran through Rachel's mind. *How can the man be so happy about maple syrup?* That he would be was the reason she had some on hand. That he felt that way was the problem. A poverty-stricken man like him shouldn't take so much pleasure in maple syrup, but that was how things were, deacon or no deacon.

"I'm glad you like it," Rachel said.

Reuben eyed the precious brown liquid she set on the table and quickly said, "Let's pray. The food is getting cold."

They bowed their heads in silent prayer, for which she was thankful because she did not want to hear Reuben pray out loud at the moment. Her stomach was queasy again, and she was trying hard to keep her roiling emotions under control. It was all much easier to handle when he was just quiet.

His silent prayer done, the sound of Reuben's fork on his plate brought Rachel back to the present.

"It's enough," his eyes told her when she looked at him.

She accepted his rebuke without protest, inwardly glad Reuben had caught her praying longer. This might irritate him at the moment, but later when it mattered, Reuben might consider the extra holiness to her credit.

After he had taken his pancakes, Rachel handed Reuben the egg plate. She then cleared her throat to speak. The moment was arriving when the words should be said. It bothered her that Luke was here, but she supposed it couldn't be helped.

What she had to say was best said now, at

this opportune moment when Reuben was enjoying his pancakes and eggs. After breakfast Reuben would not want to wait before heading outdoors. Then in the afternoon, before he left for his deacon rounds, the effect of the pancakes and eggs would be well worn off.

"You remember about last night?" she asked, broaching the subject carefully, checking his mood with a quick glance at his face. It seemed safe enough.

Just to be sure Reuben remembered the right thing, Rachel stuck the information into the next sentence. "Keeping the *ordnung* — when you go on your rounds this afternoon."

He nodded, his mouth full of maple syrup-soaked pancake, a look of pleasure on his face.

"Last fall I saw Ezra using the tractor," she said, dropping the news, "to pull his wagon back to the wheat field."

Reuben stared at her, his eyes blank. "Using his tractor?"

"Yes," Rachel said.

"But Ezra —" he said and paused, digesting the information.

Rachel knew what that meant. He didn't want to hear this charge against Ezra. Her brother was reasonably well-off, even without the lost inheritance from their father. Ezra was also a vocal supporter of Bishop Mose. He often spoke up at council meetings as well as any inbetween members' meetings when church matters were brought up.

"You think it's that serious?" Reuben finally asked.

"I saw him," Rachel said, leaving no room for maneuvers in her voice. "He did it right out in the daytime."

"Maybe he had use for the tractor in the wheat field?"

"Yes . . ." Rachel let the word flow off her tongue. "The tractor maybe . . . the wagon maybe. But not the two hitched together. You know the rules."

"Yes," he said with resignation.

"You need to talk to him."

"The bishop hasn't been told," Reuben countered.

"He doesn't have to be," she told him firmly. "You know the rules. Anyone can turn in a complaint."

"It's Ezra," Reuben said, as if that explained everything. "I'm not going without asking Bishop Mose first."

"You know what's going to happen then." Rachel glared at him.

"I suppose," he allowed. "Maybe Mose

will talk to him privately."

"Like that will do any good." She tried to bring her anger under control. "He'll just talk to him. Nothing will be done."

"That's up to Mose." Reuben was staying tightly in his refuge, then ventured out with something Rachel didn't expect. "Why are you so interested in this all of a sudden?"

Knowing she had to say something, she pulled her trump card. "Reuben, I'm with child."

He stared at her, his pancakes forgotten. "A child?"

"Yes," she said.

"After all these years?"

"Yes," she repeated, glancing at Luke, wishing this was not being discussed in front of him.

Luke was eating his eggs and pancakes, his eyes on his plate, saying nothing.

"Da Hah sei lobhdt," Reuben pronounced, a smile spreading across his face again. "The fruit of the womb is a blessing from heaven. *Da Hah* has seen fit to visit us again . . . and that in our old age."

"Yes," Rachel said, not wanting to dampen his feelings, though she doubted now whether this would help her mission much. At least her husband would no longer question her motives.

"So," Reuben pronounced, understanding spreading across his face. *Her newfound concern for church rules is connected to the desire for the spiritual welfare of this child.* "You are with child," he said reverently, remembering his pancakes again.

She could almost see his feelings about himself grow before her eyes. He would again have a child to take to church, to sit on the preacher's bench with. Even if it turned out to be a girl, she knew he would take her.

There would be cleansing for him with this child. Her barrenness had been the will of the Almighty, and it had reflected on him as a leader of the church. Unable to produce offspring, he had felt diminished and set back from the other ministers with their benches full of little ones.

"You are no longer childless. *Da Hah*'s blessing has returned."

Rachel glanced at Luke, wishing Reuben would quit his outburst. She felt embarrassed in front of Luke. She wondered why *he* wasn't embarrassed.

"I'll talk to Ezra," Reuben said so suddenly, it startled her.

"Really?" She couldn't keep the pleasure out of her voice.

"For the child's sake," he said. "It will be

for the future of the church — for him."

For her, she felt like adding but restrained herself. He would accept a girl too, she knew. It was just his way of saying it.

"This afternoon," he said, as if arriving at a firm conclusion. "You'll need to go to town this morning," he spoke in Luke's direction.

Luke nodded his head.

"We need a couple bags of oats for the horses. Co-op in Rushville would be best."

"How much have we left?" Luke asked, speaking his first words all morning.

"Not but a half bag."

"Kind of expensive right now," Luke commented. "Was cheaper in September."

"Yah," Reuben said, nodding, "I didn't have enough money to stock up then. We'll just have to buy it as we need to."

Luke nodded again. Reuben then got up, breakfast over. As Luke followed him outside, Rachel kept her anger in check. *Why had the man not purchased enough feed in September? Even Luke seemed to know enough to do that.* She bit her tongue to keep from speaking aloud.

No sense in upsetting the applecart now, besides she had her day's work cut out with baking. There was another batch of bread to be made. Then there was the child to consider. Who knew how the time of carrying would go. Luke had caused disturbances only in the morning, as this one seemed to be doing, but one never knew.

She sighed, gathering up the loaf of bread she had worked so hard on yesterday, preparing it for disposal as soon as both Luke and Reuben were out of the way. The flour, she decided, would go to the chickens.

CHAPTER
TWENTY-FIVE

At the Keim breakfast table, Rebecca was happily taking in the sights and sounds of home. Her thoughts, at the moment, distracted from thinking about John or her upcoming planned Sunday with him. She hated keeping thoughts of John at bay but figured it was not entirely her fault. John had not behaved the best last night.

"Mom cooks real good when someone's come home," Lester pronounced for all of them to hear, as he took another biscuit, poured creamy white gravy on it, and then gazed rapturously at the sight.

"Mom's always good," Matthew spoke up.

"You just want to come back from somewhere so *you* get some attention," Katie told him.

"He's got to leave first," Viola said, sharing a look with her sister.

"I'm leaving as soon as I can." Matthew made a face at both of them.

"No kann nimmand uns foahra," Ada, the seven-year-old, said with concern about the possibility of losing their driver if Matthew were to leave.

"She means to school." Katie supplied the interpretation, glaring at Matthew.

"Now . . . now." Lester let his voice remain mellow as he took charge. "Matthew's not going anywhere."

"Goot," Ada proclaimed, slicing her egg in half.

"Someday?" Matthew dared ask.

"Maybe." Lester qualified his statement.

"Only in *Gottes villa,*" Mattie said quickly.

"Yes — only that way," Lester agreed.

"What is *Gottes villa?*" Matthew asked.

"That's God's will for you — *Dat,*" Mattie said, getting up to leave the table for more biscuits, the supply getting low. She stepped toward the oven where more were being kept, lest they cool off too quickly.

Lester cleared his throat. "The book," he said, nodding toward the living room where they all knew the family Bible was kept, "that first — then the council of the church. With those two, you will be kept safe."

Rebecca wondered if she dared, then decided she would by saying, "The English say we must go by our own judgment too."

"That's the English," was her father's only

response.

"You can do better than that," Mattie said, from over by the oven.

"It's not us," he said, more curtly than usual.

"I wasn't trying to make trouble," Rebecca said quickly, sorry she had brought it up. Discomfort around the family table was one of the last things she wanted at the moment.

Her father seemed to ignore the remark, making her think he was more upset than she had imagined. Visions of John from last night flashed in front of her eyes, but this was not John. Lester had never spoken to her with such anger.

Apparently having found the answer he was looking for, Lester said slowly, "We are different. Yes, we think our judgment ought to be used but only to decide if we are understanding the Word correctly." He played with his spoon and continued, "Also to decide if the church is teaching the Word. But," he said, laying his spoon down, "not to decide our own rules. That is where we are different."

Breaking into the conversation, Mattie, who was standing at the window, asked, "I wonder why Esther's here."

"I wonder what she wants," Matthew asked.

Mattie went to the front door to meet Esther. A moment later, the family heard a muffled greeting and then silence as the front door shut.

"They went outside," Katie stated the obvious.

"Why can't Mom talk inside?" Viola asked.

"Sh. They probably have woman things to talk about," Lester told them.

"What are woman things?" Viola continued.

"You don't want to know," Matthew said. "It's trouble."

Glancing at her father, who seemed at a loss with what to say, Rebecca helped him out. "Maybe someone had a baby and . . ." Rebecca said and then hesitated herself, "they might be having trouble."

"It's *always* trouble," Matthew muttered, his mouth full of egg and biscuit.

"Did you have trouble — with baby Jonathon — in Milroy?" Viola asked.

"She likes babies," Matthew chuckled.

"Yes," Rebecca replied, smiling, "I do — but there was no trouble with Jonathon." Yet her mind flashed back to that evening and night of the birth. There easily could have been, and it also easily could be what the two women outside on the front yard were talking about.

They heard the front door open again, followed by Mattie's quick steps across the living room. She stopped in the kitchen opening, her face drawn. "Rebecca," she said, in a strained voice, "come outside."

"Is something wrong?" Rebecca asked, rising from her chair. Everyone around the table was looking at her, surprise on their faces. Rebecca felt a sudden fear grip her.

"Just come," Mattie told her.

"Trouble," Matthew said ominously, as the door opened and shut again.

"Be quiet," Lester told them one and all. "Finish your breakfast. It could be anything. Mom will tell us when it's time."

"I want to know now," Viola protested.

"Just eat," Lester told her, as silence settled on the room, except for the sound of their eating.

Outside Esther was standing by her buggy, her head bowed. Mattie hadn't said a word since leaving the kitchen, walking briskly in front of Rebecca.

"Rebecca, it's John," Esther said, her eyes rising to Rebecca's face.

Rebecca felt herself go cold. "What is it? What about John?"

"He's in the hospital," Esther said. "He has a fractured skull. Aden thought I should come tell you."

"What happened?" Rebecca asked, still cold from the news. "How is he?"

"Someone hit him while he was driving his buggy. The horse made it home on its own." Esther was saying, hesitation in her voice. "He was coming home from here — we think."

"Did they find the person?" It was the next question that came to Rebecca's mind, sounding inappropriate to ask, but everything felt inappropriate at the moment.

"No." Esther shook her head. "It must have been a hit-and-run. He hasn't recovered consciousness yet — at least that we've heard."

"He's in West Union," Mattie volunteered. "I'll take you down as soon as we can."

"He was going home from here," Rebecca said, noticing that her hands were shaking.

"Nearest we can figure." Esther's voice sounded strained.

"I see," Rebecca said, wishing again last night had never happened.

Esther looked intently at Rebecca and then to Mattie, "They didn't break up — did they?"

Mattie shook her head. "Just a little — well, disagreement — I think they had. Nothing serious."

"We all have those." Esther smiled grimly.

"All of us being human."

Rebecca was silent, listening, feeling detached.

"Was he driving on the wrong side of the road?" Mattie asked, and Rebecca figured she knew why. Her mother wanted to know if maybe John had been distracted by their argument.

"Not that I know," Esther said, her eyes meeting Mattie's. "The officer would have said so, I'm sure. Isaac talked to him — at least that's what Aden said — there was no blame put on John."

"Do they expect him to recover?" Rebecca asked, now that the question of blame was answered.

"I think so," Esther told her. "Doctors are doing a CT scan this morning."

Rebecca nodded, still feeling a little cool flush, but calm otherwise.

"Thanks for coming over." Mattie was concluding the conversation. "The family's still having breakfast."

"A Saturday morning." Esther smiled for the first time.

"Fixed a little something special for Rebecca's first morning home."

"Yah," Esther said, "I'll be getting back now."

Esther climbed into the buggy, as they

stepped back toward the house and gave her room to turn in the driveway.

"Now isn't that a shock to one's system." Mattie stated to no one in particular. "Looks like you two are having some big troubles already."

Rebecca still felt numb, like crying but not able to.

"That wasn't really serious last night was it?" Mattie asked, now seeming uncertain about the answers she had given.

Not feeling like giving all the details, Rebecca told her, "John was upset, but he seemed okay. I told him we would discuss it fully Sunday night. Oh, I wish we had just talked about it right there. Now he's in the hospital."

"Did he think you were quitting him?"

"Not that I know of. I certainly wasn't."

"Did you give him that impression?"

Rebecca shook her head. "I didn't think it or show it," Rebecca stated simply, meeting her mother's eyes.

"The officer said it wasn't John's fault," Mattie replied, sounding more like she was trying to convince herself than anyone else. "We'd better get inside and let the others know."

Walking back in, Mattie went first, took her seat at the kitchen table again, and then said, "Esther brought the news that John was hurt last night in a buggy accident. He's in the hospital." She then turned back to the care of her family. "This gravy's good and cold now, isn't it?"

"How bad is he hurt?" Lester asked.

"Unconscious, but they have good hopes for him."

"You'll be taking Rebecca down?" Lester asked next, the last of his breakfast already done and scraped off his plate.

"As soon as I can," Mattie told him. "You think the children will be okay while I'm gone?"

"Should be for a Saturday," Lester said, looking at them. "They should learn to take care of themselves, if they haven't already. Matthew can work with me on cutting wood."

"Katie and Viola can do the dishes . . . Martha and Ada, dry them," Mattie said, without much further explanation. "We can get going right away. Rebecca really should get down to see John."

"I'll be in the living room then," Lester told them. "When you two are done eating, we can have morning prayer."

As her father left, Rebecca found that none of her food would go down anymore.

"It's okay," her mother told her, noticing,

as she finished her own breakfast. "Let's go in for prayers."

They rose to follow her, Rebecca scraping her chair on the floor. Still none of the other children were saying anything, a hush seeming to have fallen over them in the face of this unknown.

CHAPTER
TWENTY-SIX

Isaac walked out of the house soon after the officer left with her husband. He thought of harnessing his horse and using it for the trip to town, disregarding Aden's offer of a fresh horse. After considering how exhausted his horse probably was from last night, he decided to take up Aden's offer. His own horse would likely complete the trip to West Union, doing what it was told, but there was no sense in making it suffer.

Tomorrow was Sunday, the Lord's day, when he would need not only a fresh horse, but a fresh conscience, clear from offense to man or beast. Even if Aden hadn't offered, Isaac might have gone and asked, considering the rest his horse sorely needed.

Stopping at the barn, Isaac dropped a quarter bucket of oats into the horse's feed box and checked its hay too. The sound of the sliding oats got its attention. With a whiny, it came swiftly into the barn, halted just inside the door, and then made its way to the grain, nuzzling its nose deep into the fluffy oats.

"Hungry, eh?" Isaac asked it with a gentle chuckle. Pausing to watch the horse's teeth working so diligently, he whispered softly, "Enjoy your oats then. I guess you're off for the day."

Walking briskly up Wheat Ridge toward the Miller's complex, Isaac's thoughts ran back over the night's events. How quickly things could change. Only last night John had left the house, full of life and vigor, anxious about Rebecca. Now John was lying in a hospital bed and facing an unknown future.

It was all in the hands of God, Isaac knew. God would know what was best, yet he bowed his head from the weight of what he felt was ahead of them. Something about the way John appeared, his head swollen on the one side, made him uneasy. The doctor had seemed to be optimistic enough, but they were trained to be optimistic, he figured.

Wishing now that he had asked the officer's husband how fast he had been driving, Isaac regretted the missed opportunity. Perhaps it would have given him a better understanding of what lay ahead. Then remembering the scene from earlier in the morning, he was glad he had not remembered to ask.

Such a question would have caused Andy unnecessary grief. What good would it have done anyway? It would not help John now, and trying to make himself feel better at the other's expense didn't really help either.

He walked past three cars already parked in front of Miller's Furniture, entered through the front door, and found Sharon at the front desk. "Using the phone," he told her, his steps not slowing much.

She nodded, her attention focused on one of the customers in the store. "Our main floor person had an accident last night," she was saying.

He shut the outside door and any sounds of the continuing conversation inside. Reaching for the phone, he dialed the hospital's number that was listed in the phone book Aden kept on the shelf. It rang three times before someone answered, "Adams County Medical."

He gave his name and John's name, asking to be transferred to room 201. He hoped Miriam was there to answer the phone.

"Just a moment," the voice said, followed by two short beeps.

Miriam answered with a weary, "Hello."

"It's Isaac," he said, not certain if she would recognize his voice over the phone. "How's John?"

"He's doing about the same," Miriam answered in the same tired tone.

"You get any rest?" he asked, concerned.

"Waiting room chairs aren't very comfortable to sleep in," she said dryly.

"Doctor stopped by yet?"

"Yes. The scan's at ten. Nothing new till then . . . I guess."

"Aden's letting me use their horse. I'll be starting out soon."

"Could you find anything for breakfast?" she asked, concern in her voice.

"Cold cereal," he said scornfully.

She chuckled. "It'll keep you alive."

"Not by much."

She chuckled again. "Keeps you young."

"Really," he said, forgetting for a moment that he was on a phone, calling a hospital. Her face came into focus. He was a bit surprised at how much he missed her. After all, it had been only last night they were together.

"A little need — it's good for a man. Keeps his senses and tastes sharp," she said, with tenderness in her voice.

"I'll be on my way," he said, returning to

the subject at hand. "Should get there before they do the scan."

"I'm worried, Isaac," Miriam said.

"It's in the hands of God."

"He's our baby," she said, the words catching in her throat.

"*Gottes villa* is what's best," he told her, trying to comfort himself too.

"Yes . . ." she said, the weariness back in her voice, "He's not known for sparing though — even those He loves."

"He gave us His only Son," Isaac said, thinking about that act, not finding the words too comforting, considering the implications. "We must trust Him," he added resolutely.

"Yes," she said, meaning it.

"I'll be down soon," he said softly. Hearing her hang up, he did so himself.

"Any news?" Aden asked, as Isaac stepped back inside.

"No . . . still the same. They're doing the scan at ten."

"You want the horse?" Aden asked Isaac, getting up from his chair.

Isaac nodded, motioning for Aden to remain seated. "I can get it myself."

Aden accepted and settled back down. "Harness's just inside the barn door, left-hand side. Take the brown gelding. It ought to make the trip in good time. Shoes are in good shape."

"Thanks." Isaac took his leave, knowing they would pass on the news of John's condition to those of the family who ought to know.

Walking back up the road and across to Aden's place, he pulled the single buggy out of the barn, finding the harness and horse easily. He harnessed the horse and was on the road quickly.

Pulling back on the reins at the stop sign on the state road, Isaac stopped short, giving himself a few extra feet just in case the strange horse should act up. The horse stood there calmly, while Isaac waited for two cars to pass, starting instantly again when Isaac let out the reins.

They made good time going south till Isaac felt himself relaxing, becoming comfortable with driving the brown gelding. Aden would have told him of any dangerous habits the horse might have, but he still needed to get to know the animal personally before he totally trusted it. A simple mistake on a main highway could have disastrous results.

He thought of Rebecca, John's girl. She would, no doubt, be showing up, perhaps even before he got there. *How is she taking this?* Her reaction might be a good indication as to the quality of girl she was.

They wanted the best for John, both he and Miriam did. They wanted a girl who would be a credit to John, as well as a solid mate. She must be a good Christian girl, one with no leanings toward leaving the faith. Life among the Amish was hard enough, without being married to someone who was always complaining about the preachers or the hardship of the Amish life. A good wife would not be thinking the requirements of the *Ordnungs Brief* too high.

This he knew from being a minister, remembering past family problems. A woman who always complained could wear a man down and send many a good man to the liberal churches, where he might otherwise not have gone.

Isaac reminded himself, the man could do the same thing for his wife, but in John's case there had never been any signs pointing in such a direction. The boy had always given every indication, both by his willingness and desire, of staying in the Amish faith. That being true, it would be a disaster for John to marry a girl who would push him away from his present leanings.

Running his thoughts over what he knew of the Keim family, he remembered what he had told Miriam only the evening before. It was strange how little he knew about the family. With the family's move, there was a positive church letter from Milroy forwarded to Bishop Martin from Bishop Mose, giving a good word but nothing else.

Shouldn't there be something else? No news was good news. But Isaac wasn't sure in this case. A lot lay at stake with the marriage of John because once married, like all Amish, John was married for life. Never, outside of death, would he be able to do anything about another choice.

Isaac tightened up the reins on the brown gelding as a semi roared past, going the other way. The boy sure seemed smitten with the girl, which could well be a problem. It could be blinding John's eyes to her faults. Yet this was a sticky problem, which even concerned parents might best stay away from.

With a searing suddenness, Isaac remembered John's present state, lying in the hospital. Why in the world was he thinking about the girl? He ought to be thinking about John and whether he was worthy of the girl. What if John was a cripple now, brought down with such a handicap?

Shame flooded Isaac at the thought, shame for what John's state might mean to them and him, and shame that he had been judging Rebecca. He really had no right to do so, he told himself.

Perhaps this was why *Da Hah* had allowed this accident to happen, to bring them back from the deadly sin of pride. Miriam and he thought so much of John, their only son. Had their love been blinding them from seeing their own sin?

Isaac remembered the words from Scripture, that one was to remove the beam from one's own eyes before trying to remove the splinter from another's eyes. He hung his head over the realization of his own shortcomings.

He was approaching the town, and he turned his attention to driving the buggy. The gelding proved to be okay, as they navigated the West Union streets, pulling up to the same streetlight he had used last night.

If this is from the hand of the Lord because of our sin, then there is nothing we can do until His anger is satisfied. Isaac climbed out of the buggy, sorrow heavy on his heart for what might lie ahead.

CHAPTER
TWENTY-SEVEN

After prayers, Mattie and Rebecca got up to go get ready but were delayed when ten-year-old Katie, pale in her face, told Mattie she was afraid of being left alone.

"Is it the kitchen — the dishes?" Mattie asked, looking at Katie. "Being left with them by yourself?"

Katie nodded. "The little girls will make nothing but trouble, and I don't know where all the things go."

"They'd better behave." Mattie looked severely at the little faces seated in the living room. "Viola will help with the dishes. Martha and Ada can dry them."

All heads nodded solemnly, even little Ada, who was too small to have a clue what she was nodding about. Katie, though, looked unconvinced.

"It's expecting a lot from her," Rebecca said, remembering her own feelings at that age. "A lot can go wrong. Dad and Matthew will be back in the woods."

As if to confirm her words, she watched Lester drive the team of horses out the barnyard gate. Matthew was hanging onto the back of the rattling wagon. The chainsaw and oil and gas cans bounced around but were held in by the wagon sideboards.

"But John . . ." Mattie said, watching the two through the living room window.

"I can wait," Rebecca said resolutely. "I'm worried, but this is important."

Her mother had looked strangely at her but left it at that, rushing about, putting actions to work instead of words. With all four girls helping as much as they could, they tackled the kitchen.

Viola let a plate slip. It crashed to the floor, the pieces flying all over the place. Instead of scolding her, Mattie immediately seated the weeping girl on the kitchen bench until she could calm down.

"It wasn't your fault," Rebecca assured her sister. "Things like that happen."

Mattie silently nodded her agreement, which caused the tears to cease much quicker than Rebecca's words alone would have.

Martha, though, couldn't resist "She should be more careful. Breaking dishes is expensive."

"I didn't do it on purpose," Viola snapped. "It slipped — right through my hand."

"You could have hung on more tightly," Martha said.

"See what I mean about the younger girls?" Katie said.

"She does seem to have been right," Rebecca agreed, scraping the gravy into a plastic bowl.

"I see my parenting isn't done yet," Mattie said wearily.

"Is it ever?" Rebecca asked, feeling irked with her sisters, knowing it was not entirely their fault.

With the kitchen finally under control and her mother giving final instructions to her sisters, Rebecca had gone out to catch the horse. They would need the younger black mare for the trip. Their older driving horse might handle the long drive, but there was no sense putting it to the test when a younger horse was available.

Not everyone was able to keep two driving horses, but Lester insisted on it, even when money got a little tight, as it had last year just before the fall harvest. Lester claimed they could actually use three driving horses. Mattie had nixed that idea in the bud. Two horses were plenty and enough, in her mind, to have to pay the upkeep on.

When Rebecca opened the door to the barnyard, the black mare had its own ideas. It threw its head in the air, acting as if it was reading Rebecca's thoughts on the upcoming long haul into West Union. When Rebecca approached it, the horse took off for the back pasture, kicking its heels into the air as if to show complete contempt for any travel plans.

This required a weary trudge after the horse, halter in hand. Apparently the run had taken all the foolishness out of the horse because it now hung its head, meekly accepting the halter once Rebecca reached it.

Rebecca felt like giving the mare a good tongue-lashing but decided not to. Even a horse must be a horse once in a while, she figured. The real reason, though, for her restraint, was one she did not wish to admit even to herself. She too felt like running away — away from town, away from the hospital. She wanted to see John but not in this condition. Like a heavy blanket, the emotion hung over her.

Rebecca marched back to the barn, tugging on the halter when the mare slowed. "You're going," she said firmly, "just like I am. Me because I love the boy, and you because you are told to."

Pushing her thoughts aside, she hastened to harness the mare. Mattie rushed to help at the last moment. "We're so late already. I'm so sorry, Rebecca," she said all breathless.

"That's okay," Rebecca told her quickly. "I want to see John, but it's going to be hard."

"You're being so good about this. If Lester had been in the hospital . . . when we were promised. There's no way — no way — I would have helped clean up the house like you just did."

Rebecca felt guilty but told herself she was not putting words into her mother's mouth. Her mother was saying these things without any help from her.

"And now the mare runs to the back pasture. How they know that they have a long pull ahead of them, I never could tell." Mattie started placing the tug strap on its side, pushing hard until the latch clinked into place. "At least we're on our way now."

Rebecca waited until her mother was inside the buggy with a firm hand on the reins before she let go of the bridle and climbed in herself. Once they were on the way, the mare simply plodded along, her earlier friskiness gone.

"No rush . . . once we're on the road,"

Mattie said sarcastically.

"It didn't want to go to town." Rebecca stuck up for the horse, knowing she hadn't wanted to go either.

"No excuse for not doing one's duty," Mattie retorted, obviously speaking about the horse but including Rebecca.

After a few moments of silence, Mattie noted, "Rebecca, you're sure taking this well."

"I'm trying." Rebecca covered her bases truthfully.

"He may be hurt bad," Mattie said, in a lower tone of voice. "You have thought of that, haven't you?"

"I know." Rebecca now felt tears pressing, knowing she had been keeping those fears back too.

"I had hoped so," Mattie told her. "It might be best to be well-prepared."

"Could it really be that bad?" Rebecca ventured, reaching for hope.

"Only *Da Hah* knows. But thrown that far . . . many have been paralyzed for life." Mattie just blurted it out, letting the words hang in the air.

There was silence in the buggy. The only sound was that made by the wheels humming on the pavement.

"You'll have to be faithful to him, regardless," Mattie said, her voice firm. "One must not forsake a promise because of something like this."

The dread of it all filled Rebecca. She felt her mother's eyes on her but couldn't do more than squeeze her own eyes against the tears.

"It would be *Gottes villa.*" Her mother approached the subject from another angle. "A promise is a promise — for better or worse."

"But I'm not married to him," Rebecca said, speaking the words without thinking, the thought suddenly occurring to her.

"But we must be faithful," Mattie told her. "If unfaithfulness starts now, where will it end?"

"Wouldn't faithfulness start when you're married? That's when you promise for better or worse." Rebecca couldn't believe she was saying this.

"Faithfulness to a promise starts with what you've already told him — that you'd marry him. You shouldn't change that just because he's hurt."

"No matter how bad?" Rebecca felt like she was sliding off a cliff but couldn't stop herself. "I guess it's all a little too much at the moment. But I do love him."

"It'll look better — maybe once you see

him," Mattie said reassuringly. "Our people don't forsake each other just because they get hurt. John will need you now more than before."

CHAPTER
TWENTY-EIGHT

Before turning right and driving toward the center of Unity, Mattie slowed down. "This is where it happened — I think," she said quietly.

Rebecca felt no desire to stop, hoping her mother didn't either. To her the place had a gruesome feeling surrounding it. Finally, glancing out of her side of the buggy, she looked around but could see nothing in the ditch.

"It's over here." Her mother motioned with her head toward small pieces of wood and black oil cloth lying in the yard. "The house must be over there."

Looking, Rebecca shivered, almost seeing John flying through the air.

"They cleaned up pretty good," her mother noted, letting the reins out again. The mare shook its head, as if sorry they weren't coming to a complete stop. Turning right on Unity Road, Mattie and Rebecca were each lost in her own thoughts.

Once in West Union, Mattie found the correct street and pulled into the hospital parking lot.

Seeing another buggy tied up, Rebecca said, "Looks like someone's already here."

"Isaac, I'm sure. I wish we weren't so late."

"We can just tell them what happened if they ask."

"I'm not offering an excuse. Sometimes that just makes it worse."

"You don't have to, Mom," Rebecca said, trying again. "They'll understand." For some reason she was certain she was right. Not that she knew John's parents that well, but on this point she was confident.

"I guess you know them better than I do," Mattie allowed.

The receptionist greeted them with a "Good morning. May I help you?"

"We're looking for John Miller's room," Mattie said.

"Oh, the Amish boy," she responded with a smile. "He's still in room 201. That way." She nodded toward the hall.

Rebecca followed her mother, feeling like the walls were getting smaller the farther they went. She must be strong, she told herself, for her mother's sake if nothing else. To shame Mattie in front of the Miller family by running back out to the buggy as she felt like doing, would be horrible.

Rebecca forced herself to stop thinking about the hospital. Room 201 was coming next. Mattie's brisk step slowed as they approached, her hand reaching for the knob, the door already ajar. She gently pushed the door inward.

Behind her, Rebecca couldn't see what her mother was seeing, but Mattie nodded her head, indicating someone must be in the room other than John. "Good morning," Mattie said softly.

It was clearly Isaac's voice that echoed the greeting as they stepped inside. Miriam was standing in front of the hospital bed, both hands on the rail of the bed, where John's still form lay. She hadn't turned around yet. Isaac had his hands behind him, clasping them lightly, his face turned in their direction.

He looked grave, the air heavy in the room.

"It's Rebecca," Isaac whispered to Miriam.

"Oh." Miriam acted startled, as if she were expecting it to be someone else.

"Good morning," Rebecca said, to say something.

"I thought it was the nurse," Miriam said

softly. "It's been a long night."

"She stayed all night in the waiting room," Isaac added, his eyes piercing as he looked intently at Rebecca.

His look made her freeze inside, made her wish even more that she was not here. *What am I supposed to do in this situation? Cry? Go touch John with everyone watching?* She felt completely at a loss, but since motion still seemed to be in her power, she moved forward. Doing so she saw the intent gleam in Isaac's eyes soften.

Past her mother she moved slowly in soft steps, up to where Miriam was standing, and then even closer until her dress touched the bed. What was she to do? Reach out? Instead Rebecca placed her hand near Miriam's on the bed rail.

To do more, to reveal their former intimacy, here before them all, did not seem like the right thing. It could easily be misunderstood. *No,* she must give no opportunity for any besmirching of John's good name.

He had waited until she was promised to him before he ever dared reach out for her hand. Even then she knew he had wondered whether it was the right thing to do.

No, she told herself again, feeling a tear forming and sliding down her cheek. They had loved with a pure love, and it would stay that way. At least as much as was within her power, regardless of what lay ahead.

"He's so white." Miriam's voice sounded as if it came from a long distance away. She reached out and gripped Rebecca's hand, which was still on the bedrail. "I haven't seen him move — not once since we came in last night."

Rebecca couldn't find words, sensing her mother moving close to the bed.

"Has the doctor been in this morning?" Mattie asked.

"Yes," Miriam said, "he seemed puzzled — I thought. Said John should at least be coming around some, if it is just a skull fracture."

"So it's something more serious?" Mattie asked in a matter-of-fact tone.

"He said that they would know more after they did the scan," Miriam said.

"We must submit ourselves to what *Da Hah* has planned," Mattie replied, in the same tone of voice.

Looking at John's still body, unmoving except for the slight rising and falling of his chest, Rebecca remembered how he had been. Her memory was not of last night and his anger, but of that Sunday afternoon down by the bridge. John had been so alive, so full of life, his eyes longing for her, his hand reaching out.

Her sobs came silently, shaking her shoulders as she felt the future press down. There was something about the color of John's skin, the closed eyes, the shallow breathing. This was no little problem that tomorrow would just blow away. Rebecca was scared. Scared for the future — both John's and her's.

She finally let the emotion rise up and push out in gasps. To her side she felt more than saw Isaac moving closer to Miriam. His voice reached her, deep and solemn, the one he used for preaching on Sunday's.

It filled the hospital room, as he quoted by heart. "When thou passest through the waters, I will be with thee; and through the rivers, they shall not overflow thee. O God, Father of us all, we pray now for strength and for Your holy power. Give these weak bodies of ours, frail and made from the dust of the earth, the ability to walk in Your will. Dear God, we pray, in the name of the Father, the Son, and of the Holy Spirit."

Rebecca let the sobs continue partly because she couldn't stop them, but mostly because she knew she was being accepted by Isaac and Miriam — even here, even with John hurt. That was the best feeling of all.

Isaac had prayed with her in the room. He and Miriam were offering her a high honor. They were accepting her as a part of the family.

Somewhere, and she was not sure where, she had passed the test with Isaac and Miriam. As the girl who was promised to their son, she had shown the proper respect and response they were looking for.

The right responses had come naturally. Remembering how she had felt during the trip to the hospital — wishing she didn't have to come — she now was glad to be here. John was badly hurt, but already God was bringing good to pass. John had been very angry with her last night, and wrongly so, yet she loved him deeply — deeply enough to promise to marry him.

"Excuse me." The voice of the nurse came from behind her. "We need to take Mr. Miller for his scan."

"Of course," Isaac said, quickly taking Miriam's arm to move her away from the bed.

Rebecca and Mattie followed. Sitting on the chairs, they watched the nurse swiftly move John out of the door, his single IV line swinging slightly as he disappeared down the hall.

CHAPTER
TWENTY-NINE

Luke was driving up to Rushville to pick up the bags of oats his father wanted. Something about his mother's actions that morning wasn't sitting well with him. He had been trying to figure it out on the drive up but with no success.

What is it? He pondered the question, keeping the old driving horse moving at a brisk pace even when it wanted to slow down. *Is it the confusion that surrounds the letter to Emma's lawyer?* He thought on that for a bit, counting the telephone posts going past his buggy door, trying to distract himself into finding the answer.

It all seemed so long ago now, even though he knew it had been only last night. *A long night,* he told himself, *tormenting too.* He had thought he could bring the letter home with a clear conscience because it was for a good cause. That was how he had seen it yesterday, but after last night and now this morning, things were looking different.

How he wasn't sure. Everything was changing. Maybe even he was changing. He felt as if temptation had come knocking yesterday and that he had answered the door. *Opened it,* he felt like telling himself, *welcomed the intruder in with open arms.*

Tomorrow was Sunday. He would not be seeing Susie and wished he was. His mother would not approve of his enthusiasm if she knew how he was feeling. A little emotion was fine with Rachel, but with how much he had enjoyed himself last Sunday night, Rachel would most certainly not give her blessing. *There is the matter of the money to think of,* she would say. *Can Susie fit that? Is she suitable for our family?*

If the truth be told, Luke was certain Susie fit the family perfectly. It was his mother who was trying to change the family, for the better of course, but change it nevertheless.

How strange that was. The very thing his mother did not like — their poverty — had just calmly gone ahead and taken root, creating its own life for them. They were what they were, and his mother was now the interloper, bringing in the unknown to the known.

That he was being unkind to his mother crossed his mind, but for the moment, he didn't care. Perhaps it was the trip this morning that was giving him the courage to strike out on his own. His mother had acted strange with this talk of Ezra's tractor being used in the fields. Never in his life had he ever known her to care one wit about who used the tractor where, regardless of the church rules.

Only this fall she had urged him to use their tractor for hauling some things back to the lower field. He had refused, knowing the consequences if someone saw him and knowing he, not her, would be the one making the confessions at pre-communion church. The fact he was the deacon's son would, in the eyes of fellow church members, only make matters worse.

Mother should have known that, he told himself, still feeling irritated after all this time. It was even stranger that she would now want her own brother doing a church confession for the very thing she had told her son to do. A church confession it would be, Luke knew, if his dad got involved. There was hardly any other recourse one could take to settle matters with the church once your error was exposed by a deacon's visit.

He supposed his dad could simply drive away in his buggy, after his uncle privately confessed his error. But would his father do that? After all *stretching the fence,* as the Amish called it because that was what their cows did when they saw greener grass on the other side, was not that uncommon when it came to illegitimate tractor usage.

Yet Luke doubted if his dad would take the chance on damaging his own reputation by letting Ezra, brother-in-law that he was, off the hook too easily. Word would have a way of getting around and lessoning the gravity of his future deacon visits. His father's way out of the predicament would have been to refuse to go unless the bishop asked him to. It seemed to Luke that he was now committed.

It was all quite confusing. *Why is Father going to Ezra, and why does Mother want him to go?*

One thing Luke was certain of — this was changing him in some way, that and the talk of another baby in the house. He still blushed at the plain conversation around the kitchen table.

"Susie," he said out loud to distract himself, letting the sound of her name settle in his ear. It sounded good to him. She certainly wasn't beautiful, he reminded himself, hearing his mother's voice in his ear. But last Sunday night had been mighty *gut.* Like a warm coat in the winter, which one could wrap around one's self without fear of it doing any harm.

IIc heard her laughter again. He remembered hearing it during his visit with her in the living room of her parents' home. He remembered the sound of her voice, the taste of the food she had obviously made herself, and felt again the warmth of her presence surrounding him in that room.

"My," he said, leaving it at that. It seemed to kind of sum it all up.

With Rushville in sight, he got his mind back on watching for traffic in the rearview mirror. There was little danger of the old driving horse doing anything rash, even if a big, noisy semi should pass them from behind. The fast cars were what bothered Luke.

Here along the main highway, the shoulder was just a little wider than the county roads. There was enough room to get halfway off the road but not enough room to drive comfortably without getting jarred by the uneven and rutted ground on the right. He could and would get off though, if an approaching car was coming up too fast.

Luke had never driven an automobile and so knew nothing about how fast the approach to a buggy happened. It was only from his perspective that he understood the experience. An approaching automobile that was going too fast or pulling out to pass was a chilling sight in his little oval mirror. There would be little left of him or his buggy, he knew, if he got hit. So he made a habit of pulling over on a state road, bumps or no bumps, when things looked iffy.

It had been awhile since he had been in Rushville, but he found the co-op without any problem and went inside to pay for his oats. While loading them into the back of his buggy, he noticed Henry Stuzman arrive in his surrey. Luke knew it was Henry before he even saw him because he knew the surrey. He recognized it as the one that often held Ann Stuzman on Sunday mornings.

Many a time Luke had watched Ann climb out of this buggy at the end of the house walks, accompanied by her mother and older sister. He had watched Ann, wearing a bonnet and black shawl, walk toward the house. No one noticed him looking because the long row of boys and men always faced toward the house. Inside the church house, he had never felt right looking at her. She was kind of, he thought, above his reach, as some of the boys from the youth might say. And so he never paid her much attention.

He knew though that she had just turned eighteen. Why she wasn't dating seemed strange to him. Certainly, he figured, some boy had already asked her. It was simply the logic of things. Why then had she turned the boy down, which was what surely must have happened.

Sure, he reminded himself, *Susie was twenty when she went home with me last Sunday — on her first date. But Susie isn't Ann, and neither am I the boy asking her.*

With the thought of Ann came the thought of the money, his mother's money, and it bothered him. *I've got to quit this. Susie's just fine. I don't want the money. I like her.*

But try as he might, his attraction to who might be in Henry Stuzman's surrey wouldn't go away. Might Ann be in the buggy? He needed to find out.

Henry had already gone inside the co-op, leaving his horse, its head hanging low, the reins limp, resting from the ride into town. No sign or movement seemed to be coming from either the front or backseat of the buggy. Neither had anyone gone into the co-op with Henry.

He needed to find out if Ann was in that buggy. Likely she wasn't, but he wanted to know. He also knew, much to his embarrassment, that he would never be doing this if it weren't for the money his mother was so certain should be coming their way. The promise of the money seemed to give him a confidence with someone like Ann Stuzman — confidence he wouldn't ordinarily have.

He closed the backdoor of his buggy, got inside, and drove toward the hitching rail. *If Ann is not in the buggy, I will continue on. I won't pause, and no one will be the wiser. I'll be glad if she isn't there,* he told himself. He would be spared this burden, this unknown possibility that was haunting him.

He almost went on by the parked surrey. Yet the compulsion to know for sure made him pull up and park beside it. He looked out his door window and saw nothing. But it was possible that he wouldn't because a closed buggy door could well hide a person behind it.

He told himself he would just stop and step to the ground. If the surrey door did not open once he was on the ground, he would climb back in and leave. That was his resolution and as far as he would go.

Opening the buggy door, his right foot found the step and the other the ground. Turning around slowly, he faced the other buggy and saw its door open, revealing the smiling face of young Ann Stuzman.

Her bright blue eyes, her soft arms, they

took his breath away. This was not the Sunday Ann, all wrapped up in her shawl and her Sunday dress.

"I thought you wouldn't come over," she told him with a twinkle in those blue eyes. "Dad has to check on something."

"I almost didn't," he heard himself saying, his heart pounding in his mouth. There seemed no way to stop his words. "I thought you might be here."

"Oh, you did?" She was smiling again now, her eyes going toward the co-op door. He thought she must be watching for her father, perhaps uncomfortable if he caught her with him. *She is eighteen,* he told himself, *so why should her father object?*

"What did you come into town for?"

"Dad wanted some oats. I have them in the back," he said.

"You come in often?" she asked.

He felt weak from her gaze, not at all like Susie made him feel. *But then Susie isn't Ann,* he told himself. Finally finding his voice, he replied, "Once in a while, when Dad needs something and can't come in himself." And then a wild thought streaked like lightning through his mind. *Ask her home on Sunday night. I'm not seeing Susie then.*

He gulped hard, trying to straighten out his insides and make sense of this. Never had he ever thought of doing anything like this, at least not while he was still seeing Susie.

"Dad's checking on seed prices for the spring," she said.

She didn't realize that even that short comment spoke volumes about the differences between their families, but Luke did. Reuben would never look into prices until just before he bought. Her words removed any idea of asking to take her home Sunday.

"Well, I have to be going," he said abruptly, forcing himself to look away from her blue eyes and reaching for his buggy door. He was sure he saw regret in her eyes.

"Oh," was all she said.

He wanted to shout the words, *Can I see you Sunday night?* But he didn't, his tongue dry from the tip to the base. Climbing back into his buggy, he nodded in her direction, his smile stiff on his lips, and got the old driving horse headed out of town.

You, Luke Byler, are a total dumm kopp, he told himself, as he neared the fields at the edge of town. He had never felt so stupid.

CHAPTER
THIRTY

"May we have the strength to bear *Gottes villa*," Isaac said, when John had been taken from his room.

"You shouldn't say that. Not in front of Rebecca," Miriam chided him gently. "We don't really know what the doctors will find."

"It'll be bad," Isaac said with a sigh, seemingly no longer having the strength to hide his fears. "It was a bad accident."

"But we don't know that," Miriam insisted, gently brushing his arm with her fingers.

Rebecca was surprised at their talking so freely in front of her, but they now apparently considered her part of the family.

Rebecca wondered, *What would Isaac and Miriam really say if they knew about last night and how John had spoken to me? Would they stick up for their son? Would they support him if they knew how the anger had burned in his eyes?*

"We should sit in the waiting room," Isaac announced, deciding for them all. He glanced toward Miriam and said, "You know where it is — because you were here last night."

"It'll be more comfortable there," Miriam agreed, stepping toward the door.

As Miriam led the way down the hall, Rebecca felt the white walls narrowing again.

Mattie sensed her daughter's uneasiness and whispered softly, "It'll be okay."

Rebecca hoped her mother was right, but at the moment it certainly didn't feel so. "He's not dying?" she asked, wanting to know. Her concern for John's condition gripped her and made her whisper quietly to her mother, so no one else would hear.

The words must have come out louder than she intended because Isaac paused at the door of the waiting room, holding it for Miriam and then for Mattie and Rebecca.

"I don't think so," he said, as she passed him. The full length of his beard, even longer than her father's, felt comforting as she glanced at his face. He had John's eyes, the same shade of brown, and the same gentleness.

"You don't think so?" she asked him, to

cover up her thoughts.

"No," he said, "I'm afraid *Da Hah* might have another trial in store for us. Death is a great sorrow." He shook his head. "He would have given us grace for that and will give for whatever else we must bear."

"You must not speak so," Miriam turned back to say, already seated in the waiting room chair.

"It's on my mind. She's family," Isaac said simply, still holding the door.

"It's your fear talking," Miriam insisted. "The doctor will tell us soon, I'm sure."

Isaac let go of the door, as if he was letting go of a great weight. Rebecca felt compassion watching Isaac walk toward Miriam, wishing she could comfort him.

"John just told us he asked you to marry him," Miriam said softly, leaning slightly out in front of Mattie so Rebecca could hear. The statement was startling, but relieving at the same time. "He only told us last night," Miriam added, in the same wistful tone.

Rebecca nodded her head, the tears pressing again, one slipping out and rolling down her cheek.

"Others have troubles too," Miriam continued, to which Mattie nodded in agreement. "Yours are just a little harder —

275

perhaps at the start."

Maybe John will come out of his coma today. Maybe the doctor's report will be favorable. She thought of the doctor's report as having a great power in and of itself, as if the doctor could say what he wanted it to say. *Then we can talk about our problem on Sunday like we planned.* She felt some relief at that thought. *Maybe John will even be a better person for this experience.*

Miriam's voice cut into her thoughts, "We waited so many years after Bethany was born. I thought *Da Hah* had left me barren, like a cursed woman from the time of Moses, and then John came. What a sweet little one he was. Isaac was never the same again. A father of a son, he now was. A little boy to sit on the church bench with him."

"I guess having only two . . . it might make it different," Mattie said.

"Perhaps." A smile played on Miriam's face. "Isaac won't tell you, but he loves the boy even more than I do. Of course all fathers do, but having just one son makes a difference, I suppose."

"They're all special," Mattie said. "They come quickly sometimes, but they are all gifts from *Da Hah*."

"You shouldn't tell all the family secrets," Isaac said, in his best Sunday sermon voice, having been acting as if he wasn't listening.

"One can tell them to family," Miriam told him. "But perhaps I shouldn't be carrying on like this. Prattling on about my own things."

"It's good to talk in times like this," Mattie assured her.

"Yes, it is," Miriam agreed.

CHAPTER
THIRTY-ONE

Seated in the waiting room, Rebecca still felt as though she was confined within narrow walls. She thought of each room in the hospital as containing yet another story of sadness and gloom. And in their own particular story, it was as if they all were waiting for someone in authority to reveal their future to them.

Rebecca yearned to leave this place, to ride home in the buggy, to be doing the chores with Matthew, to smell the hay in the barn, to see the feed dished out for the cows. She wished she were feeling the weight of the milkers on her arms instead of the pressure of these four walls. She wanted to breathe air untainted by the smell of medicine and antiseptic. She wanted to feel the comfort of her own room, to climb under the covers of the bed and pull the old quilt tight under her chin, never letting go. She wanted to wake up from this nightmare, to see stars from her window. She wanted to feel the nip of cold air, yet unwarmed by the rising heat from the kitchen register.

Her mother seemed lost in her own thoughts. Miriam looked like she might be dropping off to sleep. Isaac, his face firm, his eyes on the hospital wall, was saying nothing.

Her thoughts were interrupted by the opening of the waiting room door. A uniformed Adams County sheriff's officer walked in with an elderly woman. *Someone else who has experienced tragedy,* she figured, glancing away and returning to her troubled thoughts.

Isaac was rising from his seat. But why? She glanced up at his face to see him moving toward the uniformed officer with what she was certain was a smile and then a cheerful greeting.

"I didn't expect to see you so soon," Isaac said, his voice gentle.

Gentleness in a man seemed to touch her deeply right now. *This must be an officer who was at the crash site last night. Surely that is how Isaac knows her. She is now, no doubt, coming in with another injured person or one of their family members.*

"I didn't either," the officer said. "Mother insisted." She turned back and said to the older woman, "This is Mr. Miller, and this is my mother, Isabelle, the one who called in your son's accident."

Isabelle, needing no further introduction, extended her hand. "Mr. Miller, I'm so sorry about your son."

Isaac nodded, carefully taking her hand in his rough calloused one. "We are glad you've come. This is my wife, Miriam, and over here," Isaac half turned and said, "is John's girlfriend, Rebecca, and her mother, Mattie."

Isabelle smiled, her eyes going around the room, then said to Isaac, "I told Beatrice I just had to come and see the young man. You know . . . after such an experience. It was awful, Mr. Miller, as you can imagine."

"Yes." Isaac nodded again.

"I just about didn't call it in — when I heard the noise — but the Lord kept after me, I suppose."

"I'm sure He did," Isaac assured her.

"I stayed with him till the ambulance came." Isabelle's face softened thinking about it. "He was such a fine man . . . lying there so still. I thanked the Lord for him."

"You shouldn't be saying all this," Beatrice interrupted. "They have enough to think about already."

"No, that's fine," Miriam spoke up before

Isaac could say anything. "Won't you have a seat? We're waiting for John's tests to finish. The doctor said he'd tell us as soon as he knew anything."

"Is he hurt badly?" Isabelle asked, taking the chair beside Isaac. "Beatrice couldn't tell me much, and I, of course, just had to see for myself."

"She's just that way," Beatrice said, in an apologetic tone.

"Oh, there's nothing wrong with that," Miriam said quickly. "We ought to be concerned about each other."

"Especially when it happens in your front yard," Isaac added.

"See?" Isabelle glared at Beatrice. "They're nice people. That's how nice people should be. My own children want to put me in a nursing home," she added.

"Mom, that's a family problem," Beatrice said firmly. "You came to visit the injured boy, remember?"

"That's right," Isabelle agreed, not looking too chastened by her daughter's rebuke. "I do speak out of order sometimes."

Miriam didn't let the nursing home subject pass by without comment. "You live in Unity, right? Just down the road from the top of Wheat Ridge?"

Isabelle said, "Yes."

"I just thought," Miriam continued, "perhaps Isaac could give you the number at Miller's Furniture. They're only there during business hours. Maybe that wouldn't be good for all things, but during the day at least. If you'd call when and if you really need something, one of us could perhaps run down and help. Just a thought." Miriam smiled. "It might be of help — when you're by yourself sometimes."

"You would?" Isabelle asked, surprised at the offer.

"Sure," Isaac said, adding his weight to Miriam's offer. "We can't do everything, of course, but knowing someone close by is always a good feeling."

"That would be wonderful," Isabelle said, deeply moved. "That way you wouldn't have to worry so much," she added in Beatrice's direction.

"But . . . that would be a bother," Beatrice said. "You can't just go imposing on people."

"It wouldn't be," Miriam said quickly again. "Really it wouldn't. We would love to."

"See," Isabelle said, still in Beatrice's direction.

Behind her the door opened, letting in Dr. Wine. "The Miller family?" he asked, looking questioningly toward Beatrice and then Isabelle.

"Friends," Miriam said. "You can talk in front of them."

Beatrice, who had started to rise from her seat, sat down again. Isabelle looked satisfied, never having made any effort to leave.

Dr. Wine glanced around the room. "I've looked at the CT scan we just did. The news isn't too good, I'm afraid." His eyes found Isaac's face, then moved on. "John has a comminuted skull fracture, which we knew from the X-ray last night."

"There is more then?" Isaac's spoke up, his voice tense.

"I'm afraid so." Dr. Wine was taking his time. "There is bleeding, as I was afraid there would be. A *subdural hematoma,* to use the medical term." Dr. Wine glanced around, and when no one said anything, he continued. "The hematoma consists of a swelling where blood vessels broke from the injury to your son's head. With no place to go, that blood is accumulating and pressing in on the surrounding brain tissue, and may grow for some time yet."

"Is it serious?" Isaac asked.

"Yes," Dr. Wine said. "How serious? That depends on how large the hematoma becomes from the bleeding. If your son's swelling keeps pressing on the brain, a lot of damage can result. We're going to try to keep him stable, and relieve the pressure by medication first. Hopefully surgery can be avoided. There is no way though, to tell how much damage is being done until after the hematoma stops growing. This happens once the blood clots. The hematoma will then decrease over a period of time. When your son regains consciousness, we will be better able to tell his condition."

"Can there be aftereffects?" Isaac asked.

"Yes," Dr. Wine said with some hesitation. "It's possible a subdural hematoma can leave the symptoms of a stroke, among other things. Of course there may be nothing wrong when the swelling has fully gone down."

"How long before we know anything?" Miriam asked.

"I wish I knew, Mrs. Miller," Dr. Wine said, "but with this condition, I would not venture to guess."

"Are you keeping him in the hospital?" Miriam asked.

"I would recommend that," the doctor answered, "at least until John regains consciousness. He really needs to, but . . ." He paused, his meaning clear to them all. "I wish to respect your people's wishes."

"Yes," Isaac bowed his head. "But we don't have medical insurance."

Beatrice cleared her throat before Dr. Wine could respond. "I believe, Mr. Miller, that your hospital expenses will be covered."

"Thank you, officer." Dr. Wine nodded his appreciation to Beatrice. "She is correct. We have been contacted by the party's insurance company, the one that represents the person at fault in the accident, and they are paying all your expenses."

"Not more than that," Isaac quickly said, half rising in his seat. "We don't want any money."

"That's between you and the party who injured your son," Dr. Wine said. "Our concern is for our own bills, of course. They are being paid."

"Then John should stay," Miriam said, slowly this time. "It would be better."

"It would be," Isaac agreed.

"Should the family stay with him?" Miriam asked.

"It's not necessary," Dr. Wine said, "but you are welcome to stay if you want."

"Is John in critical danger?" Miriam asked.

"There is always danger. We have excellent care here at Adams, I believe. So it's just a matter of how much damage has been done and will be done as the bleeding continues. I assure you we will monitor your son's condition with great care. Beyond that — I'm sorry — Mrs. Miller, but we will just hope for the best."

"It's in God's hands," Isaac said for all their benefit. "It's out of ours."

"We will do the best we can," Dr. Wine assured them again. "It never hurts to have people praying though."

"We already did," Isabelle said. "Sunday there will be some more. These are God's children."

"We all seek to be," Isaac said quickly, his voice uncomfortable. "We'll pray that what God desires, will be done."

"I will see you later then," Dr. Wine said, dismissing himself. "The nurses can answer your questions, I'm sure. If you have some, just ask." And then he was gone.

"Who is paying the medical bills?" Miriam asked, glancing toward Beatrice.

"I'll tell you later," Isaac told her.

"I just wanted to thank him."

"Consider him thanked," Beatrice said, figuring she should say that much. "I'll pass on the word."

"She was the officer on the scene last night," Isaac said so Miriam could make sense of the exchange.

"We really have to be going," Beatrice

said, standing up. "Mom needs to get home, and I'm on shift before too long."

"It's nice meeting you, and maybe I can see the young man the next time," Isabelle got up to follow Beatrice out.

"Oh, I'm sure you can now," Miriam said quickly. "Perhaps John's back in his room."

"Later," Isabelle said. "He just got back from his tests. Beatrice can bring me in sometime."

"Oh, yes," Isaac said remembering, "the phone number. I can give it to you now."

"That's not necessary," Beatrice told him. "I'll help Mother find it in the phone book. Miller's Furniture. If not, I know where you live."

"That's so kind of you," Isabelle said to them both, as Beatrice held the door open for her. "We'll be praying for you and John."

As soon as the two women had left, Mattie said to Rebecca, "We should be going too. I'm sure if there's any change, you'll let us know," Mattie said to Miriam.

"Yes." Isaac and Miriam nodded.

Following her mother out, Rebecca said nothing as they got into the buggy and drove out of West Union. It was well north of town before Mattie spoke. "This is a time for you to be strong for John, no matter what happens," she said firmly.

"I want to," Rebecca told her, hoping the strength would be there to fulfill her intentions. That she was not feeling so strong, she couldn't help. She was doing the best she could.

CHAPTER
THIRTY-TWO

Later in the afternoon, Reuben was harness-ing his old driving horse, while the faithful animal switched its tail in vain protest. He was getting ready for his Saturday afternoon church rounds. It wasn't always necessary to take these Saturday afternoon drives. Sometimes there weren't any church mat-ters to be dealt with, but today there were.

He was going, not just to the one he had agreed to look into for Rachel, but to the ones Bishop Mose had left him. Those came from last preaching Sunday — two items that needed looking into. That made three stops, if more did not come in, and at this hour of the afternoon, Reuben doubted any would.

Rachel had seemed subdued all day. It baffled him. The change had come over her during the past few days. It must be the child who was coming because no other answer made much sense. Still while Rachel was carrying Luke, there had never been such a big change, but maybe it was her older age.

After getting his horse under the shafts and the tugs hooked up, he set out. Amman Yoder's place was his first stop. It had to do with the possible medical needs the family might have because Nancy had been diagnosed with breast cancer.

Reuben got the old driving horse moving smartly down the road. The quicker he got going, the sooner he would be done. Saturday afternoon church work was not exactly enjoyable to him but necessary, if things were to be kept running smoothly in the church.

Amman's place was also the easiest stop, and because Reuben liked doing the easiest thing first, he had so organized his afternoon.

Coming up on Amman's driveway, he saw that Amman must be out in the barn. Amman's manure spreader was parked half in and out of the backdoor. The team of Belgian workhorses waited patiently, shuffling occasionally, their feet lifting up and down on the frozen ground. He could see the steady pitchfork loads of manure coming out of the barn door, the occasional one overshooting the intended aim and ending up over the side of the spreader or hanging on the edge.

How like Amman, always a little off on his aim In more ways than one, and now his wife has cancer. Not that sickness couldn't happen to anyone, but Reuben was still convinced that going to Mexico for medical treatments was the wrong thing to do. Because Amman was apparently in favor of such measures, it seemed to Reuben a little like one of those missed throws coming out of the back barn door.

Now that he was reminded of the point, Reuben thought perhaps he should bring up the issue on Sunday with Bishop Mose. Maybe a trip to Mexico should not be included in the expenses the church was willing to help with. It might do no good to bring the matter up, but right now he felt strongly enough about the subject to at least suggest such a rule.

Dismissing the thoughts about Mexico, Reuben brought his mind back to the task at hand. He needed to find out what Amman's medical needs were and report back to the bishop. That was as far as his authority went. Pulling up in front of the barn, he got out and tied the old driving horse to a ring in the door.

"Hello," he hollered into the barn, to let

Amman know he was coming in.

"Back here," Amman hollered in return.

Cheerfully, Reuben thought, not sure how cheerful he would be if it was Rachel who was sick and the deacon was showing up to offer financial help.

"On your Saturday rounds?" Amman asked with a smile.

"Yes." Reuben grinned good-naturedly. "Someone has to . . ."

"True enough . . . true enough," Amman replied, grinning back. "You checking up on our money condition with Nancy's illness?"

"Yah." Reuben nodded, resting his arm on one of the horse stanchions. "You doing okay?"

"As those things go," Amman said, as he stopped his work and leaned on his manure pitchfork. "Doctors think she'll be able to pull out of it."

Reuben couldn't help himself and asked, "You're not going to Mexico?"

If Amman knew about Reuben's feelings on the matter, he didn't show it. "Only as a last resort."

That made Reuben feel better and got him thinking that it was probably all Nancy's idea to go to Mexico and that she must have told Margaret, which was how it got into *The Budget.*

"I wouldn't go either," he told Amman, now that he was sure that going to Mexico didn't come from Amman's head.

"Not my idea." Amman shrugged his shoulders, confirming Reuben's conclusions. "Depends how bad it gets, I guess."

"You think you'd go then?" Reuben asked, thinking of donkeys braying in the dirt streets and standing in front of filthy huts.

Amman glanced up from the concrete floor where his eyes had been resting. He pushed his manure fork into the yet untouched part of the horse stall and answered, "I suppose so. If your wife's sick and can't get help, wouldn't you do everything you could?"

Put that way, Reuben wasn't sure what to say. "But it's Mexico," he managed.

"Maybe they know something we don't. The government here and all . . . with its controls." Amman leaned on his manure fork again. "They have their fingers into everything. How do we know they aren't up to something?"

Reuben was vaguely familiar with this argument, enough at least to respond intelligently. "They wouldn't keep a good drug off the market."

"Yah." Amman glanced up again, more sharply than necessary. "They are the government . . ." he said, as if that answered everything.

It was obvious that Amman's sympathies lay firmly with crossing the border for medical help, whether the idea had originated in his head or not. "I'm not sure I'd go," Reuben said cautiously.

"Even if Rachel had no other help?"

Amman was scrutinizing him now, which Reuben didn't appreciate. This was his deacon call, and he was the one supposed to be scrutinizing people. Yet something would have to be said and said quickly, or Amman would spread the word around that Reuben would rather leave Rachel to die of cancer than chance going across the border. By the time the matter was done, Reuben's motives would not be noble, whether they started out with sound reasons or not.

"We should do everything we can," Reuben said because he did feel that way. It was just that Mexico was not in his book of things to do. He felt sure Bishop Mose would agree, and he figured Sunday morning might prove a more agreeable audience than Amman Yoder. Any conversations they had at the Sunday morning minister's gathering would have the protection all their ministerial proceedings did — a sort of Amish immunity from prosecution because no decisions made could or ever would be traced back to one man. It was their code of honor.

"I think so too," Amman said.

"You'll let me know then when the hospital bills come in?" Reuben was ready to continue on with his Saturday afternoon.

"Yes." Amman nodded. "Should be around ten thousand, from what we know so far."

"I will tell Mose then," Reuben said. "*Da Hah* will provide."

"Him and His people — we are most grateful," Amman let his eyes fall to the concrete barn floor again, adding, "we are unworthy."

"Yes," Reuben said, making moves to leave. "All of us are."

Amman was already pitching manure onto his spreader before Reuben got out of the barn door. The soft thuds from the pitchfork loads sounded in his ear, as he shut the door behind him.

The old driving horse, standing there waiting, lifted its head in weariness when Reuben came out.

Steve Weaver's place was next on his list. Only a year married to his wife, Becky, the young couple had taken up housekeeping on the old Ben Byler place. It needed lots of repairs, having fallen into a dilapidated state in Ben's waning years. Ben's wife had passed away ten years before he did. That left the old man with a sense of wandering. Though Ben never went anywhere, he just visited places in his mind — mainly memories from his young and growing up days.

Ben's youngest daughter, Rose, who had never married, came home from Wisconsin to take care of her dad until he passed away. The family had then sold the farm to Steve and Becky, and Rose returned to Wisconsin.

Steve and Becky now seemed well capable of doing the extra work the place needed and were turning things around quite smartly. A nice couple, Reuben considered them to be, Becky already well into her first pregnancy.

It did all the ministers good to see the way Steve had turned his life around from only a few years prior. He had given up his wild ways to take a decent wife and get right down to the business of keeping a place, raising a family, and becoming involved in the church.

All of that brought Reuben to the reason for his visit. He was not expecting any trouble. Steve was just not that sort of person. But Bishop Mose had thought something should be said, even with how well Steve was doing. Apparently Steve was still holding on to some of his bad habits, picked up from his wild days.

Bishop Mose had been sure a simple stop on a Saturday afternoon would be enough to solve the matter, and Reuben had agreed. The problem was, Steve still cut his hair. *Thinning it out* was what Reuben thought it was called. No matter what the style was called, it was against church regulations.

Pulling into the driveway, Reuben thought the barn, freshly painted a bright red, a pleasant sight. He pulled up to a new hitching post, placed conveniently at just the right spot for occasions when visitors would come. Certainly not planned for the purpose of a visit from the deacon on a Saturday afternoon, he grinned wryly to himself, but it served the purpose whether anticipated or not.

Tying the old driving horse, Reuben wondered whether to walk toward the house or the barn. There seemed to be no sign of anyone around. His problem was solved when Becky opened the front door, her round form filling the opening.

"He's in here," she hollered, assuming it was Steve Reuben was after.

"I made him come in for a lemonade

break," Becky told Reuben, all smiles as he approached. "He works so hard."

"I can see that," Reuben told her, the pleasantness of this young family sweeping over him. He didn't like the news he was bringing to them, but the church's work must be done, even on a pleasant Saturday afternoon.

"We're not in trouble?" Becky asked him, holding the door open, not waiting for his reply. "Steve's in the kitchen."

"Why would we be in trouble?" Steve asked, apparently not as familiar with Amish customs as his wife was.

That might be because of his wild days, Reuben thought. "No," he said, wishing he could talk with Steve by himself. "Just a little matter — no trouble."

"Then have a seat," Steve told him. "Lemonade?"

"No — no. I'm fine," Reuben assured him, taking the offered chair. "I can't stay long."

"So there *is* trouble," Becky said.

Reuben wished she would sit down beside her husband. It would sure make him feel more comfortable, but Becky stayed standing, looking at him, her eyes steady.

"No," he said again, hoping against hope there weren't any bad feelings from past deacon visits on Saturday afternoons in Becky's memory, memories that might be waiting to leap out and pounce on him, the hapless deacon.

"Oh, in that case I'll sit down," Becky concluded, pulling out a chair and lowering her swollen body gingerly onto it.

"It's this month," Steve said, obvious joy in his voice.

"Yes," Reuben agreed, feelings of pleasantness returning a little. "You are both doing well?"

"That we are," Steve agreed, while Becky only smiled, more relaxed now.

He cleared his throat. "The ministry is very pleased with how you are coming along with church life," he stated, trying to smooth the path and wishing he didn't have to continue.

"Yes," Becky said, not looking at Steve but at Reuben.

He squirmed in his seat, deciding to get this over quickly. "There is no trouble, just a concern," Reuben said, keeping his eyes on the table top. Neither of them was saying anything, so he plunged on. "We're happy — what with your past." He paused to catch his breath, which was coming harder than he wished.

"Yes?" Steve said this time, puzzlement on

his face.

"They have something against you," Becky said, filling him in. "You're doing something they don't like."

"No — no," Reuben said quickly, and then, "well, yes, but it's nothing serious." Neither Becky nor Steve said anything.

"You see, your hair, it's not supposed to be thinned out." Reuben just blurted it out. "We thought it might be a habit from your former days," he said, clearing his throat to give the words their proper meaning, "which you were unaware was against the *ordnung*."

"He cuts his own hair," Becky said, concerned now, looking Steve's hair over. "I never noticed anything."

"Why," Steve answered, running his hand across his head, his fingers combing his hair from front to back, "I just thin it out a little. Always did."

"That's what we thought," Reuben said quickly. "We figured you didn't notice."

"I guess you do thin it out at that," Becky said, looking at Steve's hair again. "You'd better let me cut it from now on. I've wanted to anyway."

"I guess I'd better," Steve allowed slowly. "I didn't know."

"That's what we thought," Reuben assured him, breathing easier now.

"I'll make sure he gets it right from now on," Becky said, running her fingers through Steve's hair. "I guess he does things to it — just never noticed."

"I'm sorry." Steve was all apologies now.

"Does he need to do anything?" Becky asked.

"No," Reuben said quickly. "We figured it was an accident, but it leaves a bad example for the young boys. They notice such things."

"What would I have to do?" Steve asked in Becky's direction instead of Reuben's.

"Oh," Becky said, wrinkling her brow, "maybe a confession at pre-communion church."

"No," Reuben said even quicker this time, "that's not necessary. The ministry is so appreciative of how you're doing."

"See?" Becky was smiling now, running her fingers through Steve's hair again. "You're doing okay. He works so hard," she said in Reuben's direction.

"Yes, I can see that," Reuben assured them. "We're thankful for that. But now I must be going."

"No lemonade?" Steve questioned, trying again.

"I have another stop," Reuben said, then wished he hadn't. It wasn't good to share church plans with others.

They made no attempt to rise, so Reuben stood, leaving them sitting there. The picture of the two — such good sound church members and so obedient — stayed with him until he pulled into Ezra's driveway.

Ezra was washing his buggy in front of his storage garage, which Reuben thought was a little foolish for someone his age, but this was his wife's brother, so he kept his thoughts to himself. The matter he had come for would be difficult enough.

"On your Saturday rounds." Ezra grinned from ear to ear, as if he were sharing an uncomfortable secret. "Rachel wanted you to stop by for something."

Reuben didn't comment on that because Ezra didn't know how right he was with his guess.

Not used to a lot of words from his brother-in-law, Ezra didn't find Reuben's silence surprising. "Elizabeth's in the house," he said, apparently assuming Reuben wanted something from her for Rachel.

Sitting inside his buggy and not wanting to get out unless it was completely necessary, Reuben cleared his throat. Because Ezra was right here, his garden hose in hand, they might as well have this conversation from where he sat instead of standing on the ground. "I came to talk with you," he managed, raising his voice to make sure it carried all the way over to Ezra

"With me?" Ezra couldn't have looked more surprised.

"It's just a little matter," Reuben assured him. "Easily cleared up — I'm sure."

"Really?" Ezra didn't look happy at all, as he walked over to Reuben's buggy door, leaving his garden hose on the ground.

"It's really nothing," Reuben said.

"Then why are you here?" Ezra asked the obvious.

"It's just a little thing," Reuben said quickly.

"Did Mose send you?" Ezra asked.

There was no way Reuben was going to answer that question. "It's not much," he said instead.

"So what is it?" Ezra placed his hand on the buggy side wall, waiting.

"You were seen using your tractor to pull the hay wagon back to the fields — this fall." Reuben wished he could make his voice louder, but it wasn't working quite right at the moment.

"So?" Ezra wasn't looking at the ground.

"It's against the *ordnung*," Reuben told him. "You know that."

"Maybe." Ezra still wasn't looking down. "I just did it once."

"It's a bad example for the young people," Reuben replied, searching for the high ground and noting that Ezra's bold, direct eye contact indicated the conversation was not going well.

"Maybe," Ezra allowed again, "but no one saw me — except family." A suspicious gleam turned in his eye.

"You shouldn't have done it." Reuben was trying to keep the conversation going in the right direction.

"Rachel wouldn't have anything to do with this?" Ezra's eyes were not happy.

"You shouldn't have done it," Reuben repeated himself.

"Maybe we'd better just forget this." Ezra moved his hand downward on the buggy. The sound made a smooth rasping — a gentle yet insisting sort of noise.

"It's a bad example for the young people." Reuben was not about to be caught backing down. Ezra would be sure to pass the matter around if he did. *Backed right down,* he could hear Ezra telling the story. *Just come and talk to me when you need to know what to say,* Ezra would add with a chuckle.

No, there could be no backing down now that he was committed. "I would advise a confession next pre-communion church." Reuben dropped his ace line. "You wouldn't want this matter getting any bigger than it already is."

Ezra laughed, not seeming to be offended at all.

He is that way, Reuben thought, *confident and careful in all he does.*

"Well, we'll just leave it like it is. You and Mose and I. It'll probably all work out, don't you think?"

Reuben wasn't sure about anything at the moment, so he said nothing, keeping his eyes straight ahead while he thought of a proper response.

"What's Rachel up to anyway?" Ezra asked. "She's not usually like that."

"She's expecting again," Reuben said, figuring Ezra might come to the same conclusion he had.

"Still doesn't explain it." Ezra shook his head. "If you can't trust family anymore — what's the world coming to?"

"You still shouldn't have done it," Reuben told him, refusing to let the matter go.

"How about I talk to Mose tomorrow?" Ezra suggested more than asked. "Maybe we can get this matter cleared up right and proper."

That was the last thing Reuben wanted

Ezra doing, but what was there to say? Certainly telling Ezra he shouldn't talk to the bishop wouldn't help matters at all. "I'd just do my confession and get it over with," he said.

"We'll see." Ezra clearly considered the conversation over. "You have any more stops to make?"

"No," Reuben said before he thought better of it, then had to finish the sentence, "this is the last one."

"See you tomorrow at church then." Ezra nodded his head briskly. "Got my buggy to finish washing."

Reuben nodded, slapping the reins, waking the old driving horse out of his stupor, and moving forward as Ezra hosed his buggy with water. He had a deep concern for what might happen tomorrow if Ezra actually talked with Mose.

That evening Rachel seemed at peace around the house, and Reuben was thankful for it. As she served them supper, Luke sat across the table, lost in thought over something.

"You get the oats at the co-op?" Reuben asked him.

"Yes," he answered, nodding, "got home sometime after lunch."

Rachel thought she saw a slight redness creep up Luke's neck but decided not to mention it. Things were going too well with what Reuben had done this afternoon to disturb anything. There was no sense in making trouble where there was none. Whatever Luke was embarrassed about likely involved a girl, probably that Susie creature.

With *Da Hah* soon to be pleased with them, Susie would be a thing of the past. Reuben was on her side now and the world was looking rosy.

CHAPTER
THIRTY-THREE

The brisk Sunday morning air moved across Rebecca's face, as she walked to the barn. She was ahead of Matthew, who had been stirring in his room when she left the upstairs. Her father was always the first out to the barn — unless he wasn't home — but that was seldom.

She had gone to sleep last night thinking about John and their future together. Poor John was still unconscious, she assumed. Rebecca doubted she would have been told if he had awakened. That chance would come this morning — at church — the first real opportunity for Miriam or one of the other relatives to pass on any news.

It crossed her mind that because she was promised to John, that made her — in a way — a Miller relative. Yesterday Miriam and Isaac had fully accepted her into the family. They would have eventually, but the accident had sped the process up.

There was so much about their relationship that still needed addressing, and they
had planned to talk about it today. But now
that was impossible.

She opened the barn door to the familiar
smells and sights of the morning milking.
Its very simplicity and earthiness flowed
around her.

*Why can't all of life be this simple? Why
can't all of life have this solid rhythm and flow
about it, like milking the cows or tilling the soil
does? Here the sun comes up each morning
when it is supposed to. Here the cows drop
their milk on schedule, bawling in pain if they
aren't relieved on time.*

*Does everyone really think I am just sup-
posed to go on living in the same way as
before, even if the world changes so abruptly
around me? They certainly seem to. Am I to
bear up and keep on with the plans and act
the same regardless of the pain?* It hardly
seemed fair to her, and she felt like telling
the world.

If she spoke her thoughts aloud, her father
would be the only one to hear, and maybe
Matthew. *Trouble,* he would say, or *Girls.*
The thought of Matthew and his simplistic
solutions made her smile. How like the
young to think they knew everything, that
all of life could be summed up by one or

two sentences.

"Good to see you smiling," Lester said, having come in from the milk house. "There's always something to smile about — isn't there?"

"Just thinking about Matthew," she told him, "and what he would say about my problems."

"You do have some big ones," Lester agreed soberly, "but *Da Hah* will see you through."

"Does He always?" Rebecca asked, more to make conversation than because she doubted.

"If we let Him," her father said.

"How do we let Him?" she asked, this time sincerely wanting to know.

"By doing what is right — then waiting."

"What if I don't always know what's right?" she asked.

"Then you wait — doing what you *do* know, of course. Maybe others can help."

She nodded. Behind her the barn door swung open, letting in Matthew, his face brightening when he saw her.

"Thought you had to do the chores by yourself?" she asked, teasing him.

"I'm capable," he retorted. "Dad knows I am."

"Yes, you are," Lester said, "but extra help

doesn't hurt anyone."

"I did it all by myself when she was gone," he replied.

"And a good job too," Lester said. "Now take the help while you can and be thankful. You never know how long things will last."

"Is Rebecca going somewhere again?" Matthew asked.

Rebecca wasn't sure whether the concern was from the thought of her leaving or from the extra work it would leave him with.

Deciding to lead him on, Rebecca said, "I'll get married someday."

"When?" he asked skeptically.

"We'll see."

"You think too much," Matthew told her, waiting for the cows, which had just come in, to settle down.

How fast he is growing up, she thought, *so quickly turning into a young man, and he, my little brother.* She could remember changing his diaper not that long ago, feeding him with a spoon on the highchair while her mother tended to other household duties. *So quickly time passes,* she told herself. *Will this pass too? John and the accident?*

It didn't seem to be passing quickly. The last day and night had stretched out like an eternity, and this day wasn't looking any better. *I probably need to go see John this afternoon,* she thought, wondering if her mother would take her or if she would need to drive herself.

As her father walked by, she asked him, "Can Mom take me down to see John this afternoon?"

"I don't know why not. You ought to go — even sooner if he gets worse. I can watch the girls if you go with Mom."

"I'll ask her," she replied and then added, "I ought to go in and help with breakfast. After the next round."

"We need to be on the road by eight ten," Lester said, just to be sure everyone remembered. "Church is clear on the west end — Jacob Byler's place this week."

Arriving late for church wasn't only frowned upon, it was embarrassing. Not only could everyone watch you pull in late, they could watch you the whole time it took to walk in and find your place. There was no backdoor to enter unnoticed.

"I'd better go then," she said, loosening the last milker from the line of cows.

Matthew was waiting to release the cows from their stanchions. As he did they pushed and shoved their way back out to the barn-yard.

Rebecca left just as Matthew hollered at

the cows, pressing to move out of the barn all at the same time. Outside she took a deep breath of the fresh winter morning air, letting her eyes feast on the bright dawning of the sun in the east. Great streaks of red, orange, and blue went skyward, accented by low hanging clouds on the horizon.

With a sigh she went into the house, stopping to leave her coat in the front closet.

"Good morning," Mattie said. "Can you get the girls up for me?"

"Sure," she said. "I thought you might need help."

"I've almost got the eggs and oatmeal done. Lester probably wants to leave early."

"That's what he said. Can you take me to the hospital this afternoon? I probably should go."

"If Lester watches the girls."

"He said he would."

"Shouldn't be any problem then. You get the girls up. We might be running late already."

Rebecca went to get her sisters up, making sure they got dressed in their everyday clothing for breakfast. "It's Sunday morning," she told them to keep the orientation correct in their minds. "After breakfast you'll need to change into your good clothing."

Gathered around the kitchen table by the time Lester and Matthew came in from the barn, breakfast was eaten mostly in silence. After the second prayer of thanks, everyone scattered to their tasks. The girls helped in the kitchen and then ran off to change again. Lester went to the barn to get the driving horse ready.

While Lester changed, Matthew hitched the horse to the buggy. At fifteen minutes after eight, they were on the road, and by twenty till nine, they were pulling into the Byler's already fast-filling barnyard full of buggies.

"Made it in time," Lester said, relief in his voice.

"You always do," Mattie reminded him. "You have a good sense of timing."

"Whoa there," was all Lester said in reply, talking to the horse, pulling up to the sidewalk to unload the womenfolk.

CHAPTER
THIRTY-FOUR

Outside of Milroy at Ben Yoder's place, Reuben arrived at church on time. Pulling in he eyed the long line of men standing in the barnyard facing the house. He had hoped against hope, he wouldn't see what he was now seeing — or rather not seeing. Bishop Mose was missing from the front of the line. He was never late. That meant that the bishop must be in the barn talking to someone. Who that was, Reuben had little doubt.

To distract himself, he asked Rachel, "How's the baby doing?"

Rachel looked surprised, even happy, Reuben thought, but she had been looking that way since yesterday when he had agreed to approach her brother Ezra about the tractor driving.

"Good," she said, before the buggy stopped in front of the walk.

Behind him, three other buggies were

pulling in from the road. They slowed down, waiting until he moved on. Rachel never looked back or sideways, gathering her shawl tightly around her shoulders in the chilly morning air and strode quickly up the walk.

Watching her go, Reuben wondered again how he had let himself get talked into this situation with Ezra. Not much could be done about it now though. He would simply have to live through it. *Surely things won't get too bad,* he told himself, feeling a little hopeful, even if Ezra was out in the barn complaining to the bishop.

Executing a sharp left, Reuben maneuvered into place, along the line of parked buggies. Amos Troyer, a young man about Luke's age, came over to help unhitch.

"Nice morning," he said, taking the tugs off his side as Reuben removed his own. "Luke here already?"

"Should be," Reuben told Amos, his mind not on the conversation. "Left before we did."

Amos glanced around. "Yah, he's here," he said, having spotted Luke's buggy. "Taking that Susie home now," Amos stated, chuckling.

"You weren't wanting to do that yourself, were ya?" Reuben teased, his mind temporarily distracted from his troubles.

Amos grinned. "Nah, I had my chance, but — you know — it didn't suit."

"There'll be someone for you," Reuben said. "Just don't get too old. Youth only comes once."

"That's what Dad says, but I'm not that old. Luke waited awhile too, didn't he?"

"I suppose so," Reuben allowed. "Wanting to be sure, I guess."

"Oh, I'm sure," Amos said quickly. "It's just that . . ." He held the shafts of the buggy as Reuben lead the horse forward.

"Little young?" Reuben guessed, then remembered his deacon responsibilities, "Behave yourself."

"I always do," Amos said, which Reuben knew was the truth or close to it. Amos's family caused little trouble in the church. Reuben couldn't remember when the last time was he had stopped in at the Troyer residence on Saturday afternoon.

"Just keep it that way," Reuben said, remembering that pride was the biggest pitfall a man or woman could fall into.

Leading his horse toward the barn, his worse fears were realized. Bishop Mose was coming out of the barn, taking his place in the line, greeting several of the men closest to him. Ezra Miller came out just behind the bishop. Reuben was sure he saw a smug look on his face.

There was nothing to be done. The matter would just have to run its course. Trying to talk to Bishop Mose now would only create a scene and accomplish nothing. It would be better to face the bishop in the minister's gathering once church had started.

Composing himself, Reuben tied his horse and waited a few minutes to see if any bad feelings would develop between the horses. When everything remained quiet, the horses occupying themselves with reaching for scraps of hay, Reuben left.

There was still time to greet a few of the men before they began moving toward the house. Bishop Mose led the way. Someone motioned for Reuben to take his proper place. Speeding up his steps, he did so, slipping in behind Manny Coblentz, a visiting minister from one of the other districts.

Moving in the line, Reuben hung his head, signifying his humility and his reliance on God, while accepting this exalted place of leadership among brethren. Filing in, the men took their places on the hard, backless benches, the women doing the same on the other side of the house. Following that, the young folks came.

When all were seated, the first song number was given out, and the service began. At the start of the second line of the song, Bishop Mose got to his feet and moved toward the stairs, where the minister's morning meeting was to be held. He paused momentarily to receive a whisper from Ben Byler. Ben was telling the bishop exactly which upstairs bedroom to use. Otherwise the entourage might be led into a bedroom containing sleeping young babies.

Reuben kept his steps as soft as possible, climbing the stairs with the others, a long line of men in straight-cut black dress suits. Once in the bedroom, chairs scraped on the hardwood floor, as the bishop took the first seat. Reuben, the last one through the door, closed it softly behind him.

"It's good to have Manny with us." The bishop nodded in Manny's direction, before Reuben barely got seated. "He'll be working hard for us today." A murmur of laughter went around the circle, as they all knew what that meant.

Manny squirmed on his chair but said nothing. What was there to say? Custom was custom, and he had run the risk by visiting that day. Any visiting minister was subject to being assigned to preaching the main sermon, an hour long affair without notes or a Bible to read from.

"We shouldn't have too much to talk about this morning," the bishop continued, the low sound of the singing downstairs rising around them. "Everyone's behaving themselves, I think." This produced smiles around the circle, especially Reuben who was feeling better the longer the bishop talked. Maybe Ezra hadn't done too much damage.

"Our Scriptures are Matthew five and Luke eleven," the bishop continued, for the benefit of anyone who had forgotten the announcement two weeks earlier and for Manny, who hadn't been there.

"Easy enough to preach out of — plenty of material — it's good to be reminded of." Mose paused as if thinking. "Maybe Reuben can tell us what he found out from Saturday's work. He had two things to look into, I think."

Reuben cleared his throat, deciding quickly it was best to play it straight. With that decision behind him, he mentioned Amman Yoder's hospital bill of a possible ten thousand dollars.

Then because he was feeling better, he brought up the issue of paying for Mexico medical expenses. "About this going to Mexico. Amman said Nancy might — if things got worse — want to go to Mexico for treatment not given in the States. Is questionable treatment something that should be paid for by church help?"

It all just kind of came out in a gush, surprising even Reuben. He knew it was a bold question, but surely it was safe here to say such things.

"Well," Mose said, sitting back in his chair, "I guess if you're sick — if someone can make you better — why complain?"

"It usually doesn't though," Reuben said before anyone else could comment. "It's usually wasted money."

"I see our deacon has opinions." Mose smiled, not looking too irritated. "Maybe he has gotten too close to the situation."

"Or not close enough," someone else said, at which they all chuckled again.

"We better just leave that one alone," the bishop concluded. "There was something else, wasn't there?"

"Steve Miller," Reuben said, not feeling like giving any more details. If Mose wanted more, he could ask. "He was very easy to work with — as we expected."

"I thought so," Mose said, seeming satisfied. "The issue is concluded then?"

"I think so," Reuben answered, nodding his head.

Mose was silent, as if waiting.

After a minute of silence, Reuben decided he had better say it. "I stopped in at Ezra Miller's too. He —"

Mose cut him off with a raised hand. "I know. He talked to me this morning. Rachel wouldn't have had something to do with this?"

What was there to say? He would have to admit this. "Yes," he said, knowing no one else around them had a clue what Mose and he were talking about. But it was not his place to explain.

"I see," Mose said. "She saw him?"

"Yes," Reuben said again.

"Well, we'd better leave family out of this, I think." Mose nodded his head to his own conclusions. "That would be best. Things get sticky with family in such matters, and so we'll just leave it. Ezra said he'd be more careful in the future."

Reuben nodded, thankful the rebuke wasn't any worse. Mose was letting him down easy, and he resolved right then and there this wouldn't happen again.

The others, who still had no clue what was being talked about, decided to leave the matter too, as the bishop moved on to other subjects. Fifteen minutes later, they all filed downstairs again. The singing stopped by the time they found their seats.

Reuben, who had no assigned part in the service that day, sat thinking about what he would tell Rachel on the way home. He would be nice to her, he decided, because Mose had been nice to him. That way no harm would be done, the matter would be behind them, and they could go on with their lives like before, but there would be no more Saturday projects from her.

Church dismissed by ten after twelve, and the noon meal was served soon after that. Around one thirty, Reuben got his horse out, hitched it to the buggy, and picked Rachel up at the end of the sidewalk.

Reuben got right to the point. "Mose didn't like what I did on Saturday."

There was no need to tell Rachel what that was. She already knew.

"He didn't like it?" She turned toward him, shock in her voice.

"He said family shouldn't be involved in things like this. It gets sticky. Ezra talked to Mose, I guess," he said, checking both ways for traffic, then letting out the reins when no vehicles were coming down the road.

Reuben took a closer look at Rachel's face once they had made the turn and the old driving horse was moving along well. He thought he had figured out why Rachel had wanted him to go to Ezra on Saturday, but the look in Rachel's eyes caught him by surprise. He read fear and hopelessness, emotions that didn't seem associated with the conclusion he had arrived at.

"So why did you want me to go?" he asked her.

There was only silence, her bonnet no longer allowing him a clear look at her face.

"I figured it might help," she finally said.

"Help what?" he asked.

She said nothing, not moving on her side of the buggy.

He thought about asking again, but then remembered what Mose had said about letting this one go. That was for the best, he decided. No serious harm had been done yet.

"You feeling okay with the baby?" he asked instead. "When's it due?"

"It'll come when it's ready. Not for a while . . . but soon enough," Rachel said.

Reuben let that subject go too, slapping the old driving horse's reins, urging him home.

"Emma was to see the heart doctor this week," Rachel said, her voice low. "Martha Kemp said so."

"That's too bad," Reuben said. "Anything

serious?"

Rachel didn't answer.

CHAPTER
THIRTY-FIVE

At church, west of Wheat Ridge, Rebecca received no news on John's condition. She half expected someone to whisper an update while she worked her way along the line of women that morning. She greeted them, one by one, including Amanda Troyer, who had come on the van load Friday. At first John's mother seemed not to be in the room, but once the line of girls and women filed into the living room for the start of the service, Rebecca saw Miriam ahead of her, but there was no chance to talk.

The lack of news, she assumed, was good because bad news would have been brought straight to her by Miriam or John's aunt Esther. After the ministers left for their meeting upstairs, the singing settled into its slow and normal routine. In the middle of the third song, the bishop's black dress shoes came into view on the stairs as he reentered the room with Isaac Miller close behind.

Rebecca wondered at their quick return. They had been away a mere forty-five minutes, according to the clock on the far living room wall. The lead singer led out for two more lines and then stopped at the end of the stanza.

Bishop Martin had the opening sermon, followed by Isaac with the main message. Rebecca found herself paying close attention to Isaac's sermon. She watched his eyes as they moved across the room, listened to his words, and finally realized she was checking to see if the gentleness she had seen yesterday was still there. It seemed important to know if what she had seen was just a passing thing, or was Isaac always like that?

Although an Amish minister hardly ever announced what his topic was, Rebecca picked up on a thread of a topic along the lines of forgiveness. Isaac said that Jesus was calling us all to forgive those who trespass against us, no matter how great that trespass was. As he spoke, she watched his gentle eyes. She realized that, yes, this was Isaac's nature. It almost seemed as if tears weren't far from his cheeks and his voice was disrupted by a slight catch.

Isaac said that the evil in the world was bound to affect all our lives. He said we are all called as children of God to forgive the person who did the evil, knowing that he needed God as much as we ourselves do. He said this was what it meant to forgive — to grant others the same mercy we had received ourselves.

Rebecca wondered if John would have those same tender eyes when he grew older. Would they have that special softness? She found herself remembering John's eyes, right there in the middle of the sermon. They did have a little of his father's gentleness, but they also had a hardness, a lurking storm, like the one that erupted in front of her house on Friday evening.

Was she supposed to forgive and forget all of that? Isaac wasn't saying anything about forgetting evil, but she wondered if that wasn't part of it. Could she just forget what had happened on Friday night? It seemed a strange and terrible thing to be asking of herself.

She turned her attention back to Isaac's sermon. He was telling the story of the Pharisee and the publican who went up to pray together in the temple. The Pharisee, who thought of himself as a good man, removed himself to his own corner lest he be contaminated by his corrupt fellow men. There he began to name his virtues to God. The publican, on the other hand, just stood with all the rest of the people, beating his chest and begging God for mercy.

"Now we all know the story," Isaac said, "but we must also live the story. It's not the Pharisee who went home that night right with God, but the publican. Oh, how heavy it lays on us to learn the lesson. How easy it is for us to become proud in our own virtues. How easy it is for us to tell God how good we are. Yet what we need to do is beat our chest." Here Isaac thumped his chest lightly for emphasis. "We need to ask God for the same mercy everyone needs."

Rebecca listened, but she was really looking at his eyes again. She wanted to know if the hard eyes of the son had come from the father. Half expecting to find anger, she felt a tear slip down her face at the sight before her.

What she had seen in the hospital doorway was magnified. Isaac was looking toward the ceiling, seeming to see straight through it to the glory of heaven. His eyes shone with pure softness, the zeal from his soul reaching upward, and saw things she could only imagine.

"We must be the children of God," he was

saying softly, never taking his eyes off the ceiling. "It is what we are called to be — a holy people."

She felt like brushing the tear on her cheek, but she couldn't move, the knowledge of her own heart gripping her. This was the standard she must live by. To forgive John, to forget it all, to accept whatever condition he was in down there in West Union on that hospital bed. She would, she decided.

Isaac now had his eyes off the ceiling. Rebecca couldn't see them anymore, but the memory stayed vivid in her mind. If this was what God was like, then He would have mercy on her for not forgiving John right away.

Mercy, she thought. *Mercy even for my lack of proper feelings. Mercy for my inability to always do what is right. Yes,* she was certain of it. She had seen hope in Isaac's eyes. Hope that mercy was real, available. As to offering it to others — especially John — well, she would try. That much she now knew.

Rebecca shifted on the hard bench as Isaac wrapped up his sermon. After asking three of the older men to give testimony on what was said, he took his seat on the bench. To the drone of their voices, saying that all they had heard was within the will of God, Rebecca gave testimony — silently of course — and thanks for what she had heard. It was the living out which would be hard. *But one step at a time.*

With the testimonies from the three men concluded, Bishop Martin dismissed the service. Rebecca filed out with the line of girls. Forty minutes later she helped tend two rounds of dinner tables and still had not received any information on John's condition.

Several of the girls her age had made inquires of her. She responded with what little she knew. That John had been hit from behind by an English driver while driving through Unity. That John was still in the same unconscious state as when she last saw him yesterday. That the doctor didn't know much beyond that yet.

The general consensus among the girls, as they carried bowls of peanut butter and cheese to the tables, seemed to be that the roads were getting ever more dangerous for anyone driving a buggy. Wilma, who with her brother Will often picked up and drove Rebecca on youth nights, said they had just had a close call last Sunday night.

"Someone nearly ran us off the road near the bridge in Harshville," Wilma said. "Driving fast too. Thankfully Will saw it coming and could pull over."

"They still don't know for sure who hit John," Rebecca said, unaware of Isaac's encounter with Beatrice's husband. "I guess John's the only one who knows for sure."

"How long's he going to be unconscious?" asked Wilma.

"The doctor didn't know that either," Rebecca said. "It could be awhile till the pressure on his brain goes down."

"He must have been hit really hard," one of the other girls commented.

"I suppose so." Rebecca nodded, thinking about it. "From what I picked up, he was thrown quite a distance."

"It must be *awful* . . ." Anna Yoder let the sentence drag out meaningfully. "You've been going with him for a while."

Rebecca searched for the right words. "Yes, but we have to accept the Lord's will."

At least she could say the right thing, she thought, as the buzz of conversation continued.

"It could happen to any of us," Wilma said in Anna's direction. "Even after we're married."

"I suppose," Anna allowed. "It's still hard."

"Yes, it is," Rebecca said, wanting the

conversation to move on. Talking about John and remembering how he looked in his unconscious state at the hospital were difficult.

"I heard that with injuries like that, he could be paralyzed . . . maybe for life," Anna half-whispered, as if she didn't want anyone else to hear.

"You don't know that," Wilma broke in quickly. "You shouldn't be saying things like that. It's hard enough for Rebecca already."

Rebecca felt the words cut.

"Oh, I didn't mean to be harsh," Anna said softly. "I was just saying what I heard."

"Well, you shouldn't say it. You don't know," Wilma said in Anna's direction.

Apparently feeling regretful, Anna said quickly, "I'm sorry. I should be more careful."

The other girls started moving away, and Anna soon followed them.

"Come on. You need something to eat. The third table has room," Wilma nudged Rebecca gently in the direction of the long table where a few stragglers and table waiters were finding their places.

Numbly spreading the peanut butter on her bread, Rebecca chewed without tasting much. Wilma spread her own sandwich silently, saying nothing and staying with Rebecca until her mother came over at the end of their meal.

Mattie whispered to Rebecca, "John's still the same. Miriam said they're going down this afternoon — between three and five. We should go too."

Rebecca nodded, the tears slipping down her face again. Wilma squeezed her arm before getting up to leave. "Will's hitching up," she said, leaving for the kitchen and her bonnet and shawl.

"We're going soon," Mattie told Rebecca, before leaving to walk back toward the living room. Catching sight of her father coming out of the barn with the horse, she went to the kitchen for her own wraps and waited for Mattie to join her. Together they walked out to the end of the sidewalk.

CHAPTER
THIRTY-SIX

After arriving home, Lester unhitched the horse from the buggy while Matthew got the younger driving horse harnessed for Rebecca.

"He's ready to go," Matthew told Rebecca, as he brought the horse out from the barn. "Raring," he added. "You'd better drive."

"Mom can drive," Rebecca said, as Mattie came out of the house, having dashed in to pick up a small satchel.

"You're driving," Mattie said, taking one look at the pawing young horse. "It's feeling its oats."

"That's what I said," Matthew said, happy to have his conclusion supported.

Rebecca climbed in, took the reins from Matthew, and kept a tight control on the horse as they dashed out of the driveway.

"What's gotten into him anyway?" Mattie muttered, hanging on. "We should have taken the other horse."

"Dad would have let us, if church hadn't been way over on the west side. The horse is tired."

"He still could have made it." Mattie was obviously questioning the wisdom of this, as the young horse pulled them speedily around a corner out on the open road.

"He'll calm down by the time we're halfway there," Rebecca said. She then let the horse have its head, as they clattered across the open bridge at the first bend.

"If we're not in the ditch by then," Mattie said, hanging on tighter as they approached the Harshville covered bridge.

In the din of the crossing, both women fell silent and remained so until they approached the edge of West Union.

"How long do you want to stay?" Mattie asked.

"Not too long, I suppose."

"Hospital's aren't the most comfortable place."

"It's not just that. It's like you can't do anything — you know — about it. And with him unconscious, I can't really talk to him."

"Maybe he'll come out of it soon."

"I still don't like hospitals."

"We bear the burdens given to us," Mattie said. "You're doing pretty well."

Rebecca wasn't sure if she was or wasn't, but she did know she was trying, and her mother would, no doubt, count that for something.

"I hope he's awake," Rebecca said because she suddenly wanted to talk to John. This pressure of not knowing, of being left hanging without going forward or backward was stressful. "I'd like to talk to him."

"I suppose you would," her mother agreed. "You never did talk again after he left the house on Friday night?"

"No, but I was thinking about more than that. Things like hearing his voice again."

"I guess the argument just makes it all the harder now."

"It wasn't all John's fault," Rebecca said quickly. "I guess I'd like to tell him that too."

"I didn't say it was," Mattie said. "We all share blame sometimes. It's just a lesson in not letting the sun go down on your wrath. One never knows what could happen in the nighttime."

Rebecca pulled up to a lightpost in the hospital parking lot, the Miller's buggy already tied nearby.

"I see Isaac and Miriam are here already," she said, letting her mother's comments go unanswered.

"That's better than going in by ourselves,"

Mattie replied, stepping down out of the buggy and taking the tie rope with her. "I don't like hospitals either, especially going in by myself."

Walking inside, the two found Miriam and Isaac in the waiting room.

"We've just been with John," Miriam said. "Why don't you two go on in by yourselves and have a few minutes with him."

Mattie nodded, moving toward the door.

Rebecca followed her mother, but not before noticing that Isaac's eyes were weary. The tenderness from the morning was still there, a softness lingering, but now he looked as if the vision he had seen was fading.

Rebecca followed Mattie down the hallway and into John's room. Mattie stepped in first, stopping in front of John's bed. Rebecca joined her, feeling a great sadness filling her.

John lay there as he had been before, the IV line still running into his arm, his breathing shallow, his face the color of the hospital walls.

Rebecca said nothing.

"I'll leave you with him," Mattie whispered.

"You can stay," she said quickly.

"No," Mattie said firmly, "you need to be

alone with him."

Rebecca steeled herself as her mother quietly left, closing the door softly behind her. The stillness of the room descended on her, broken only by the occasional beep of the monitor beside John's bed. She wished she wasn't so nervous.

She moved a bit closer, and summoning up her courage, she forced herself to whisper, "John . . ."

"John," she repeated, forcing herself again. She reached out to lay her fingers on his hands. They were cold and unmoving. She remembered how they had felt before, the life flowing in them, the feeling they transmitted, the love they left lingering on her own fingers. She remembered, and she let the tears come. With the flow came release, and warmth gathered around her heart.

"John," she said again, wanting what they used to have to come back, to reappear from this awful nothingness into which it had gone.

She reached out again. This time her fingers brushed gently across his cheek, feeling the growth of his beard.

Someone had tried to shave his cheeks but missed some spots. She felt a desire to kiss his cheek, wondering if that would bring him back. Gathering her courage, she kissed him, letting her lips linger. She wondered if John knew how much she cared and that she had forgiven him.

Will John come back soon? The question burned in her. How long she stood there, she wasn't certain, but she finally wiped her eyes and turned to leave.

Those in the waiting room noticed her red eyes, their obvious satisfaction in her reaction embarrassing her, but it also felt good.

"I'm ready to go," she told her mother.

"You'll let us know then," Mattie said in Miriam's direction.

"Yes, we'll send word if anything changes."

With that the two left, mother and daughter walking out to the buggy together. The young driving horse was again raring to go, this time in the direction of home. Rebecca was ready too, only she was not certain whether home would be any greater shelter from her thoughts than here.

"He'll come around soon," Mattie told her.

"Yes," Rebecca agreed, hoping it was true.

CHAPTER
THIRTY-SEVEN

Nothing had changed by Tuesday.

After an early supper, Isaac and Miriam drove to the medical center, arriving sometime before six, the winter daylight almost gone by then.

"Aden and Esther might be coming too," Miriam said, as they approached the outskirts of town.

"That's nice," Isaac said, his mind obviously elsewhere.

"It might be a little later though. Esther said Aden had some things to do at the store. They really miss John because of the holiday season approaching and all. Aden said he isn't hiring anyone else on. Do you think he's just being kind by not replacing John?"

"Maybe he likes the work John was doing. John's a good worker."

"It's got to be more than that," Miriam thought aloud. "Maybe he thinks John will get better soon."

"Don't we all," Isaac said, leaving it at that.

"But John's still not even out of his coma," she protested. "How can he assume that John's going to be able to work again soon?"

"Aden doesn't. He's doing what we all have to do. Wait and see. If we guess, it'll just be wrong. I'm sure Aden is wise enough to know that."

"Why is life like that?" She shivered under the buggy blanket, pulling it up tighter around her waist.

"Not all of it is," Isaac said. "Just enough to keep us from feeling too at home on this earth. *Da Hah* knows what He's doing."

Miriam said nothing as Isaac pulled to a stop at an intersection. The light was red. The vehicles crossed in front of them, rushing by each other in a hurry to go somewhere.

She wished she were in a hurry to go where she was going, but she wasn't. The evening ahead seemed like a load too heavy to carry. The days that had gone by had done their damage, like clouds that dropped their rain but still hung leaden in the sky.

"There they come now," Miriam said, turning around to look down the street behind them, having heard the faint sound of horse's hooves on pavement.

"It is a buggy," Isaac agreed, after a moment's silence in which the distinct sound became louder. "I'm not sure it's Aden's though. There are others who come into town."

"This time of the night? It must be them."

"Aden must have gotten done early then."

"It *is* them," she repeated, as the buggy pulled to a stop two cars behind them, her eyes catching a glimpse inside.

When the light turned green, Isaac let his horse go with a jerk. Both horses trotted across the intersection, the buggies following tight behind each other as the two cars turned right.

"You know what time we're going back?" Isaac asked, pulling to a stop again before turning into the hospital parking lot.

"Not too late. Visiting hours aren't that late," she said, as he brought the buggy to a halt at the lightpost.

"You think anyone else will come down to visit?" he asked.

"I doubt it. Weekends — maybe they would. Most people will wait till John is home."

"That shouldn't be long," he commented, having tied up the horse. They stood together, waiting for Aden and Esther to join them from farther down the parking lot.

"Oh, I hope so," she said.

"It's just the way things are," Isaac said. "It has to happen sometime. When the swelling goes down, then he can start getting better and come home. Then things will be much easier. Home is where things like this should happen."

"But we should be thankful for what hospitals do for us," she said quickly.

"That's true," he agreed, "but the best is still the best."

"I'm just thankful for all that these doctors and nurses are doing. They really care here."

"I am thankful," he said.

"Good evening," Aden said, as he and Esther approached.

"Good evening," Isaac said with a nod.

"Thankful the weather's not too cold," Aden offered. "Makes the drive down easier."

"Yes," Isaac agreed. "I thought of that too. Guess we would have put the visit off — if things had been too bad."

"You think we'll have snow for Christmas?" Aden asked.

"Sounds like a schoolboy," Isaac commented, chuckling. "I see your parking lot is full — most days anyway. Suppose you could be using John."

"Sure. But it can't be helped." Aden's face was all sympathy. "I guess you could fill in for him a few days, if you wanted," he added, holding the front doors of the medical center open for the rest of their group.

"But what about my harness shop?" Isaac said from just inside, the front doors swinging shut with a soft thud.

"I know." Aden shrugged his shoulders. "It puts all of us in a pinch."

"Why don't you hire someone part-time?" Isaac asked.

"Takes too much training — wouldn't be fair for either of us. We'll just muddle along the best we can."

"Well, maybe I could come over a day or so."

"It would help," Aden shrugged his shoulders again. "Even an afternoon would do wonders. You know your way around. Some of the sales, Sharon just can't make."

"I could work at least till Christmas sales are caught up," Isaac thought aloud.

"Things are busy, though, till the first of the year," Aden reminded him. "Maybe John will be better by then."

"That's probably asking a lot. He's a long way from that," Isaac said.

"You never know. People recover fast

sometimes."

"It's all in *Da Hah*'s hands."

"Yes, it is," Aden agreed.

As the four walked up to the empty front desk, Miriam said, "A nurse should be here soon."

"Can't we just go back?" Isaac asked.

"I always let them know when I come in," Miriam said.

"We're not waiting too long." Isaac made his decision quickly. "If no one shows up soon, we know where the room is."

As if he had been heard, footsteps sounded in the hall. The attendant appeared around the corner, walking briskly. "I thought I heard someone," she said, greeting them with a warm smile.

"You're still here?" Miriam asked in surprise, used to seeing the familiar nurse she had come to know as Mrs. Madison during the daylight hours.

"I'm on second shift today. It varies," Mrs. Madison said. "You can all go on back if you wish."

"Any changes?" Miriam asked, unable to keep the hope out of her voice.

"Nothing that you can see," the nurse said. "But don't give up hope. Sometimes they come out of it just like that," she said, snapping her fingers. "But really no one knows."

"It's in the Lord's hands," Isaac agreed.

"We're praying for him at our church," Mrs. Madison said. "Put him on the prayer list right after they brought him in. Been praying for a miracle. He's such a nice boy." There were tears in her eyes now. "Faith can raise the boy up — I just know it."

"If it's the Lord's will," Isaac said quickly.

"Healing's always the Lord's will," Mrs. Madison said with conviction. "With the doctor's hands or with His own divine hands. That's what I believe."

Isaac heard Aden's feet shift on the floor beside him. He searched for a way not to offend this obvious expression of concern for his son with any statement of disrespect.

"Thank you," Isaac finally said. "We believe the Lord heals too, in His time and in His way. We will continue praying that the Almighty's will be done."

"We will too," Mrs. Madison agreed. "We'll keep on taking good care of your son too, Mr. Miller."

"Thank you," Isaac said.

"Thank you too," Miriam added. "Maybe we'll see you on the way out?"

"I'll be here somewhere," Mrs. Madison assured them.

With that they walked back to John's room, Miriam opening the door softly and leading the way in. They gathered around the bed and stood standing single file at the rail. Somewhere the steady, rhythmic beep of a monitor sounded, its noise seeming to grow louder the longer they stood there. The pale IV line hung limply down toward John's arm.

"He looks a little better," Miriam said quietly.

"There's good color, anyway," Esther agreed. "I haven't seen him since the first day. He's better now — certainly."

"He's got to wake up soon," Miriam half-whispered the words, then said louder, "John — it's Mother. Wake up." She reached out and touched his arm but received no response.

"It will be in *Da Hah's* own time," Isaac told her gently, laying his hand on her arm. "We must wait for His will. It's always best. Always."

"I know," Miriam whispered. "He'll be awake soon — if *Da Hah* wills it."

They all stood at the rail for a few more minutes, and then Isaac suggested they should sing something.

"Like what?" Miriam whispered.

Aden answered by beginning a favorite

hymn, "Farther Along." They began with the chorus, "Farther along we'll know all about it . . ." and continued through two stanzas, singing softly and allowing the beautiful sound to fill the room.

When they were finished, they all were quiet until Isaac led the way out. Outside the halls were empty, as they found their way to the waiting room. There too only a few people sat, leaving plenty of empty seats available.

Sitting against the wall, the low sound of their conversation in Pennsylvania Dutch went back and forth. Twenty minutes later, when no other visitors for John showed up, Isaac suggested they go.

Putting action to his words, he got to his feet. As they found their way out, there was no Mrs. Madison in sight at the front desk or in the halls. Minutes later they were both in their buggies, turning their horses homeward. The hoofbeats clattered on the pavement as they left the hospital parking lot.

CHAPTER
THIRTY-EIGHT

Wednesday morning dawned as if making a dramatic attempt at awakening and then giving up, surrendered to the deep gloom of heavy storm-laden clouds. The anticipated snow started before Rebecca's alarm clock went off, its soft swirl brushing her window.

She reached out, shutting off the racket, getting no rush of energy from the cold air in the room. Her spirits as low as the weather, Rebecca got dressed and went out to help chore. Thoughts of John and his condition had been with her all night.

Matthew said nothing to her when she entered the barn, apparently feeling the effects of the weather too. Halfway through the chores, she told him she was leaving to help with breakfast. He mumbled some version of an assent, telling her to shut the barn door when she left.

Rebecca felt like telling Matthew she would not have forgotten but decided not to. There was no sense in making feelings worse on this gray morning. When she opened the barn door to leave, she found snow falling heavier. The large flakes seemed to dangle in the air, taking their time to decide where to land until they were pushed on down by their fellow falling mates.

When Rebecca entered the kitchen, her mother told her she needed help with the bacon, the girls needed to be awakened, and the breakfast plates and silverware set out. By the time they all sat down to eat several minutes later, Rebecca was already tired and certain it was not just the weather.

"You still troubled?" Mattie asked, as they ate their breakfast.

"Yes," she said.

"It was hard for you to see John Sunday," Mattie said.

"I can imagine," Lester agreed.

"We need to write to Leona," Mattie stated matter-of-factly. "Tell her about John."

"Why her?" Rebecca asked.

"You just came from there. It's not like all the aunts and uncles need to be told. I expect they'll find out soon enough, but Leona deserves a personal note."

"Whatever." Rebecca didn't care one way or the other at the moment.

"I'll write a note after the dishes are done," Mattie decided.

"You think the mailman runs today?" Lester wondered.

"The snow will quit after a while," Matthew said, as if he was an authority on such things.

"Are you the weatherman now?" Lester asked, chuckling.

"No," he said, "but we still have to get to school. Can't have any more snow days this year."

Rebecca felt like telling Matthew that things like the weather didn't always concern themselves with human needs, but she decided not to. Let Matthew keep his innocence as long as possible. Hers was being taken away fast enough.

After the breakfast dishes were done and kids sent off to school, Mattie sat down to write her letter. Lester had decreed, after a glance outside, that Matthew was probably right. The snow would be stopping soon.

Mattie's letter told the story of John's accident in great detail. When it was finished, Rebecca took the letter to the mailbox. Walking back up the driveway, she saw the mailman coming. He was an hour later than usual and bounced along the snowy road in the old beat-up pickup truck he used during bad weather. Skidding to a stop, he pulled up to the Keim mailbox.

Turning back to get the mail, Rebecca wondered what it must be like to be a mailman, to carry both sad and joyous news at the same time. Did the one perhaps outweigh the other? She quickly decided this was silly thinking, as if the mailman could tell what was in the letters.

Glancing back she saw the mailman stop before crossing the little bridge to the east, waiting on a buggy coming from the Harshville direction. Certain it wasn't coming to the Keim house, Rebecca resumed walking, drawing her coat tighter.

When the crunch of buggy wheels on gravel sounded behind her, Rebecca stepped aside to let whoever it was pass. But instead of passing her, the buggy stopped and the door slid open.

"Good morning, Rebecca," Miriam said, her face stretched with a thin smile.

There was news, Rebecca knew at once. Otherwise Miriam would not be here in person.

Sensing the worst, Rebecca gasped, "It's bad news, isn't it?"

Miriam shook her head. "No, it's good news, really. A little too good, but the hospital assured us it was true."

Rebecca stood, waiting for Miriam to continue.

"John's awake. Moving around and cheerful." She tilted her head in Rebecca's direction at the look on her face. "I know . . . I thought the same thing. But maybe *Da Hah* has decided to bless us with a fast recovery. We must not doubt His will or power to do what He wishes."

"But . . . that soon?" Rebecca finally managed. "Oh, it's such good news. Are you going down to see him?"

"Yes. And I thought maybe you'd like to come along." Miriam glanced back toward the house. "Unless you have other things to do?"

"No, of course not. I would love to." Rebecca said quickly. "I was just dropping off the mail. And then the mailman came, and so I was on my way to pick it up. After I take it inside, I'm sure Mom won't mind if I go with you."

"I'll drive you up to the house then," Miriam said. "You'll need a thicker coat for the drive. Unless this snow quits soon."

"I'll get my Sunday coat," Rebecca agreed, quickly running out to the mailbox, then climbing onto the buggy step, being careful not to slip on the wet metal. Sitting back in the seat as Miriam let out the reins, her emotions struggled to catch up with the news.

"I'm surprised too," Miriam said, aware of Rebecca's shock over the news. "One doesn't really know how to feel."

"They really said he was well?" Rebecca asked. "It's so wonderful."

"Sharon took the call this morning," Miriam said. "I had told them to call at the store if there was news. I guess that's what they did. They told Sharon that John was awake and moving about. Said his mood was good. They are very optimistic now about his prospects."

"Sure changes how I was feeling this morning."

"A little low?"

"Yes," Rebecca admitted. "Mom just wrote to Leona about the accident. That was one of the letters I was just dropping off. Maybe that stirred up the thoughts again. That and the snow."

Bringing the buggy to a stop by the house, Miriam waited as Rebecca went inside.

Mattie had noticed the buggy drive up and was waiting when Rebecca entered.

"What's Miriam want?" Mattie asked.

"Oh, its wonderful news. The hospital called. John's awake and moving about. She wants me to go down with her."

"Well . . ." Mattie let her relief and joy show fully on her face. "I guess that's one crisis over for you. Now just take care of the other one."

"I'll try to," Rebecca agreed. "I hope John understands. Miriam's waiting. She didn't say when we would be back."

"Take whatever time is needed," Mattie told her. "We can handle things here. Just thank the good Lord He is helping you out. Things could have been much worse."

"I know," Rebecca agreed. Quickly she got her coat and left the house.

In the buggy with Miriam, she settled in for the drive, listening to the wheels squeak in the snow. Miriam's attention to the driving meant for a quiet ride, at least until they started climbing the hill toward Unity.

"You've been handling all of this really well," Miriam said tenderly. "Many a girl would have fallen apart with what John has gone through."

"I don't know about that," Rebecca demurred, knowing Miriam couldn't know everything she had gone through. "Maybe I just don't show it."

"You still did well. Isaac and I couldn't be more thankful with the choice John's made."

Rebecca said nothing, her gloved hands wrapped up in her Sunday coat, wishing

Miriam wouldn't be so open with her praise.

"Many times I was thankful *Da Hah* gave us a girl first — so John wasn't an only child. Without that, no doubt, we would have spoiled him completely. Even now," Miriam said, smiling again, "I wonder sometimes. But we do our best. I know Isaac does."

"You try, I know," was all Rebecca could get out.

"Maybe the accident was a maturing point for John," Miriam wondered aloud. "Not that we thought John needed it, but *Da Hah* must have. Now He has given him back to us so quickly, and that after all of our fears. I feel so ashamed at how we have acted and even thought."

"I didn't think you had such thoughts — I did too," Rebecca assured her.

"We're all human," Miriam said, sighing. "Now to get John home and on his way to full health. Even with this good news, I suppose there will still be a recovery time."

"I imagine the doctor can tell us," Rebecca said.

During the rest of the ride, the silence resumed between them. Rebecca felt comfortable enough with the quiet ride, for which she was glad. It was a good sign, she figured, of things to come. At least she was getting along with John's mother, if not totally yet with John himself.

Miriam tied up at the lightpost, and the two of them headed up the walk to the hospital front doors. Their steps made a crunching sound, although the snow had stopped falling.

"What can I do for you?" a cheery young receptionist asked, greeting them.

"My son is here," Miriam said. "You called us about him."

"What's your son's name?" the receptionist asked.

"John Miller."

"Miller." The receptionist tapped the keys on the computer. "Yes. We have two John Millers. A head injury, and then they just brought in a case last night. Appendicitis. A young boy. I believe Nurse Bethany called his family this morning to update them."

"What about the other John?" Mattie stepped closer to the desk.

The receptionist tapped a few more keys. "Dr. Wine's the attending physician. There's nothing new on the case that I can see."

"Then why did the hospital call us?" Miriam asked, a little upset.

"Who called you?" the receptionist asked.

"The hospital. They called our number,

358

saying John was awake and moving about."

"That call would have to go through me. No one else was handling the desk this morning." The receptionist was tapping away on the keyboard.

"But they *did*," Miriam insisted, her voice firm.

The receptionist seemed to have found what she was looking for. "I gave Bethany this phone number," she said, pointing to the monitor, "and asked her to call the parents of the appendicitis case."

"That's *our* contact phone number," Miriam said, her voice alarmed.

"*Your* phone number?" the receptionist said with surprise.

"Yes. It's our phone number."

"But . . ." The receptionist's hand was on her mouth. "I can't see how. I must have gotten the phone numbers mixed up. I'm so sorry."

"So John is still in the same condition?" Miriam asked, stepping back from the desk, her face showing no emotions.

"Yes . . . I'm so sorry," the receptionist said with genuine regret.

"Can we see John then?" Miriam asked, making as if to head in that direction whether she had permission or not.

"Of course," the receptionist said quickly.

Rebecca followed Miriam down the hall, waiting as Miriam softly opened the door to John's room and glanced in.

"Nothing's changed," she said quietly, her hand swinging the door inward so Rebecca could see too. "I guess we might as well go on home."

"I guess so," Rebecca agreed, feeling numb. "It was all just a mistake."

"I guess it was," Miriam said, her voice low, pulling the door of the room shut.

They walked out silently. Rebecca climbed into the buggy and held the reins as Miriam untied the horse and then got in and took her own seat. The snow began to fall again, as they reached the outskirts of West Union and continued all the way home.

CHAPTER
THIRTY-NINE

Rachel Byler filled the sink with the hot water and prepared to wash the breakfast dishes. There had been nothing special about the breakfast, just the usual fare she fixed on a weekday morning — oatmeal, scrambled eggs, toast, and a slab of homemade sausage.

Reuben was still in the house, lingering over his coffee. Rachel let him enjoy the coffee, its steam rising over the rim of the cup, spreading its warmth. Reuben appreciated the rich aroma with every sip of the dark delight. Rachel had made sure to add pure cream to his cup, though she could ill afford to spare it.

This morning at just the right moment, she had another plan to implement, and she felt that this one perhaps had a better chance of success than the last one. At the very least, she figured, it was high time they had a long talk.

There was now a great sense of urgency because she knew she was with child. That she should be bearing a child again at her age was still a mystery to her, but those were things best left in the hands of the Almighty.

The women at church would soon notice her condition, and with it would come approval and admiration. She was certainly looking forward to that.

"Do you want something?" Reuben asked, startling her.

Her mind spun, as the proper moment had not yet arrived. "Ah, yes — no," she managed.

"It must be something," he said dryly. "It wouldn't be another sin you've seen in the church? You know I told you no more of that. Only the bishop — he will assign those things from now on."

His voice had an edge to it and cut painfully. The morning was already threatening to spin out of control, as this was not going as planned. Yet the matter simply had to be discussed. She plunged forward. "But the baby. What about the baby?"

"What about it? It's going to be born. *Da Hah sei lohbed,*" he said in a voice reflecting the praise he just offered so reverently.

"How can you preach to me?" she asked, her voice rising in frustration. When she caught sight of his astonished look, she lowered her voice. There would be no winning this way. "You shouldn't use that tone," she tried again.

"I wasn't preaching," he said simply. "We are just blessed."

This brought a rush of emotion. She struggled to keep it out of her voice as she asked, "How can you say we are blessed? We are as poor as church mice. Even they might have peanut butter to eat once in a while. How are you going to feed another mouth?"

"Children are a blessing of the Lord," he said, paraphrasing a familiar Bible verse.

"You ought to think about us once in a while. About me and Luke and the kind of girl he's bound to get with his meager life. What has he got to offer a girl? He'll have to end up settling for that Susie Burkholder. What is she? Her parents have less money than we do. And all the while Emma sits over there with all our money and you preachers do nothing. And now she's not in good health. Why can't you be of some good for once, when it really matters?"

"I see," Reuben said knowingly. "So that's what the little Ezra event was about. You have concluded that Emma's inheriting your father's estate is a result of sin in the congregation? No wonder *Da Hah* keeps women out of running the church, to say nothing of the world." He sighed and rolled his eyes.

She glared at him with fire in her eyes, but he held her gaze, his eyes steady as a rock. *Confound his deaconship,* she thought bitterly. *He never dared look at me like that before. Little poor farmer's boy that he is.*

"I was just trying to help," she said out loud, keeping her voice down. "The baby's coming, and we have no money — not even for the midwife."

"Why is Emma's money such a big thing all of a sudden?"

"It belongs to us. It has always belonged to us," she said.

"You shouldn't be so eager for money. Riches — ill gotten — bring no good."

It sounded like another quote to her, and her temper flared again. "So we just sit here and do nothing? Isn't that what we've done all these years?"

"Really?" He raised his eyebrows, his cup of coffee almost done. "That's what you think?"

Something in his tone warned her to be careful. The man wasn't angry, but he was annoyed. Whatever it was seemed best left unprovoked.

"So you want to do something?" he asked it another way.

"Yes," she said cautiously. "I think Emma should make things right with her *own* will and give the money to the family as it was supposed to be done all along." Watching his face, she almost started to hope. He at least seemed to be thinking.

"I wasn't suggesting we do anything about Emma," he finally said, draining the last of the dark liquid, his face serious.

She felt disappointment flash through her, "Then why torment me like this, if you're not going to help?"

"I want to do something about our money situation." Reuben wasn't looking at Rachel now but at the top of the tablecloth, moving the flowery piece back and forth under his fingertips. There was hesitancy, frailness, and vulnerability wrapped up in his body language, all at the same time.

If Rachel hadn't been so disappointed, the words might not have made it out of her mouth, but the syllables came out in a gush, "When have you ever been good at making money?"

He didn't flinch, and she was a little astonished. In fact he seemed to be gathering his courage, "It's true the baby is coming. That we need money. That we don't have any. I've been bothered by that too, but we don't need Emma's money." He paused as the tablecloth moved again under his fingers and noticed that she waited with an air of skepticism on her face. "I would like to do something about this. Something . . . like making money. Maybe by raising goats. Nubians. I think we could make money at it. Extra money."

"Goats?" She was totally in shock.

"Nubians," he repeated. "They're good for milk."

"*You* . . . raise goats? You can't do that," she said, suddenly realizing he was serious.

"We need the money," he admitted. "They practically raise themselves. That's what Mose Stuzman said the other Sunday. His nephew in Ohio started raising them last year. Said Nubians were the only way to go. The milk sells at a great price. They ended up going into the business full time. The money was that good. Of course I wouldn't do that."

"But you don't have any money." She had forgotten her dishes. "And they *don't* raise themselves."

"They're hardy creatures, and we have the room here," he said. "They work good on pasture with meat cattle. Eat the weeds and stuff."

"Money." She couldn't help herself as her voice rose. "To buy these stinky things? Where's that coming from?"

He shrugged his shoulders. "We've been making steady payments on the farm. The bank should give us good marks. With that record, there might be money available to borrow."

"No," she said firmly, "we're not borrowing money."

"We have to," he said, "if we want to make more. It would be necessary to buy the goats and the feed."

A thousand images of late payments, dying goats, animals lying around the barnyard as skinny as rails, money being spent while they starved, and Reuben sleeping through it all flashed through her mind. "No," she said. "No goats."

"We have a child coming and not enough money," he said flatly, not looking at her. "I'm just not going to sit here and do nothing."

"You can add a few more cattle this spring."

"There's not enough money in cattle alone." He looked up, his eyes flashing with an inner light. "We have to make more money."

The thought flashed through her mind,

and she spoke it, "You think the Lord will bless you because you're a deacon? Even with an impossible task like raising goats?"

He said nothing, his eyes on the table again, his fingers not moving.

She thought he was finished . . . that she had stopped him cold.

Then Reuben said quietly, "No. I am just like other men. I have to make money. There will be no special blessing because I'm a deacon. I am going to raise Nubians. We'll start as soon as we can."

"Well," was all she could manage.

"I'm doing the work," he said, in answer to what he knew she was thinking.

"What if we die of hunger in the meantime?" she asked bitterly.

"Then I'll be first to go."

To this she had no answer.

CHAPTER FORTY

The morning sun filtered through the hospital drapes, playing on the floor, bouncing upward to the ceiling. It seemed to hang in limbo, suspended above the patient in room 201.

John's face flushed for a moment, the slightest hint of red coloring his cheeks. One arm stirred. He opened his eyes, blinked, but remained motionless. Out of a deep fog, he sought meaning to his surroundings. Slowly his eyes swept across his field of vision, the muscles in his forehead tensing in pain from the movement.

He found nothing that made sense, nothing that indicated home or where he belonged. The stark white walls bore no resemblance to anything familiar. Trying to turn his head, the pain shot upward with a fury that brought tears to his eyes. He tried to move his fingers, his hands, and then his feet and was left uncertain of the results.

From the depths of his soul rose a fear, so nameless, so awful in its silent dread, that he felt himself spinning off into a cloudy nothingness. His thoughts swirled wildly — and then the world went dark again.

The slight creak of the opening door failed to rouse him.

The hospital's head nurse, Mrs. Madison, walked in, pushing her cart in front of her, and glanced briefly in his direction. He had been this way — motionless — for many days, and she expected nothing different this morning. She quietly exchanged his IV bag, checked his vitals, and then left the room, closing the door as she left.

The click of the door latch reached him, the sound coming from across the room like thunder. The echo of her fading footsteps registered in his mind, and he opened his eyes again. He teetered between two worlds, the pain and dread facing him in the sunlight on the ceiling and the nothingness lying behind him. It felt as if the choice were his, to go forward or to let go and slide back to where he had been.

He moved his parched and dry lips. His throat ached intensely, burning. He moved his tongue. It felt so dry and rough, no comforting moisture. But more than the unfamiliar physical sensations, there were the more urgent questions: *Where am I? What happened to me?*

He thought of letting go, of seeking relief by drifting away again. But then her name came to his mind. *Rebecca.* It came with an intensity greater than the thunder from the closing door, and it willed him to stay, to not turn back to the darkness.

"Rebecca," he said in a harsh whisper, tearing at his vocal cords. With all the strength he could summon, he called out to the light above him, "Rebecca . . . where are you?"

The thunder in his head seemed to break loose pieces and bits of his memory. But it made no sense. The darkness of the town. The sound of a horse's hooves on the pavement, sounding even louder in the still night air. A car approaching from behind. And then . . . the sound of crunching wood. The feeling of being airborne. Then that nothingness. He could remember . . . but it still made no sense.

In the midst of it all, he saw her with blinding clarity — laid against the backdrop of his pain, the image overriding everything else. She was sitting in her parents' living room just before he left for home that night. She was getting up now. He saw her so clearly. Her usually sparkling eyes clouded when they lifted to his. The gas lantern, hanging from the living room ceiling, hissed from above, the sound seamlessly joining the buzz of his own thoughts.

He opened his mouth to cry out, but no sound came out. He remembered with a clear and fierce jolt — he was losing her. It came back with a force that made the throbbing in his head go momentarily unnoticed. "Rebecca," he said again, ignoring the pain. "Rebecca."

The moisture forming in his eyes burned its way down his cheeks, leaving a trail of glittering wetness against his pale skin. He mustered all possible strength to lift his arms, to try to sit up, to even swing his feet out of this bed, but the pain prevented him. He thought of calling out louder to her, to anyone, but restrained himself.

He was Amish, and even in these conditions, he remembered that. He knew that there was honor to uphold, a faith to remember, a tradition that overshadowed his very existence. Even here, in this moment of horrible awakening, the tentacles of belief wrapped themselves around him, relieving him, supplying him with strength.

"I am John," he told himself, seeking sanity in this utter senselessness surrounding him. He remembered his father's name and said it out loud, "Isaac." He let the comfort of the sound soothe him. He searched for another name, bothered that one was not readily apparent to him. Then he found it. "Miriam," he said. "Mother."

His head still hurt. He ignored the pain, searching for an answer to why no one was here and why he couldn't move. He tried to turn his head and found it possible despite the pain.

Then the door to his room opened, letting in the white-clad nurse.

"Well!" she said in surprise. "I thought I heard something. You're back with us! A lot of people are certainly going to be glad about that."

He struggled for words, whispering, "Where am I?"

"Water," she said, offering him a cup with a straw protruding from the top.

He sucked on the straw, letting the moisture slide down his throat. *So cool and soothing.* "Where am I?" he managed.

"Adams County Medical Center," she said. "I'll let the doctor know you're awake."

"Why am I here?" he asked, the words coming out smoother, his throat now moist.

"You had an accident," she said. "Someone hit your buggy."

"When?"

"Friday night," she said.

"How long?"

"Six days," she said.

"Has Rebecca been here?" His eyes were pleading.

"There was a young girl here the first day," she said, studying his face. "Maybe the day after, but I haven't seen her since." She saw him nod slightly. "I'll be back soon. I want to let Dr. Wine know about you. Please rest now."

The door shut with its click again.

He could feel the fog clearing slightly. *Rebecca has been here but has left. She has seen me like this and did not return.* He let the thought settle into the hurt in his head.

The numbness in his body could only mean one thing — he had been paralyzed. He heard the dreaded words say themselves in his head, sounding as if some disemboweled voice were pronouncing them — *paralyzed. Useless.*

Of course Rebecca would not stay with him. What girl would want a husband who was unable to move, unable to earn a living or to raise a family? Of course she had left. It made perfect sense.

John felt like sobbing, but the tears wouldn't come. Nor were they allowed. No, it would simply not do to have someone come into the room and find him broken down. So he let the tears run silently from the corners of his eyes.

He heard the door open again, this time admitting a young man, the doctor apparently.

"Mr. Miller," the man said. "You're awake. Good. Let's see what's going on, shall we? Any pain here?" the man asked, squeezing John's leg.

John could see the hand squeezing but couldn't feel anything, so he shook his head.

"Anything here?" The man moved his hand higher.

John shook his head again.

"This leg?"

John winced.

"That's good," he said.

"Here?" The man's hand was on John's chest.

John thought his heart, from the way it was hurting, should surely have sensation from the doctor's touch, but he felt nothing and shook his head.

"This side?"

John nodded. "A little."

"Here?" The doctor's fingers touched John's throat.

John nodded again, the fingers soothing the throbbing of his still parched throat, their coolness diminishing the burning sensation.

"I see," the man said, his words full of meaning.

"It's not good," John volunteered more than asked. "I'm paralyzed."

The man cleared his throat. "I guess I didn't introduce myself, John. I'm Dr. Wine. I was on call when they brought you in from the accident."

"I broke my neck." John's voice was a whisper. "I'm paralyzed for life."

"No," Dr. Wine said slowly. "It's not a broken neck. You had a skull fracture and bleeding into the brain, a subdural hematoma. The blood had no place to go, so it pressed into your brain. The mass is stabilized now — as of yesterday — confirmed by the CT scan we did then. Apparently the hematoma must be decreasing, but we don't know how much damage has been done."

"I'm paralyzed for life," John said again.

"We don't know that," Dr. Wine said quickly. "It's more like a stroke than a broken neck. There's always hope that it won't be permanent."

John nodded because that seemed like the proper thing to do.

Dr. Wine turned to the nurse. "Schedule

another scan as soon as possible. If things are stable, we can see about when he can go home. His mother can be notified when she comes in."

Their voices trailed off as they left the room. The thought of seeing his mother should have brought him joy, but it was the name he hadn't heard that was preventing the glad emotion. Neither the doctor nor the nurse had said anything about Rebecca. It was — it seemed to him — as if she had never even come in to see him.

"I'm a cripple," he whispered to himself, as he wept silently.

CHAPTER
FORTY-ONE

As she approached the edge of West Union, Miriam let her horse take its time. The horse was fresh this morning, but there was no sense in tiring it needlessly. Plus no real sense of urgency gripped her. Yesterday's rushed drive to the hospital with Rebecca, in response to the false news of John's recovery, had left her feeling numb. She and Isaac had spent a quiet evening together, and she could only imagine what Rebecca had gone through.

John had been unconscious and unresponsive now for what seemed like ages. Today was just another day, and this was just another trip to see her son. Not that she feared John would pass on, but rather she harbored a sense of foreboding about what life held for him.

From what she knew of the doctor's opinion, he seemed to feel there was hope ahead. Dr. Wine had cautioned them to wait and not draw conclusions until after John regained consciousness. They could then tell exactly how extensive the damage was.

How that could be was a little mysterious to her. The doctor talked of possibilities and chances in medical terms, which were foreign to her. Broken bones and stitches could be easily understood, but how did one really know about damage to the brain? That the doctor, by his own admission, wasn't sure, made his hopeful attitude seem like medical training.

Isaac was trying to keep his spirits up. Miriam had seen him looking out of the living room window last night after the sun had set. His gaze wandered over their farm, over to Wheat Ridge Road, and to John's eight acres just down the hill.

Isaac must be thinking of all that could be lost if John's condition was as bad as they feared. What if John was a cripple for life? What would happen to his plans, and what about Rebecca? Would she still love a cripple?

Miriam had gone to Isaac's side, while he was standing by the window, the last of the daylight fading away, the little snow drifts still piled up by the barn. "Are you thinking bad thoughts?" she asked tenderly. "You thinking the way will be dark ahead of us?"

"He's our only son," Isaac had said. "He's a good boy. Always has been."

"Are you thinking the Lord will take John?"

"I would not tell the Almighty what to do," he had said softly. "He knows what is best."

"What if John's a cripple," she said, hearing the sound of the words grow even larger till they filled the room, gripping both of them with their icy meaning.

Isaac had said nothing for a long time. Miriam had thought he wasn't going to answer. She felt the dread of her words grow even stronger until Isaac's arm came around her shoulders.

"We must not fear," he said. "Where the Lord goes, we can follow."

"Is He with us?" she asked.

"With those that obey Him," he said firmly. "We must not doubt. Even after this morning, He knows the way."

She had let the tears fall against the solidness of his shoulder, his arm tightly around her. Miriam turned in the direction Isaac was looking, feeling comforted for the moment. Yet now she was wondering again what lay ahead and what John would be like when he regained consciousness.

■ ■ ■ ■

Slapping the horse's reins, she suddenly felt an urge to hurry. Why she didn't know, but she wanted to see John. He might still be lying in bed as unmoving as he had been for days, but he was her son, and she wanted to see him.

In the hospital parking lot, she tied up at the now familiar light post. At the front desk, Mrs. Madison was rifling though a file folder.

"Good morning," Miriam said, intending to walk on toward John's room.

"Oh, Mrs. Miller!" Mrs. Madison said, glancing up. "Dr. Wine wants to see you."

Miriam paused, fear moving through her.

"Something wrong?" she asked. "Is John worse?"

Mrs. Madison seemed reluctant to say anything. "I think the doctor would rather tell you."

"Oh . . . dear . . . but I thought he was out of danger."

"No," Mrs. Madison said. "I didn't mean that." She took a long look at Miriam's face and then said quickly, "Your son is awake, but the doctor wants to tell you."

"He's awake?" Miriam's joy evident. "He's

really awake?"

"Yes, but you'd better talk to the doctor before going in."

"I'm going to see him," she announced, already on the way. She didn't care at the moment what doctors or nurses told her, she was going to see her son.

Mrs. Madison watched her go, shrugging her shoulders. "Can't say I blame her," she said to no one in particular.

Miriam opened the door to John's room without pausing. John's head turned in her direction, his eyes searching her face. She saw fear in them.

"John," she said, her voice barely a whisper, "you've come back to us. This is so good."

He said nothing, his eyes moist.

She wanted to take him in her arms as she had when he was a baby. Wanted to brush his forehead with her hand, to tell him the hurt would go away, but the years stood between them. She knew with great clarity that even in John's present condition he was no longer a child. Acting otherwise wouldn't help matters.

"Where's Rebecca?" John asked, so low she had to lean over to catch the words.

"She's at home," she said. "We didn't know when you would regain consciousness. She will be real glad to hear this news."

"Will she be back?" he asked, still in a whisper.

"Of course. When I let her know you're awake. You don't have to worry."

He said nothing, turning his face away from her, his eyes searching the ceiling.

"She's gone," he half-whispered.

Watching him, the thought occurred to her, *Maybe John's brain has been affected. Was brain damage not on the list of things the doctor was concerned about?*

"John, are you okay?" she asked, not certain what else to say, and yet realizing he was still far from okay.

John still said nothing, his eyes silently on the ceiling.

Certain now she was right, great waves of horror swept over her. She wished now she had listened to the nurse and talked to the doctor first. He would, no doubt, have prepared her for this, making the blow much easier than simply walking in and finding out on her own.

Watching another silent tear run down John's face, the situation could not have been any clearer. She and Isaac had prepared for the wrong thing. They had seen the possibility of a cripple in their home, sitting in a wheelchair, helpless and in need.

What they had not prepared for was a mental disability — the wasted stare, the unreasoning demands, the wants that never seemed to be defined or satisfied.

Surely it could not be, yet there it was, right in front of her eyes as plain as day. John was back, but what was back might well not be John but some shadow of himself. A shadow who was unresponsive and asking strange and gloomy questions.

John now whispered something else, and she drew back, uncertain, resisting coming closer to be certain. And yet she must listen. This was still her son. Her hand went out to him, brushing his brow, the wetness of his perspiration moistening her hand.

"You'll be okay," she told him. "We'll take you home. You'll be getting better now."

He whispered again, and she bent low this time. The words were formed even slower now. "She's not coming back."

John's brain was affected. It was now obvious to her. This was the blow the doctor and the nurse wished to soften. Isaac would be broken when she told him, and she dreaded the task. Yet Isaac would carry on, just as she must carry on, with courage and faith that God was able to help. This was the path He had chosen for them.

"She's gone," John said, his lips moving.

She laid her hand on his forehead again. There was no answer to such madness of the brain. "I don't know what you're talking about," Miriam told him. "Rebecca will be very glad to see you. You'd better rest now though."

"I want to," he managed, his voice a little stronger. "My head hurts."

"The doctor will be in to see you soon."

"I don't want a doctor," he insisted.

"God help us," Miriam prayed aloud. "You are a good God, even when the valley is deep. Help John now and help us too. *Please*."

CHAPTER
FORTY-TWO

Miriam was still praying when the door opened, admitting Dr. Wine.

"I see you're here already," he said, his voice professional and to the point.

As she turned from John to face the doctor, she registered the dull look in John's eyes and felt a stab of pain, understanding what this meant. His mind had been lost. But she knew she must be strong until Isaac was here, and then she could find comfort in his arms.

"I had wanted to talk to you first," Dr. Wine said. "I guess the nurse didn't mention that."

"She did," Miriam said quickly. "I couldn't wait. I'm his mother."

Dr. Wine seemed to relax his attitude at those words and turned to John. "So how are you feeling?"

Miriam was astonished that the doctor would ask John to speak of his obviously brain-damaged condition.

"Can't move the right side," he mouthed slowly. "This arm comes up a bit," he added, lifting his left arm slightly.

Miriam was at a loss to understand John's present coherence, considering his condition moments earlier. Now Dr. Wine's hands were testing points on John's legs, pressing in as he waited for a response from John. A facial twitch seemed to communicate John's response in most cases, she noticed, yet this made no sense at all to her.

"What is wrong with him?" she finally asked, assuming that discussing the matter in front of John would be okay.

"That's what I wanted to tell you. I think John already knows," he said, turning in her direction. "He has paralysis on one side, even though the subdural hematoma was declining in yesterday's CT. We'll check it today again, and if the swelling is decreasing even more — which I would guess it is — we might have more improvement soon."

Miriam glanced at John, then ventured the question, "His mind. Is it affected?"

Dr. Wine seemed to ponder the question. "A little hazy I suppose. A little amnesia is even possible but no permanent damage." He looked at John and grinned. "You gave your mother that idea?"

"I don't know," John said, bringing his eyes over to his mother as if the effort cost him a lot.

"He's fine in that department," Dr. Wine nodded. "Responds well."

"I just want to see Rebecca," John said. "Can you tell her I'm awake?"

"That's a perfectly normal reaction, considering," Dr. Wine said. "That was one of the things I wanted to talk to you about. I don't expect the paralysis to be permanent, but we just don't know. Under those circumstances, anything can happen to even established relationships. His girlfriend hasn't been around to see him for a while."

"She was here last night with me," Miriam said. "When we got the call — the false one. She's very concerned about John."

"We should hope so," Dr. Wine said briskly. "Yes . . . and about the call. Sorry about that. I guess the new receptionist didn't check things well enough."

"Rebecca's not coming back . . . is she?" John's eyes were still on his mother's face, his voice a little stronger.

"Of course she is," Miriam told him firmly.

"I will have the nurse come in," Dr. Wine's voice broke in. "She can also tell you about any preparations you need to make once your son can go home."

Miriam nodded as Dr. Wine left the room. Relief that John was of sound mind was tempered by the knowledge that their original fears might still come true. That John doubted her opinion about Rebecca was not a surprise, considering his obvious distress, but he would get over it. It might be good, though, to have Rebecca come down as soon as possible, even before she took John home.

The memory of Rebecca's action yesterday strengthened her resolve.

"She's a good girl," she said to John, as the door shut behind Dr. Wine. "You don't have to worry."

John failed to answer, his left hand twitching.

Letting her eyes move up and down John's body, Miriam still wondered, *Should John even continue with his plans to marry? How might he support his family? Will it be fair to his wife? What if they can never have children? Is it right to deprive a girl of even the possibility of little ones?* It was all a little too much for her, but maybe Isaac would know the answers.

"Can you tell Rebecca? Tell her to come right away?" John asked.

"Maybe you shouldn't push things," she

said, wishing Isaac were here. "I'm sure you still need rest. She'll come."

"Would you have stayed on with Dad?" John asked. "If he had been . . . like this?" He still mouthed the words slowly but stronger than before. "In my condition?" he asked, his eyes on her face.

"Yes," she said because it was true.

"Is Rebecca like you?" he asked, fear in his eyes.

"We're all different," she said truthfully.

"Then she doesn't love me?" The fear in his eyes was increasing.

"Do you love her?" she asked him, searching desperately for the right words.

"Of course," he said, his lips dry again.

She reached for the glass of water beside the bed, but he refused to drink.

"Then you'll be just fine," she said, holding the glass in her hand. "*Da Hah* will help us all."

"I can't lose her," he whispered now, still refusing the water she held out to him. "I love her too much. Do you think it's possible she'll stick with me?" he asked, not looking at her.

"I think she will." She brought the glass closer to him, forcing him to notice.

"You will tell her to come to me?" He ignored the water.

"Take a sip," she finally said.

He complied but was waiting for her answer.

"I will," she told him. "I'll go to her house on my way home and tell her."

"You can talk to her . . . prepare her?"

"I think you should talk these things over with her," she said. "But for now we need to concentrate on getting you home and getting you well again."

"I'll never be well. I'm broken. I can't feel all of myself," John said, his eyes on the ceiling again. "The sunbeams are gone," he spoke his sudden observation.

"Sunbeams?"

"There were sunbeams up there this morning." His left hand came up slightly, motioning toward the ceiling. "They're gone now."

Considering there might have been, she agreed with a nod.

"They're gone," he said.

"We need to get you home," she repeated, wanting him out of here. Home was where her son needed to be, not in this hospital room with its drab walls and sunbeams playing on the ceiling. If she didn't get him home soon, he might truly get touched on the brain.

What he needed was an open window and

the walls of his own room. He needed to be surrounded by the sounds of life on the farm, the smell of winter outside, the beat of horses' hooves on pavement, and the love of his own family.

"The nurse is coming now," she said, hearing the click of the door behind her. "I'll wait and see what the test results are. If they give the okay, I can be back this afternoon with a driver."

"Sounds like you're making plans already," Mrs. Madison said, her cheerful voice filling the room. "There are some papers at the front desk for you."

"Can he go home for sure then?" Miriam asked.

"He needs to have another test. We'll know more after the doctor looks at the results. I'm here to take him to the imaging room now."

"I'll be here when you come back," Miriam told John, as Mrs. Madison began to wheel his bed out of the room.

He nodded as they left, his eyes still dull, searching the ceiling as he went.

CHAPTER
FORTY-THREE

Nearly an hour later, Miriam, sitting in the waiting room, glanced up from her magazine and noticed Mrs. Madison pushing John's bed down the hall to his room. Rather than go to his room, she wanted to find Dr. Wine first to hear the test results and then discuss plans to move John home.

When she didn't see Dr. Wine anywhere, Miriam went to the familiar front desk. She ruled out following Mrs. Madison, who was still in John's room. It would be better to speak with the doctor without John's presence.

"Can you locate Dr. Wine for me?" she asked the woman at the front desk. "My son just underwent a scan, and I was told he might be able to come home today, depending on the results of that scan."

"Dr. Wine said he would see you?"

"Yes, after the scan."

"I'll page him then," the nurse said.

"Would you like to wait in the waiting room?"

Miriam took her seat and picked up the magazine, as she heard the nurse page Dr. Wine. When the minutes passed and no doctor appeared, she began to consider making another trip out to the front desk. Just then Dr. Wine stepped briskly into the room.

"I'm so sorry," Dr. Wine said. "Hectic morning."

Miriam nodded, then asked, "How is my son? Can I take him home?"

"No," he said quickly. "There is some change, but you must understand your son was very seriously injured. Although he's making progress, he's not ready to go home yet."

Miriam waited, expecting more.

The doctor continued. "I'm comfortable with the difference between yesterday's and today's CT scan. I would have liked to see more, but it just wasn't there. Perhaps he can go home tomorrow."

"Tomorrow," Miriam managed. "If you say so. I will speak with John and then return tomorrow."

"That would be best," he agreed. Then he turned and walked briskly down the hall.

Miriam turned in the direction of John's room.

When she entered, she found that Mrs. Madison had left. John was alone.

"John," she said softly, not certain whether he was awake or not.

He stirred, turning his head toward her with great effort. "Has she come?" he asked.

Miriam approached his bed, running her hand over his forehead. John made a weak effort to shake her hand off, but the pain tightened the side of his face.

"You have to stay here another night," she told him gently, expecting disappointment to cross his face. "We'll pick you up tomorrow then."

He struggled for words. "You will let her know? Rebecca? Tell her I am here."

"Yes," she said.

"You will tell her," he repeated, "that I want to see her."

"Yes," Miriam answered.

He seemed to be thinking.

"We will pick you up tomorrow morning, if Dr. Wine agrees. I'll have things ready for you at home."

When John offered no words, she left, thinking it best that way. There would be plenty of time, once she got him home, to nurse John back to health. Only so much could be done in this hospital. She simply must get John home as soon as possible.

As she walked past the front desk on her way out, Mrs. Madison approached her. "Here are some instructions," the nurse said, offering Miriam several pages paper-clipped together. Then she added, "I'm sorry to hear the news. I can imagine how much you want him home now that he's awake."

"Yes." Miriam glanced briefly at the offered papers.

"This is just a list of instructions and things to expect and watch for with John's type of injury. Also there are phone numbers to call if you see anything unusual. I'm sure Dr. Wine will tell you more tomorrow."

"Thanks." Miriam felt deep gratitude for what this woman had done for her son during his stay here. "We all appreciate it," Miriam said. "You've done so much for us."

"I have three sons." Mrs. Madison's face was tender. "They don't live around here anymore, but I can imagine how it must feel. John's your only boy, isn't he?"

Miriam nodded, repeated her thanks, and walked out to her buggy.

Driving the back roads from West Union to Unity, Miriam got the horse going at a good clip and then let it settle into its own steady pace. Her mind was busy, running over all the things to be done, first and foremost was letting Rebecca know of John's status.

Remembering the time of day and knowing she had missed making lunch for Isaac, she slapped the reins, urging the horse on. It momentarily increased its speed. When she didn't repeat the motion, it soon settled back down to its former pace. Miriam didn't have the heart to push it any harder. They had a long way to go, she figured, and it had good reason to take its time.

Coming up to the junction at Unity, she carefully pulled to a stop and then turned left instead of the normal right. She could tell the horse was puzzled by this change, but it reluctantly obeyed, shaking its head in protest as they drove down the slope out of Unity.

"We'll be back soon. You can have your oats then," she said.

At the Harshville Bridge, she had to wait for a car coming from the other side. After making the sharp turns on the other side of the bridge, she turned right into the Keim driveway and allowed the horse to walk up the slight incline toward the house. She stopped the buggy by the hitching post and was preparing to step down when the front door opened. Mattie rushed out, her cooking apron still around her waist.

"You have news?" she asked.

"Good news," Miriam said, managing a weak smile and settling back into the buggy seat. "John woke up this morning. He wants to see Rebecca."

"That is good news then." Mattie was wiping her hands on her apron. "Sorry, I was in the middle of making bread."

"That's what I should be doing," Miriam said wearily, "but it's likely John can come home tomorrow. I have to get ready for that."

"I'll tell Rebecca right away. She's finishing some chores in the barn."

"That's why I stopped by. I wanted to let her know. John wants to see her pretty bad. Can't say I blame him, considering."

"How's his condition?'

"He's still paralyzed on the right side. Can't even move his arm." Miriam was looking out the windshield of the buggy, her lips a thin line, her hands gripping the reins, even though the horse had no intentions of taking off. "Doctor hopes for a full recovery once the swelling goes down."

"I'll tell Rebecca." Mattie smiled, relief on her face. "I suppose you have plenty to do at home — to get ready."

"That I do," Miriam told her. "I'd better get going."

"You need help?" Mattie asked.

"Sharon can help — if I do — or one of the other women close by. We'll be okay."

"You sure?"

Miriam nodded, letting the reins out on the horse. "Thanks anyway. Tell Rebecca he'll be okay."

"I will," Mattie said, stepping back as Miriam took off.

CHAPTER
FORTY-FOUR

The breakfast dishes were long done and the table cleared, but Rachel had been unable to concentrate on the day's work in front of her. There were the Sunday pies to bake, the dough already prepared and spread out on the counter. There was bread to be made for the weekend, which she still needed to stir or it would never be finished baking by evening.

If that wasn't enough, the mending pile had grown larger than she liked. Even with only the three adults, such things had a way of collecting. Its menacing presence now lay in the sewing room. And though the baby's expected birth was still months away, the coming event pulled at her like an undertow, staking a claim for its share of her thoughts.

Yet with all the work to be done, her mind simply wouldn't stay on the tasks. Her eyes constantly strayed to the kitchen window, checking up on what Reuben was doing because he left the house so abruptly.

It had been an hour since Reuben had returned from the back field, where he had been tending the cattle. If he followed his normal routine, he would be coming in any time now, as it was a little past noon. What had gotten into the man this morning, she had no idea. She had never seen him quite so . . . well, determined, and it was disturbing to Rachel.

Will he actually go and venture into a new business? A goat business? Although she thought it only natural the answer would be *no,* something about the whole thing made her nervous. Surely Reuben would soon be in for lunch and apologize for having scared her with such foolish talk and perhaps, for even daring to think of jeopardizing the little money they had. Yes, an apology was in order. And when it came, Rachel would accept it, and her world could return to normal, as it was supposed to be.

He's coming now, she thought, her heart lifting at the sight of the barn door opening. She was at the point of leaving the kitchen window to prepare food for his lunch, when the corner of her eye caught something unusual. Reuben was leading the driving horse out with him.

She stopped — startled. Reuben had no

business with a driving horse because he had no place to go. She knew his business and his schedule. There was no place he needed to be today other than home. Why then was Reuben bringing out the horse, all harnessed up? And what was he planning on doing about lunch? Never had she known him to willingly miss lunch for any reason.

Now frozen in place, she watched as he walked toward the single buggy, pulling on the bridle lines, as if he was in a hurry. *This must be serious indeed.* The thought rushed into her mind, then froze into an icy crystal on her brain. Laying there, its weight became immense, its coldness numbing her head and creeping down through her body.

Reuben paused at the buggy and reached down to pick up the shafts, lifting them high over his head. For a moment she thought his eyes had found her, but then she knew they had never stopped long enough to look. With a deft movement, he brought the horse under the shafts, attached the tugs, and to her great horror, got in and drove out the driveway.

Has the man gone crazy? No, something else was going on, something so fundamental and profound that it shook her world to the foundations.

It has to do with the money. She just knew it. Did Reuben know enough to be dangerous to her if he was going to the bishop? *Is that what Reuben is doing?* In desperation she ran the scenario through her mind. *What does Reuben know?*

He knew her anguish and distress over losing the money. He knew how badly she wanted it back, but that couldn't be held against her, she decided. He also knew she had tried to get her brother in trouble for breaking the church rules, but that had amounted to nothing. Even if Reuben told the bishop of the connection her tattling had to the money, it would likely produce more smiles of sympathy than condemnation.

No, she decided, Reuben didn't know enough to be dangerous. Her pie dough forgotten, she watched the last of his buggy disappear into the distance, turning west and out of sight. It was then she realized Reuben's destination. She knew it with great certainty, her heart pounding with the thought. Reuben was going to make good on his threat.

If he was going to Milroy, he would have gone south. Because he had not, then Rushville must be where he was going. Rushville had many things, all of which — as far as

Reuben was concerned — would require the surrey to bring them back. No, Reuben wasn't going to the feed mill or any farming supply store. Reuben was going to the bank. He was going to borrow money.

She turned from the kitchen window, her movements slow, her heart numb. How could the man risk the little they had on his crazy scheme of raising goats? This was what he was going to do, she was certain. Nothing else made any sense.

Reuben was going to take the little equity they had in the farm and invest it in goats. And a gamble it was. She was certain it was just as much a gamble as those taken by any Englishman in the gambling halls. Reuben's actions were disreputable and dishonorable, even if he was a deacon and even if the bishop backed up his plans. That the bishop would do so, she was sure.

The thought burned in her, filling her with anger. This was why Reuben would not come in for lunch. He was afraid to face her, afraid to tell her he was going to borrow on the farm. The farm she had made the extra payments on, skimping and saving.

He, with all his high airs about being a deacon, a servant of the Lord, a man's man, had sunk to using his wife's money — the equity in the farm — for his own purposes.

With a flourish, without even having to think about it, she flipped the dough into the pie pans, expertly cut the edges off, added the filling, and shoved them roughly into the oven. Adjusting the heat on the oven, she saw the whole thing clearly. Reuben would fail.

It was up to her, as it always had been, to find an answer. But what was that answer to be? She had already tried everything she knew and had been thwarted at each turn. *Am I to be doomed to failure, the money which belonged to my family lost forever?* She felt fear running through her at the thought.

There is no answer, she finally told herself. *There never was, and now we are to be turned into a goat farm. A deacon and now a goatherd. How fitting an ending to our miserable lives.*

And I am going to help him, the thought presented itself. *I suppose so,* Rachel sighed. *I suppose so, if we don't all starve.*

CHAPTER
FORTY-FIVE

John was barely awake when a nurse he hadn't seen before positioned a lunch tray across his bed.

"Time to eat," she said cheerfully. "Doctor said to give it a try. If you feel up to it, that is."

He gave no response, his eyes taking in the sight of the offered portions.

"It's not home cooking," she said with a smile. When John didn't reply, the nurse said, "I'll leave it then. Be back in a little bit."

With that the nurse was gone. John continued to look at the food without interest. There was something missing but what? It was standard food — the little glob of white mashed potatoes, the small bowl of dark gravy, the corn on a white plate, the piece of roll in the corner. A small piece of meat, presumably a hamburger.

Then it occurred to him what was missing. It was the smell . . . or rather the lack of it.

His instincts were to test it, to touch it with his fork — like he would at home — to smell the simmering gravy, to breathe in, even before it reached his lips, the rich earthy aroma of fresh mashed potatoes.

Without thinking he tried using his right hand to reach for the plastic utensils on the tray. He tried hard to make the arm move, every instinct feeling like it should work, but nothing happened.

The terror of his paralysis struck him afresh. This was no dream, as he had started to think. Faint memories of his mother — from long ago it seemed — played in his mind. She was going to take him home, he thought she had said, but then there had been nothing all day. She had also said Rebecca would be coming, had she not?

The light coming through the window beside his bed was dim. In front of him, the plate of food confused him. Was it lunch time or supper? John tried again to move his hand, frustration filling him at the continued inability, fueling not anger but despair.

His emotions spiraled downward. *You can use your other hand,* he heard his mind telling him. John heard, but the solution repulsed him, the implications obvious. There would be a need to accept, or at least to acknowledge, his right hand as useless.

This he rebelled against. *Rebecca won't marry a man with a useless right arm.* He wasn't sure whether he said the words aloud or not. He only knew they rang in his ears, in his being.

"She won't," he said, this time hearing the words come out in a rough whisper.

He tried again to reach the fork, setting his eyes on the white piece of plastic, willing with the full strength of his body and mind. But there was nothing. No movement. No feeling. Only a void, a chasm he could not cross.

His head fell back against the pillow, the softness of it folding around his head, inviting him to go back even further, to allow his body to sink into its darkness.

A cripple, the thought screamed through his brain. *A cripple who has lost what I loved the most.* He saw, as clear as if Rebecca had been there, her eyes, their tender gaze falling on him. He felt her fingers in his, the softness of their touch caressing his hand. The agony of the memory brought a groan from the depths of his chest.

In his despair, he threw his left arm in the air as if to ward off the evil that had befallen him, to drive it away with the only action available to him. He hit the tray of food in his outburst, causing it to teeter on the extended arm. It began to slide away from his control and possibly dump its contents all over his legs.

His mind stopped, like an object shot in midair. The tray became the urgent matter. It was going to fall if he did nothing.

The time before he made up his mind was negligible. He saw clearly that he could stop the falling, but did he want to use his left hand?

He knew there was time given to decide, but not to waver. He reached for the tray, deciding not from any noble impulse but from a deep compulsion within him. Lifting his left hand, he grasped the edge of the tray with his fingers, his lips opening in a great cry of agony.

Pain rose not from his body but from his mind, from knowing that he had accepted, from knowing he had gotten around the injury without being made whole first. He had not chosen to be a cripple, but he now chose to live with it. He pulled the tray back onto the extended arm, the sound of his voice filling the room.

He didn't hear the footsteps, just the door as it burst open with great force. The nurse was already inside by the time it was half opened. "Mr. Miller," she said, stopping short, taking the situation in with one long look. "Whatever was that?"

He studied her, knowing his eyes must be wild, but he was not about to tell her anything. "My tray was sliding off," he said, his voice coming out a little louder than he intended.

"You weren't trying to throw it away, were you?" she asked, giving him a long hard look.

He shook his head firmly. "I caught it with my left hand," he said, as if that explained everything.

"You're going to eat it then?"

He nodded. "Yes, everything's fine."

"Okay then," she said, shutting the door.

He studied his right hand for a moment, then lifted his left and took the plastic fork in his fingers as best he could. The fork felt strange and unwieldy, threatening to go places and do things he didn't want. Carefully he brought the fork down, picked up a little of the mashed potatoes, touched the bottom edge into the gravy, and then brought the food to his mouth.

The taste was worse than he expected, but it was food, and he needed food. That was if he wanted to avoid that nasty looking needle the nurse called the feeding tube. The red bruise on his unfeeling right arm and the round patch of crusted blood verified where the needle had been.

The thought of Rebecca returned and with it the urgency of seeing her. Surely, he thought, she would not leave him without first talking. Yet he did not know what she would do, and in that uncertainty, lay his dread. He faintly remembered his anger the last time he had seen her, his fear that her heart was being drawn to the shadowy Mennonite boy from her childhood. And with the memory, came his first feelings of shame.

Taking another bite of the food, the fork in his left hand shook. Laying the fork on the tray, he rested, shaking his head in an attempt to clear it. *What had actually happened and what had not? Had we not planned on talking on Sunday night? What Sunday night was that, and when had it passed? Have I acted unreasonably?*

Searching his mind, he became certain that he had. Yet what was he supposed to do about it? He thought of what his mother had said earlier and felt ashamed again. He didn't deserve his family or Rebecca. The thought troubled him.

Picking up the fork again, he brought

more food to his mouth and swallowed it slowly and carefully. So focused was he on trying to eat, he didn't hear the door open again.

This time it was not the nurse.

He looked up just as he heard her say, "You're awake."

She was more beautiful than he had remembered, her face soft with concern as she moved across the room toward him.

"You're awake," she repeated.

Her words stirred emotions from the past, memories from a day when the sun had been shining and he could walk on his own two feet, reach with both his hands toward her, touch her from his own strength, from the love he felt for this girl. "You've come," he managed to say, not quite keeping the surprise out of his voice, struggling to lift his left hand weakly in her direction. "I was just thinking about you, and . . ."

She smiled and reached out for his hand, but he could only lift his left hand to hers.

"I'm sorry," he whispered. It was all he could think to say.

"It's okay," she whispered. She moved closer to the rail of his bed, her grip tightening on his left hand. "How are you? It's so wonderful that you're finally back. It was so long."

He had to grin in spite of himself. "The food is terrible. Doesn't even taste like food."

"Poor fellow," she said teasingly, drawing closer to him.

He knew what she was going to do and was in the process of turning his head away . . . when he stopped. Maybe it wasn't right, but he wanted this to happen. His right hand awkwardly moved toward the other, rising to reach out for hers, as she gently kissed him.

"You're wonderful," he whispered. "How can you still love me after the way I suspected you?"

"Let's not talk about it now."

"My mind is foggy." He let go of her hand, rubbing his forehead. "But something tells me I was — well, angry with you . . . that night at your house."

"Yes," she allowed, "but you had some reason for it."

"No." He shook his head. "I'm sorry it ever came up."

"It's okay," she said, taking his hand again.

"I'll never be worthy of you. And no more kissing. That has to wait."

"Once won't hurt," she told him, a twinkle in her eye. "Special occasion. You are getting better now and will soon be home."

"My right arm just moved," he said, the realization of what he had done earlier dawning. "It must have been you."

"I'm glad I'm of some good," she said quietly. "Does your arm hurt?"

"A little," he said. "The other didn't hurt at all. No feeling. That was the problem."

"Does the doctor know what will happen?"

He shook his head slightly. "They never say for certain. I think I will be better though. You are here now."

"That can't be everything," she said with a smile.

"Most everything. You are beautiful."

"You shouldn't say things like that," she told him.

"And you shouldn't kiss me."

"Do you want me to tell you about Atlee?" she asked abruptly.

"You don't have to," he said.

"Are you sure?"

"Yes," he insisted. "I don't need to know."

"We shouldn't have secrets," she replied, making a face. "It was like this. When I was a young girl in Milroy, I liked a boy named Atlee," she said, glancing at him. "But his parents went Mennonite, and we, of course, were then in two different worlds. Before his family moved away, though, he asked

414

me to promise something. We promised we would meet again when I was twenty-one. At the bridge. That we would wait for each other till then."

"But you didn't?" he asked.

"No, I met you."

"Did he wait for you?"

"No." She smiled gently.

"Do you wish he had?" he asked.

"No," she said, bending over the bedrail, kissing him on the cheek this time. "I love you now, and the past is the past. I'm no longer a schoolgirl. My heart is larger, and you have filled it."

"Even if I'm a cripple forever?" he asked.

"Yes," she said, a tear in her eye, "even then."

"But I'm not going to be one," he said confidently. "I'll get better. You'll see."

"I know you will, John," she told him. "And, yes, I did go back to the bridge when I was in Milroy. I had to see. To settle the matter."

His eyes found hers. "He didn't come back? Did he?"

She shook her head.

"Would you have gone with him if he had?"

"No," she mouthed the words.

Tears stung his eyes as he whispered, "You

really are too wonderful. I don't deserve you. But I *am* going to get better. And I really was wrong. Very wrong to act like I did."

"I should have told you sooner," she said, as the door opened behind them and let in the nurse.

"Am I interrupting?" she asked.

"No, we're finished," Rebecca said, to which John nodded.

CHAPTER
FORTY-SIX

Rebecca left some twenty minutes later, wanting to get home before too late. Dr. Wine stopped by soon afterward for a final check on John, finding him still awake and quite cheerful.

"Well, I see you're looking better," he said not sounding surprised. "The visit with the young lady do you good?"

"That was my girlfriend," John said, a silly grin on his face.

"The nurse mentioned it." Dr. Wine was checking John's chart and scribbling notes. "How are you feeling?"

John got an even bigger grin. "Both hands work now. At least better than before!"

Dr. Wine came over and ran his hand down John's side, squeezing and seeming pleased when John winced. "Good progress already, I would say. You're not quite where you need to be, but you're well on your way. You might need some more visits from that young woman."

To which John only smiled.

"Get some sleep then. Tomorrow you're going home. Is that good news?"

"Very good news. Twice good now. All in one day," John said.

"You've been through a lot," Dr. Wine said. "I guess it's time for things to turn around for you. You settle in now. Sleep can only do you good."

After Dr. Wine left, John had no trouble falling asleep, and his first thought, when he awoke the next morning, was that of going home. Even breakfast was bearable with that on his mind. The egg, toast, and small bowl of oatmeal sat before him only momentarily before he started eating.

With breakfast done, John noticed his right leg alternating between stings of pain and a tingling sensation. When the nurse came in for the breakfast tray, he told her of the strange sensations in his leg, and she told him this could only be good news. That any feeling in the leg was good news.

Miriam came for him around eleven, having found a driver with a handicap accessible van from across the river in Maysville. John felt a little embarrassed, rolling out of the hospital in the wheelchair, but was happy to be going home.

■ ■ ■ ■

Isaac walked in from the harness shop when he saw the van approaching, meeting them in the driveway. When Isaac rolled open the van door, John saw tears in his father's eyes.

"You are home, son," Isaac said, taking both of John's hands in his. "It has been *Da Hah*'s will that we should see you this well again."

"I'll be better soon. All the way," John said.

"You must accept what will be," Isaac told him quickly, taking the handle of the wheelchair and gently rolling John down the ramp.

John nodded.

After making their way across the rough, graveled drive, Isaac wheeled John into the house, where John saw that the bed from his room had been moved downstairs to the sewing room.

"But your sewing things," John said to his mother, alarm in his voice. "I don't have to sleep down here."

"You'll be much more comfortable down here, where I can take care of you," Miriam told him.

"And I sure wasn't going to pull this chair up the stairs," Isaac added.

"I'm getting better fast," John said. "You shouldn't have bothered."

"Well, until you *are* better, you're staying down here," Isaac said firmly.

When Miriam served lunch, Isaac pushed John's wheelchair up to the kitchen table. The sight of his mother's sandwiches made him even more certain the restoration of his body would come quickly.

"Nothing like your cooking," John told his mother, after they had paused for prayer. "The food at the hospital was awful."

"I'm sure Rebecca's food will be just as good," Miriam said. "Did I tell you? She held up real well during this time."

"She's a very wonderful girl," John said, meaning more than his parents would ever know.

"It's good things turned out well," Isaac said, satisfaction in his voice. "We learn and then we go on living. And always we must give thanks."

"She would have stayed with me even as a cripple," John said. "I don't deserve that."

"No man deserves a good wife," Isaac told him. "It is *Da Hah*'s mercy on us men. That is all it is."

"Well!" Miriam exclaimed. "It goes both ways. You are a good man, Isaac."

"Sometimes," Isaac allowed. "That also is mercy."

His sandwich done, the excitement of the homecoming fading fast, tiredness creeping through his entire body, John said, "I think I'd better lie down."

"Oh my!" Miriam said. "Here we are talking, and you're still a recovering boy. Let's get you settled in."

"I won't be recovering for long," John muttered under his breath.

True to his intentions, John tried walking the next day. The steps were hesitant, the two he took, and he had to hold on to the side of the bed, but they were steps.

Mattie and Lester came to visit on Saturday night with Rebecca. By then John had already walked across the sewing room twice and that morning managed to make it to the kitchen table for breakfast on his own two feet. He had raised the question of when he would be moved upstairs, to which Miriam had informed him the time had not come yet.

With the three visitors there for the evening, popcorn was called for, and Isaac brought cider from the basement. While the older folks sat in the living room, Rebecca and John were served their popcorn and cider in the sewing room, where they talked at length about nothing in particular, simply enjoying the pleasure of being together.

Finally John suggested they join their parents in the living room. Miriam jumped up to get John's chair ready when she saw him coming. He was still a little shaky on his feet but wanted the progress he had made to be on display for all to see.

With the gas lantern hissing above their heads, the three couples emptied the popcorn bowl and the gallon of cider, talking far into the night.

ABOUT THE AUTHOR

As a boy, **Jerry Eicher** spent eight years in Honduras where his grandfather helped found an Amish community outreach. As an adult, Jerry has taught in Amish and Mennonite schools in Ohio and Illinois, has been involved in church renewal, and has conducted in-depth Bible study workshops. Jerry lives with his wife, Tina, and their four children in Virginia.

LP FIC EIC
Eicher, Jerry S
  Rebecca's return

5CLY0014083

DATE DUE			